PRETTY SAVAGE BOYS

PRETTY SAVAGE BOYS

A DARK NEW ADULT ROMANCE

LAYLA SIMON

Cover Photograph: Cadwallader Photography www.kcpclients.com
Cover Model: CJ Lockwood
Cover Design: Katherine Hayton
Developmental Editing: Emerald Edits www.emeraldedits.com

ISBN: 979-8-3960-6251-1

PREFACE

Content warning: this book contains scenes or references to child abuse, dub-con/non-con, image-based abuse, physical assault, illegal surveillance, sexual assault, torture, and murder

CHAPTER ONE

ROSA

"You're such a good girl," my mother says as I curl onto the bed next to her, trying to hold her in a way that doesn't knock a vital component free.

There are a dozen different attachments I need to steer clear of. The saline drip keeping her hydrated, the gastrostomy tube keeping her fed, the colostomy and catheter bags draining everything away. The lines to draw blood, the port to inject drugs. The EKG stickers spotted across her chest and ankles.

To give her a hug is like embracing an android, part human, part machine, all of her slowly turning grey and dry.

Despite it all, the love she injects into each touch, each kiss, is one hundred percent my mother. The warmth from each piece of praise edged now with the terrifying thought it will be the last.

If it is, I want to wring these occasions dry, slurping up every drop.

"How's your course going?" she asks, her voice cracking on the last word.

I reach for some balm to coat her chapped lips; no matter how many bags of saline they pump into her, none of it ever seems to make it through to her skin. Her lungs are clogged with an ocean of fluid while her skin flakes every time she changes position in bed.

"It's good." I'm studying engineering and design with a focus on textiles. Clothing design would be the absolute dream but even with a hefty dose of reality playing its part, interior design is a good second-best landing place. "The lecturer is so enthusiastic about textile processes you can't help but be excited. Even listening to the stuff that's dull as dirt."

"You're not too overloaded?"

"Nah. Sleep's overrated," I state, following it up with a gigantic yawn because if there's one thing my body likes to do, it's betray me. "I'd rather go without for the next eighteen months than rack up another year's worth of fees."

"And your flat? How's it going with your flatmates?"

"Finley's a doll, as usual. Did I tell you about Aroha?"

I have, but my mother shakes her head.

"She found a better job up north and left us for the greener pastures of the Kapiti Coast."

"Are they replacing her?"

"We have our fingers crossed the caseworkers are so overloaded they forget. The past week, with just the two of us, we're actually getting a decent length shower every morning before the hot water runs out."

She laughs along with me, then moves to the next item in her rota. "What about work?"

I press my forehead against her shoulder, smiling at the question. The first time I told my mother about the sex work I was doing to pay for university, my heart had been in my throat. But instead of disappointment, I got acceptance and an overload of advice—most of it sorely outdated.

My main impetus in telling her had been the worry another of her friends would beat me to the task. Better it came from me with context than from a gossip, even a well-intentioned one.

Now, I'm glad I told her. She's one of the few people I can talk to about it. Someone to share commiserations when things are awful or rejoice with me when I have a good day.

"It's fine."

"You're staying safe?"

That prompts a small laugh. "Yeah. You know it." After a pause weighted with her expectations, I add, "The other girls there look out for me."

'There' is a share house in a poor but tidy suburb, currently repurposed as a brothel.

Nothing you can tell with a passing glance, but the neighbours know. No matter how tidy we keep the front garden and driveway, we can't hide the multitude of cars that pull up and leave with regularity throughout the day.

"No one's getting rough?"

I laugh for longer at that one. The client list I bought from a retiring worker is mostly middle-aged submissives with a few vanillas on the side. Being domineering without crossing the line into an actual domme is something I practised beside the retiree for a month to ensure it was a good fit.

The control over another person was something I'd never experienced before. The need to put myself in their place, think about their wants, their tolerance, their boundaries, exposed me to an intimacy far beyond my previous sexual encounters.

It gave me a thrill that still lingers, even now the newness has gone. Being in charge became immediately addictive and the only person getting rough at my sessions, is me. "No. Nothing like that. Nobody's giving me any grief."

"You girls are so lucky. Back when I started, we wasted so

much time and money staying on the good side of police, and I still clocked up two convictions for solicitation."

I've heard it all before, but I snuggle in closer against her side, happy for the chance to hear it again. The reform act that decriminalised sex work is twenty years old now, but I still hear horror stories from the women who were working at the time.

The lack of protection, the proliferation of pimps. The way you couldn't go to police to report an attack without the fear you'd be the one who ended up with a conviction, allowing violent men to flourish.

If things were still that way, I wouldn't be able to finance my way through university. The worry that I'd rack up a permanent blot on my record would scare me away.

And if I couldn't pay for it outright, I wouldn't go.

I learned early on the pressures of living outside your means. The debt that taught me might have belonged to my father—now deceased and may he rest in hell forever with demons pegging the shit out of him—but he left the payment of it to my mother and me.

"At least you didn't have to pay tax," I counter, falling into the swing of the repeat conversation like pulling on a favourite pair of old boots.

My flatmates gave me pitying looks when I told them my mother is down to around a dozen topics of conversation and she just repeats them over and over. They think it makes her harder to visit with, when it makes it easier.

There's so much comfort in this familiarity, I don't know how I'll get past the loss when it's finally time to let go.

"You don't have to pay tax, either," she says with a soft giggle. "That's the advantage of working in a cash economy."

"You're out of touch, old lady. Most of my fees are paid by credit card." The billing statement displays the bland business name of Fenn Ltd so nobody casting a casual eye across a bank

4

statement discovers something they shouldn't. "I wish we were still a cash society."

Mum makes a disgusted noise as her head tilts to the side, eyes closing. "That's so lame."

"Yeah, it is."

"I need to tell you something important," she whispers, and I check her face, wondering if she's talking to me or has disappeared inside a vivid hallucination; something that happens with increasing regularity now the cancer has metastasised to her brain.

"What's that?" I prompt when she's remained silent for close on a full minute. "Something nice, I hope."

"Your uncle..."

Her voice trails into a whimper and my body stiffens, icy cold slush filling my veins. Of all the things we don't talk about, my uncle rates at the top of the list.

Not my real uncle, even if I thought of him that way back when I was a girl of seven and eight. He was a client of my mother's, then her pimp, then her abuser, then...

But I don't like to go down the road of what he was at the end. Meant to stay away from us for one. Meant to still be locked up in prison for another.

"He's out?" I ask, my voice a squeak sounding nothing like its usual self.

"A friend called me." She raises her head, squinting around the room. "They heard it during a prison visit and thought I should know."

My muscles soften again. Prison gossip. Not the most reliable source of information in the land.

"He's not allowed to contact us," I remind her. "The protective order spells out all that stuff."

But she's gone. Making the small snorts and snuffles that happen because her airways aren't up to the task any longer.

The oxygen tubes under her nose make a small hiss as I lean over to kiss her on the forehead. I wait for a few minutes, but she's obviously fast enough asleep that she won't be rousing anytime soon.

I extract myself with the same amount of care I took to lie down before gathering my things and heading out the door.

Despite having late-stage ovarian cancer, my mother isn't staying in a hospital or a hospice. Her physical state deteriorated to where palliative care was the only thing that made sense, but there wasn't an appropriate bed available.

The district health board was apologetic when they moved her into the hospital unit of an aged care facility instead. *Just until a bed comes free.*

Fourteen months later, my mother has outlasted every prediction for her imminent death and that proper hospice bed never eventuated. When she was stronger, she didn't mind as much. Now her sight is mostly gone, her chief distraction and entertainment is conversation. To be surrounded by people of a different age group, with no common references, wears on her. She enjoys her chats with the nursing staff more but they're busy.

I keep trying, keep reminding people she's in the wrong place, but each month that passes meets with less hope she'll be able to be moved.

They're waiting for her to die, so they don't have to field my phone calls any longer. The awareness makes me warm with a dull anger, but there's nothing more I can do, except be there for her.

Something my courses and work don't leave a lot of time spare for.

As I wait at the bus stop a few houses down from the retirement units, my mind drifts back through the years since her diagnosis. She's always been tougher, offered more of a fight than the doctors expected. Each time the cancer struck, she struck back, handling the increasingly aggressive bouts of chemotherapy to beat it into retreat.

But it always returned, like a stalker who'd found their fixation. Once my mother got the diagnosis, she never clawed her way to the freedom of remission. The cancer is her longest staying companion.

By the time I was fifteen, she wasn't able to care for herself any longer, let alone me. Although it devastated us both, I was bundled into the care of Oranga Tamariki, the Ministry for Children. I stayed under their supervision until earlier this year when I aged out of the system at eighteen.

It wasn't as bad as we both feared. A couple fostered me along with some other late arrivals. The family was a good enough resting place that I still call Astrid—my foster mum— occasionally, and I remain close friends with Ben, a teenage boy who was under their roof for nearly as long as me.

The flat I'm currently in is partially subsidised by the department, a way to transition foster kids into adulthood with limited support. It's a godsend—albeit one I'm always terrified will be stripped away from me. Finley is an even bigger gift. As someone who's always struggled to make friends, to make one so easily and so unexpectedly is a treasure.

As I clamber into the late-arriving bus and take a seat, my mood sinks. I hug my arms across my chest and close my eyes, pretending it's the lingering embrace of my mother.

A trick that doesn't fool me one bit. It's only after getting off at my stop and walking home that I find the energy to paste a smile on my face.

"You're late," Finley tells me the moment I'm through the door. Her riotous hair—as a platinum blonde she's forever dabbling with streaks of colour not seen in nature—seems even more varied than it did this morning.

7

"No, I'm not. For what?"

"We've got a new flatmate." And my hope for long showers is gone. "She's pretty."

My previous coffee is already long forgotten by my blood-stream. I flick the kettle on as I stare at my lesbian flatmate with open suspicion. "No hooking up inside the house. That's part of the rules."

"What?" Finley's faux outrage twists her face into a grimace. "Where are these rules? I demand to know what's in them."

I point to a fridge magnet with an illegible scrawl across it in wipeable marker.

"That doesn't count," she immediately retorts. "Anyone could scribble on that. Unless there's an official form on official letterhead, I refuse to comply."

"Is she in the room right now?" I ask, eyes narrowing at Finley's continued high volume.

"Yes, and in answer to your next question, yes, that's why I'm talking loudly. So, she knows we don't bite and—"

"And our conversation is completely asinine."

"There are no arses involved at all. Believe me, I've been keeping tabs."

As usual, five minutes into a conversation, and Finley has me in stitches. I bite my lip to stop laughing and say, "Instead of talking loudly at me, why don't you knock on her door and ask her if she wants a hot drink?"

Finley stays right where she is, hopping from foot to foot.

"Are you nervous?" I ask, gleefully. My flatmate usually has such mountainous confidence that I'm resigned to never getting the upper hand. "Are you scared of the pretty new girl?"

"No. Don't be ridiculous," she snaps, colour flaring along her cheekbones in direct contradiction.

"Fine. I'll knock on the door. You make the coffees." I walk halfway to the bedroom door, then creep back to whisper, "What's her name?"

"Lily," comes a voice from behind me, sending my heart into my mouth and leaving my nervous system lodged somewhere near the ceiling.

"Nice to see you again," Finley says, recovering first. She sticks her right hand out, twiddling a lock of her multicoloured hair around her left forefinger and sucking her cheeks in until her bone structure looks practically regal. "I'm Finley and this here's Rosa."

It takes half a second to see what Finley means about her being pretty. The mousy hair and rumpled clothing make her look like a street urchin. It takes a few moments for the overall picture to hit right, showing her as quietly gorgeous instead.

"We were just talking about flat rules," I happily announce while spooning out my coffee and pushing the container of instant towards the new girl. "Finley thinks we should be able to hook up with our flatmates and I'm against. Want to be the deciding vote?"

"Not really," she says, her voice soft but not lacking in confidence.

That fits. By the time you age out of the system, you've either got brazenness to spare or you're stamped so far underfoot, no one can see you.

She chews on the side of her thumbnail, eyeing us both with a hefty dose of caution. "Are you the extent of the flatmates I'm not allowed to hook up with if I vote no, or are there more?"

"It's just us," Finley says, recovering from her earlier bout of shyness. "Unless Rosa's stored one of her conquests under the bed again."

"That was one time," I say, rolling my eyes at the new girl to include her. "And if you passed on information about scheduled home visits, I wouldn't need to stash boys away at short notice."

9

Lily frowns. "Who does home visits?"

"Some transitional officer funded by the government to make sure we don't have too much fun," Finley says, looking like the entire system is a personal affront. "And our case workers whenever they want."

"Just call us grand central station," I jibe. "You want a drink of anything?"

"No, I'm good."

"Food?"

"I had something already."

"Oh," Finley exclaims, tapping me on the shoulder. "Forgot to tell you, Ben dropped by with a party invite. Some rich guy's house, over in Fendalton."

"For me or for all of us?"

"The more the merrier, he said. There'll be free food and booze, so dinner's sorted."

"Is Ben your boyfriend?" Lily asks.

"No, he's a friend from my last foster home." I turn to Finley. "How're we getting there?"

"The magic of public transport."

"And home?"

"The magic of hire scooters."

"Doesn't your girlfriend have a car?"

"I'm single."

My eyes flick up and down Finley's length, understanding why she's added the new blue streaks in her already multi-coloured hair. "When did that happen?"

"Yesterday, maybe the day before. I've sworn off women for the foreseeable."

"Well, that was appalling timing. Couldn't you put out for longer to save the rest of us from ruining our feet by walking in heels?"

Finley purses her lips, trying to make eye contact with Lily and finding absolutely no help from that quarter. "You coming?"

Lily tips her head forward so her curly hair hides her face. A neat trick. I should see if the hairdresser can work some magic to make mine do the same. "Can't. I've got a visit with my sister tomorrow and I have enough black marks against me without adding a hangover to the mix."

"Right." Finley turns. "Just you and me, kiddo."

"What's this?" I ask, picking a white envelope off the bench with my name written on it.

"I'm no expert, but I think that's mail. Your mail, to be precise."

"There's no stamp."

Finley shrugs. "Could be one of those motorcycle dude thingies."

"DX mail is still mail." I turn it over again. "They have ink stamps."

"I don't know," Finley says, throwing her arms in the air with customary theatrics. "Perhaps someone dropped it off on foot like a stalker. It could've been sitting on the front step for the past fortnight, and I only just noticed. Who knows?"

"It was on the front step?"

She glares at me, then turns her attention back to Lily. "You don't need to drink. There'll be plenty of sober people there."

I snort with laughter at the mischaracterisation.

"Okay, fine. There'll be a couple of people there who—"

"I'm good with staying in," Lily says in a soft voice. "I'm not much of a party girl."

"Sorry," Finley says, turning back to me with something like genuine regret. "The ball's back in your court, hun. You'll have to come along."

I turn the plain white envelope over and over, trying to work

11

out where it came from. Even in the age of snail mail, hand delivery would be overkill.

"Try the flap," Finley says, apparently going for a prize at snark since neither one of us is falling over ourselves to be her date for the evening. "I find opening the envelope works far better than staring at the outside."

A shiver hits my spine, right between the shoulderblades where it's hardest to scratch. There's no reason for it. No reason at all.

Unfortunately, telling myself that does little to budge the sense of unease.

"Is something wrong?" Lily asks, and I force myself to place the envelope on the counter again.

"No. I'm fine. Where's this party again?"

Finley crows in victory, taking my hand and dragging me into a quick dance across the kitchen. "It's in Fendalton, so you'll have to dress your most la-de-dah."

"Not a clothing style I'm familiar with," I joke back to her, crossing my eyes.

"Let me into your wardrobe and I'll find you something perfect." She turns to Lily, trying to bring her into the circle. "Rosa has the most amazing outfits. She can dress in absolutely anything and look like a queen."

I shake my head. "She means I can fix a few side seams on thrift store bargains." I turn back to Finley. "Which is really not the rocket scientist level of skill you seem to think it is."

"It's magic," she insists. "When you hem something, I can't even see the stitches. They should burn you as a witch."

"Says the girl who can take apart a car engine, blindfolded." I spin away long enough to grab my coffee and finish half of it in two gulps. "Better make sure there's room at the stake for two."

Lily excuses herself before too long, heading for the safety of her room.

"I think we overwhelmed her."

Finley is busy making up dance moves and gives a shrug. "Better than underwhelming her. Go get ready."

"Yes, ma'am. Any other orders, or will that suffice for the time being?"

"Open your goddamn mail, you freak." She tosses the envelope at me. "Otherwise, I'll be forced to do it myself."

"Mail theft is a serious crime," I remind her, heading for the safety of my bedroom while the going's good. "Don't make me have to tell your case worker."

She flips me both fingers and I close the door, smiling.

Finley never fails to cheer me, even on those occasions when she winds me up as well. I have a quick shower, then pull on a short black dress, thick black tights I've hand-painted with a white abstract design, a heavy jean jacket, and tall boots as a nod to the increasing cold of early autumn.

Ready, I sit on the edge of the bed and examine the envelope again. My name is handwritten across the front in capitals, the ink a weird brown shade of crimson that makes me want to heave.

Anxiety nips at me, circles warily, and darts forward to take another bite.

I rip the seal before my paranoia can get the best of me, and a shower of bright crimson glitter explodes into the air, clinging to my clothes, my lips, my hair. I shake myself off like a dog and examine the card inside.

It's handmade from heavy stock, a watercolour heart painted on the front in pink, gold, and pastel blue.

The message inside is the same crimson ink as my name, this time a single word inside quote marks.

"Smile."

I turn it over, but there's nothing more. No name. No return address. No signature.

Brushing a few more flecks of glitter off the front of my outfit, I pick up the envelope and check the back.

Nothing.

Smile. Either an innocent word or one tinged with so much rampant misogyny that it makes my blood fizz and sputter inside my veins.

I read it again and, thanks to my mother's earlier revelation, this time I hear it in my uncle's voice.

"Smile for the camera, darling. Say cheese."

A carousel of images strike me, too many to separate, each one hitting like a physical blow. I close my eyes, my breathing hoarse. My pulse races until I can barely catch the individual beats.

My brain can't handle the influx, retreating to a safe space to huddle and wait for the rampant slideshow to end.

When it does, I'm on the floor, knees to my chest, violently shaking. Everywhere I look is glitter.

Fucking glitter.

It'll probably hang around this flat for longer than me.

Moving slowly, I uncurl and get to my feet. The change in position makes me feel better, as does tearing the thick card into pieces, tearing those pieces into pieces. I stomp along the hallway to collect the vacuum cleaner and suck up every bit of card and glitter I can find.

With that done—out of sight, out of mind—I'm back on an even keel.

Once I store the vacuum back in the closet, my heart calms to its usual pace and I'm more than ready for a drink, a dance, and as much snack food as I can cram into my face.

Anything to help forget I'm not such a good girl after all.

CHAPTER TWO

TRENT

IT'S SATURDAY NIGHT AND I'M FETCHING ANOTHER SLAB OF beer from the open garage when I hear the gunshot.

Instantly, my heart hammers so quickly I can't feel the individual beats. My eyes bulge with pressure until the world around me turns concave, like I'm staring through a fisheye lens. Hairs on my head, arms, and neck stand to attention, their thin lengths seeking feedback before they can be soothed back to lying flat.

The world pauses as I wait for the next bit.

For the blood. For the horror. For the brains to come spilling out of someone's head.

Images of Robbie flash through my mind. His body falls, heels drumming on the concrete floor of the warehouse. My mouth fills with heavy spit, the taste of metal and blood.

The sound comes again, and my muscles relax as I realise it's not a gun. Not a shot. It's my neighbour's old car backfiring as he tests the engine. The repair of the classic Aston Martin has been happening for so long now, I doubt it'll ever be complete.

I rub my hands over my hair just to move, to unlock, then finish my task and walk to the window, staring out at the back lawn, figures cavorting past as the party gets its second wind.

My chest aches and I dig the heel of my palm into my sternum, trying to rub the sensation away. Anxiety twists my nerves until they're tight enough to snap. A state they're in almost constantly since the shooting. My outwardly calm demeanour is a complete fabrication for the sake of those around me.

Not that I have any of them here now. My dad's overseas on his honeymoon. His new wife, a girl I barely know. My two best friends were invited but I haven't seen them, which means they didn't show because if they were here, they'd be the centre of attention.

I no longer want to be at this party, but that's the problem with being the host. Here I am, five hours in and sick to death of it, but I can't just leave.

"Trent," a drunken female voice calls out to me. I turn, seeing a hand waving from the mass of teens dancing and grab hold, hauling her out of the fray.

"Hey, Tina." The glassy-eyed girl sways gently back and forth, and I doubt it's anything to do with the music thumping from the sound system. "You having a good time?"

"I will once you show me your room."

The drunken giggle that accompanies the overly ambitious, excessively hopeful statement would put me off even if I were that way inclined. But, when I see the interested glance from a boy who's far too sober to be trusted, I take her under my arm, pulling her close. "How about we show you to a nice seat outside?"

Where the chilly night air will revive her. Especially if I

make her next drink sans alcohol. I pluck the half-finished one from her numb hands.

"Sounds good. Then you can cuddle to keep me warm."

Her arms are around me and I laugh, stroking her back and waiting to see if she'll detach herself or if I'll need to pry her fingers off me.

As real girls go, she's delightful. Short, dark hair, cut in a style like a pixie. Enormous eyes, even without the panda circles from an earlier crying jag, and her lips pucker up like a tempting bow as she catches me midway through my examination.

"I'm already taken," I lie to her, the easiest way to offset anyone's interest. "But you're so pretty I'd love to grab a photo."

"Ugh. Not like this," she says, pushing away from me and stumbling along the hall.

I tense for a second, staring after her, then see her grab the elbow of another girl who happily takes her under her wing.

She's fine.

Everyone's fine.

No one's being shot. No one's being drugged. No one's having their intimate videos uploaded to the masses.

All those good times are in my past and fingers crossed, they stay there.

With no other grand ideas occurring to me, I head to my father's security suite to hide from everyone for a while. I can watch from afar without the awkwardness of interacting when I'm not in the mood.

I've just sat down when my phone buzzes and I slide it out, staring at the message with a burgeoning smile.

A cam girl has followed through on one of my requests. The freeze-frame cover shows her in the company of two very well-endowed friends.

Turning my back on the security camera feeds, I put my feet

up on the desk and lean back in my dad's studded leather chair while I swipe through to the footage.

Carlotta—gonna take a wild punt that isn't her real name—beams at me from her account photo. The uploaded video sits waiting for my review. Half the money has already been paid with the other half due once I approve the final file.

I loosen the belt on my jeans, wriggling my arse in the over-stuffed chair, getting comfy. The noise from the rest of the house and outside is muted here, the thick walls screening all but the most determined sounds.

My thumb hovers above the play symbol, moving it back and forth, getting a tinier bit closer with each sweep, the curve of my phone smooth, silky, warm to the point of sensual against my skin.

The fit of my jeans is suddenly too tight, providing increasing friction with even the slightest motion. There's a low throb in the curve of my spine.

I gave crystal clear instructions, but I've been let down before. The men and women enacting my scripted directions with such wooden performances, it steals away any enjoyment from the central act itself. Or they set the camera, then forget the good angles, obscuring everything of interest, used to having an operator controlling the view.

The anticipation. That's where it's good. In this part, before I watch the actual recording, the script I sent them could still be completed with pitch perfect skill, catering to all my needs.

A tiny slice of perfection.

But if my imagination were enough, I wouldn't have to pay copious amounts to have sex workers in foreign countries act according to my specifications.

I click play.

The girl fills the frame. Nice looking, but the longer she's onscreen, the older she appears. Age shouldn't matter, but it does. There's a pucker in the skin around her underarms when she turns to the side, a relaxed angle to her breasts, even in her bra and the flimsy top.

Her teeth are jumbled in her mouth, like an AI image engine tried its best, but didn't really understand the assignment.

The mounting list of imperfections wipes away as the first man enters the room. He strides over to her as she turns, feigning surprise.

The way he grips her, fingertips sinking into the slightly doughy flesh of her upper arm, is perfect. He tugs her firmly back against him, securing her arms behind her with one hand while placing the opposite over her mouth.

She struggles and my jeans are way too tight now; I press the heel of my hand against my bulging cock, not wanting to jerk off to it, not yet. Not with a houseful of teens downstairs, ready to burst in at a moment's notice.

He manhandles her backwards, toward the bed, jerking in surprise when another man enters the room, then his posture relaxes. His relaxes, and hers stiffens further.

The new arrival crosses to the pair, tilting his head as he stares into the woman's eyes before taking the front of her blouse in his hand and tearing it apart in one rough motion. She struggles and tries to scream through the clamped hand, but all that emerges are ragged grunts.

He grabs hold of her bra and flips it down, exposing her breasts. The nipples harden in the cold air, and he grabs himself a handful, then another, grinding his pelvis into her as he does so, ignoring her wild hair and pleading eyes.

He lets go long enough to drag down her long skirt, pulling it to her ankles before reaching back up to snag the elastic of her underwear and yanking them to her knees.

She fights harder, body bucking, legs kicking. Caught

between them, naked against their clothed bodies, she's tiny and powerless against their far larger forms.

They can do whatever they like, and she can't stop them. The only options are to continue fighting or to submit.

I palm my dick again, then flinch as her face turns fully towards the camera. When the man behind her loosens the hand over her mouth, jamming his fingers in instead, she makes a pleasurable moan.

My dick wilts like spinach in a sizzling hot pan.

The whole fucking thing ruined in an instant.

I toss my phone away, groaning, my building lust turning to annoyance like somebody flipped a switch. The noise of the party grates. My skin is too tight and hot. The light stings my eyes like paper cuts, and I throw an arm across to protect them.

What is it about simple instructions that people are compelled to ignore?

If I wanted to see actors enjoying sex, I'd download a thousand viruses worth of free porn like everyone else.

I scowl, drag my arm from my eyes, and blink at the influx of light. With a second to adjust, I grab my phone from where I tossed it and send through what's owing.

Then I turn back to the internal camera feeds, scanning them, hoping for anything of interest. As I look, my mind travels back to another bank of monitors, in another house. Our old house. The one we left behind over a decade ago when my father's ambition outgrew its twenty rooms.

As a child, I'd watched those monitors late one night. Watched them while a woman's eyes widened in genuine terror, her struggles lessening as it became clear her only choice was to submit.

My cock gives a warning throb, and I cut off the image, focusing on the screens in front of me instead of those lodged deep in my memory.

The party sprawls across most rooms in the house. Some of those in the east wing are getting away unscathed, probably because the hallway is mid-renovation.

In my dad's study, there's a sedate cluster of teens. My eyes are immediately drawn to a slender girl with dark blonde curls bouncing over her shoulders.

She's petite, her face crafted with as much care as a porcelain doll. Her eyes are wide set, startlingly attractive, her lips plump as they press against the crystal tumbler filled with my father's secret stash of aged bourbon.

Apparently, not a secret any longer.

I cast my gaze across the other rooms in the house, but my eyes are drawn back to the study. Not just because she's attractive, so many people at the party are, but because the only other female in the room is on the arm of a goth boy, midway through leaving.

The girl at the bar doesn't notice. She tilts the amber liquid back and forth in her glass, swirling it, then taking a large sip, coughing, then laughing, when some of it goes down the wrong way.

One boy in a tight t-shirt watches the exiting couple and closes the door softly behind them before turning his back to lean against it. His gaze flicks to the black-haired boy behind the bar and the one sat next to the girl. All three checking in with one another while she remains oblivious.

My pulse quickens, my cock twitching with excitement like he senses trouble in the air.

Three against one.

There's no obvious reason to think that. Not yet. Something in their body language still feeds it out to me. An air of anticipation edged with menace.

Enough to make me wonder if bourbon is the only thing in her drink.

The cameras dotted throughout the house can be remotely controlled from any PC signed into the main server. I access the study, casting the feeds from all six cameras across the bank of monitors, adjusting their angles so they each focus on the girl.

It's been such a long time since I had suitable material.

My breathing becomes shallower the longer I stare at the screens, eagerly tracking every single movement.

If this were playing out in the same room as me, I'd intervene, but seeing the drama unfold over the monitors distances me. Even though there's more threat here than there was to Tina, it hits me in an entirely different way.

A flash of conscience glimmers in my peripheral vision but I dismiss it, arbitrarily deciding this girl can handle herself. I assure myself I'll step in before things get too far is that's how it goes. The siren call of the screen twists my mind any way it wants, trying to get what it needs.

The girl wears a short dress overtop black tights covered in white designs and I figure the jacket draped across the neighbouring stool is hers. The boy behind the counter says something, lifting a bottle from the top shelf. He presents it to her like he's a sommelier in a fancy restaurant and she just ordered their most expensive wine.

She tips her glass towards him, twisting to look over her shoulder, lips pursing. The boy on the stool next to hers is speaking and, judging by her expression, they're not words she wants to hear.

Her gaze shifts to the boy still leaning deliberately against the door. He crosses his arms, flexing his biceps, a message she can't fail to understand.

Nervousness grabs hold, the lines of her body tensing. Her eyes skate around the room and I wonder what image she's comparing it to. Wonder how many girls were in there when she first arrived, leaving in dribs or drabs small enough that she didn't realise she was the last one.

Until now.

I check the controls, trying to find a volume button for the mics I know my dad has installed. It's hard to locate since my eyes are glued to the images broadcasting from the room, but I eventually stumble across the right one.

"You don't want to leave us here alone, do you?" a rumbling voice says. There's a light teasing note to his words, but the way he tenses his muscles to make them bulge sends a completely different message.

A shiver takes hold, spreading its vibrations across the surface of my skin, increasing the intensity of each sensation.

I feel the thick layers of my jeans, the straining throb of my hardening dick, the weird metallic taste I get in the back of my throat when I'm watching something good, something titillating, something raw and powerful and visceral.

The screens are small, blocky, the images grainier than I'd like.

They're also showing me a scene I couldn't have scripted. A slice of real life with all its tantalising ambiguity.

A show of force, a power play.

My face flushes with warmth as I wait to see how these boys will turn her resistance into submission.

Their numbers and size are already working for them. Can their mouths utter the magic phrases to bend her further... or will their chosen words empower her with the urge to fight?

"No leaving the room until you finish your drink," the boy pouring says. "Otherwise, you've just wasted hundreds of dollars' worth of bourbon."

"And pouring it down my throat isn't wasting it?"

"Not if it makes you more friendly."

He puts his hand on her arm and she shakes him off. There's

a set to his jaw that sends another rush of blood straight to my groin. A twinge of pure pleasure at what's unfolding.

Her shoulders hunch, then a second later she unfurls them, straightening her spine and meeting the boy's gaze head on. The smile on her lips is cold. "This is as friendly as I get."

"Not what I heard." His lips widen into a knowing smirk that makes my breaths shorten. "I heard you can be a lot friendlier for a little cash incentive."

The girl stiffens, eyes sneaking to the side to capture the location of the other boys in the room before her attention refocuses on the one right in front of her. When she speaks, her voice sounds bored. "Oh, did you?"

"Yeah. I heard you could suck my balls dry for a hundred."

A new twist. I don't hate it.

The curl of her lip hits me in my chest. Where it pulled tight a few minutes before, it now floods with warmth.

"Because I look like a street walker? Try doubling that and you can go on my wait list for a hand job." She gives him a butter-wouldn't-melt smile. "Although, I have to warn you, there's little chance you'll reach the top before I finish school and then you're shit out of luck."

I smile at her sass, filing the information away in case it comes in handy later. A working girl, someone who might be amenable to suggestions. The proximity could work against me, but it might also be worth it to control the narrative more closely than I've managed with my overseas compatriots.

If this girl takes requests.

If she'll do anything after tonight.

"Well, we won't pay you now. Not with that attitude."

The ringleader slides off his seat to stand in front of her, crowding her, towering above her. He grips her chin in his hand, the fingers digging in so hard it'll leave bruises. He wrenches her to face him, smirking at her discomfort.

His friend moves out from the bar, circling around to close in behind her. With his left hand, he takes her hair, curling his hand around until it becomes a leash. His right lands on her shoulder, sliding down to tease at the edge of her throat.

Fuck, yes.

Now this... this is a party.

At the door, tight t-shirt is stroking himself through his jeans, smile broadening until his white teeth flash. "That dress looks like it's too warm for you," he calls out, winking to the friend standing in front of her. The boy obliges, reaching out to roll up its lower hem until it sits on her hips.

Her face is calm, impassive, but her eyes dart around the room, flickering away to the side, to the ground, over her shoulder. Trying and finding no help.

My conscience flashes again but it's weak.

She's fine. They're not even touching her, not really. If she wanted help she could scream. I'll intervene... just give it another minute. Maybe two.

"You want to suck me off while my friend fucks you?" the boy in front asks with the studious attention such a serious request demands. "Or you want to take it in turns so you can give each of us your full attention like a good little whore?"

Her left hand flashes to the side, grabbing something from the counter, then she falls to her right, hair tearing loose from the restraining hand, rolling over and scrambling to her feet like some kind of whizz at parkour.

It takes a second for me to work out what she's holding. Only registering when I see the glint of metal, then I bolt from my seat, running for the door, my spell broken.

Fuck.

It's the knife for peeling off the seals on the liquor bottles. Not big, not flashy, but my dad keeps it sharp.

I plunge down the stairs, praying I'll make it in time.

CHAPTER THREE

ROSA

THE BLADE LOOKS LAUGHABLY TINY, EVEN CLUTCHED IN MY miniature hand. A fiddly little knife for performing fiddly little chores.

Not much of a weapon to hold off three attackers. The bourbon I scoffed earlier clouds my head, even with the surfeit of adrenaline now pumping through my body.

All I wanted was to get drunk at a party, eat far too much junk food, and go home, complaining all the way about Finley's bad relationship timing and why couldn't she keep dating someone with a nice roomy car?

Now I'd kill for my feet to be blistering from walking too far in heels.

These three fuckwits who appear to think I'm part and parcel of the free entertainment on offer have officially ruined my night. A thrill of fear shudders through me, morphing into indignation, into anger. Who gave them the fucking right?

One stab wound each would transfer this lingering pull of trepidation from me to them, the place it rightly belongs.

A nice scar to remind them not to gang up on a girl. A wound just bad enough so they're the ones triggered into an anxiety attack when all they wanted was a few shots of free booze.

"We don't want any trouble," the boy nearest the door says. Like it wasn't *troubling* that he stationed himself in front of it to make it impossible for me to leave. "Just put down the knife and we can all go back to the party."

"You want to get back to the party, you're welcome to go," I tell him and thank fuck my voice stays steady rather than joining in the full body wobble that's happening elsewhere.

The boy with black hair, who apparently thought I was put on this earth to suck him off, lunges for me, retreating when I twist my arm his way.

Everything is happening too quickly. I need a plan. Beyond pointing the stabby end of a miniature knife at them.

My breath slams in and out of my chest. Sights, smells, sounds hit me in such a constant stream that I'm overwhelmed, unable to put it to use, unable to even categorise the information.

I turn towards black-haired boy, thinking he's moved a step closer. Then spin on my heel as the boy who'd grabbed my hair moves.

They're both advancing and I don't have a plan.

They're both advancing and it will be a simple thing to over-power me and steal the knife.

I scream, running straight for the boy blocking the door.

His eyes widen, hands immediately up in a defensive position.

Then he sidesteps, and the door opens, a large blond man filling the space, the whole space, and how the fuck is that possible that someone can be large enough to fill the whole fucking *doorway*, then he steps forward, grabs my wrist, pulls the knife free with his other hand, spins me, my back to his front, and clutches me against his chest, hugging hard, incapacitating me.

Three against one didn't come close to inspiring the level of terror that envelops me now. This fourth member of their rape troupe is gargantuan.

A sob of pure terror catapults from my throat before I scream, "Let me go!"

There must be a move to get out of this hold. Something to do with elbows but I can't get one free, let alone manoeuvre it back into his gut.

In a second, he twists me again, throwing me over his shoulder, stepping outside and dumping me in the hallway.

The door slams shut in my face.

What?

Everything happened so quickly, I'm dizzy. I don't really understand the sequence of events but I'm safe. I don't have my knife any longer but I'm safe.

A synapse in my brain fires wrong and I turn, pounding my fist on the study door. "Let me in."

Even though I obviously don't want to go inside. No. I *want* to be on this side of the door, but the acclimation period sped past too quickly and now I'm scrambled.

A girl wolf-whistles as she walks by and I see my dress is still rolled up my hips, leaving just my tights as cover. I adjust myself then recall my jacket is still inside. My jacket with my house keys and my wallet with my student ID and I do actually need those things. I can't stand the thought of those callous fucks pawing through them, looking at my terrible licence photo and laughing.

My palm hits against the door before I form the coherent thought to enter. "Hey. Let me in."

The door opens, giant blond man using the entire space again.

Except he's not a man. He's a boy my age.

His right hand is on the doorframe beside my head. The knuckles are grazed and spattered with blood. There are flecks across his face. Easily visible because of his pale complexion, matching to his fair hair.

"Yes?"

I swallow, heart beating with such force I can feel it in my throat. His eyes are a raucous blue, like the sea glass I used to collect from the beach when my mum took me as a child. Collect, then smash apart so I could see the difference in the worn opaque outside and the clean shine of the inside.

That's his colour. That same depth as the sharp edge.

They soften the longer my gaze rests upon them, then I give a start. I'm staring. "My jacket's on the seat."

He moves aside, letting me enter. One boy, the ringleader, is against the far wall, bent double, holding his stomach like he's afraid his insides will fall out if he pulls them away. Another boy rests with his back against the bar, legs splayed on the floor, between two stools. Blood pours through the hand he has clapped across his mouth.

"Don't you fucking move," a deep voice rumbles and I freeze, my hand outstretched, halfway towards the jacket. I'm scared to look but I have to.

I have to understand the threat.

My neck seizes in a painful muscle contraction as I turn, fear manifesting as a cramp.

But it relaxes as I see the warning wasn't for me. Big Blond glares at the boy who was blocking the door, now on his hands and knees near a large, stained wood cabinet.

The boy who's now scared. Fear is the only thing written across his face.

Once I see it, it's hard to look away. The flutter in my stomach is a new sensation. Satisfaction? The sweet taste of karma served piping hot?

Whatever it is, I want more. I could drown in this stuff and die happy.

"She's a fucking whore," says the boy on his knees, his dark eyes gleaming with menace.

Personally, I would have left well enough alone, but I guess I'm not like these boys. My mind isn't warped like theirs for a start.

He spits blood to the side before grinning, his teeth water-colour crimson. "Is that how you're getting your kicks these days, Trent? Paying hookers to come to your parties?"

"You shut your fucking mouth." The blond boy—who must be the Trent in question—hauls him to his feet, bunching his shirt and holding him inches off the ground. He then shoves him against the wall hard enough that his skull bounces off it with a crack.

The kid opens his mouth again, unbelievable, and Trent smashes his fist into it. A spatter of blood and saliva goes flying while the injured boy's smile grows wider.

"My dad's going to fucking kill you," he whispers, then stops talking as the next punch hits him in the throat.

"If anyone asks, I'll swear under oath he tripped," I say sweetly, craning my neck to get a better view of the carnage.

"You got your jacket?"

No. I got distracted by the entertainment.

I grab it now, circling the bar to grab a very nice bottle of bourbon while I'm at it, holding it aloft. "Mind if I take one for the road?"

The smile turns Trent from a menacing hulk to a giant marshmallow. I stare for a moment, licking my lips as I take in his gigantic frame once more, this time without the tint of fear.

He's so well put together it should be criminal. I wonder if Finley would object if we kept one of him by the front door to scare away case workers.

But he's probably got a girlfriend. Or maybe two or three. I'm sure he could easily handle at least three. Maybe four.

Handle them and never disappoint a single one.

I waggle the bottle as a farewell, then slip out the door, a shiver of delight working its way down my spine as I hear the crack of knuckles against bone.

I really, really, really hope that was the boy's face.

"Where the fuck did you get to?" Finley asks, bouncing from a side room and grabbing hold of my arm. "Ooh, presents!"

She relieves me of the burden, frowning at the label. "This looks old."

"It is old. That's what makes it expensive."

"Any good?"

"Buggered if I know." I stick out my tongue, eyes travelling back along the hallway just in case the blond snack has finished with beating duty for the night and wants to relax and have some fun.

No sign of him. Pity.

"My palate is about as sophisticated as the rest of me," I add, turning back to Finley with a smile. "You want to stay much longer?"

"Fuck no. My pockets are crammed with pizza, and I've tucked half a bottle of vodka in my bag for a chaser. If we don't leave soon, I'll start to attract rats."

———

A FEW HOURS LATER, we're safely home, feet up, alternating between passing the bottle of bourbon and the bottle of vodka back and forth.

"Trent?" Finley asks when I get to the end of my heavily edited story. No need to parade everything in front of her. She doesn't need to know that the evening could have taken quite a different turn. "Pretty sure Ben said that's the name of the guy throwing the party. You should have stuck around longer, girl. His dad must be loaded to own a house that size."

"Really?" I bring up the pictures of him I've stored carefully in my memory. The first, where he looked like an angry giant who'd come to break shit and take names. The second, where his smile transformed him into a gigantic teddy bear.

A teddy bear who—upon reflection—had a raging hard-on when he burst into the room. Either that or a third leg was tucked down the front of his jeans.

Whatever tipped him off to what was happening, it seemed coming to my rescue had disturbed him mid-action. I can envision the perfectly coiffed girl he must have left behind while he intervened to beat the shit out of my tormentors. Imagine having someone that large in your mouth when he suddenly turns into a white knight and gallops off to another girl's rescue.

Bet she was pissed.

"What're you giggling about, hm?" Finley reaches over to tickle me, making my laughs so much worse that I'm soon struggling to breathe.

"Stop," I blurt along with a snort. "There's no need to resort to torture."

"Shh," Finley says, eyes widening. "You'll wake Lily."

"Fuck," I say, giggling again. "I completely forgot she existed."

We collapse together, barely able to draw in air through our shared mirth. "Tell me what you were laughing at before or I'll drag her out of her room so we can interrogate you en masse."

"I might have remembered how well-endowed he was," I sputter.

"You should have got some," Finley says with the wise tonal qualities of an old woman who lives alone in a forest. "At his level of wealth, he probably ejaculates gold."

I smack my lips together and she holds a hand over her mouth to stop the gales of laughter from waking our slumbering flatmate.

"Time to call it a night," I say with genuine reluctance.

Although I'd love to stay up—it's been ages since I've had so much fun sitting on the couch—I have a shit tonne of assignments to get on top of before Monday and I can't leave them, not with work taking up four afternoons a week and visits to Mum using the rest.

It's not a lot, I remind myself as I peel enough clothes off to make it look like I've changed for bed. There are people working full time and going to uni. People not studying at all who have two or three different jobs just to make ends meet.

I'm lucky. I still have the freedom to do the things that are important to me.

Still, thinking of luck leads my thoughts back to the blond boy who looks better every time I pull out his memory. Ben probably knows his surname if I ever want to look him up. Not that I *would*, that's not really my style, but knowing I *could* still makes me happy.

I pull a toy out of my side drawer, checking my main door is fully closed before I turn it on to be rewarded with its steady hum. As I gently tease it around my clit, using wider and wider circles so I can edge myself rather than opting for a quick release, Trent fills out the visual board in my mind's eye as effectively as he filled that doorway.

He puts his hand on my shoulder, the one with blood ground into the knuckles and bruises flowering underneath, guiding me to my knees.

My fingers unzip him, freeing the full gloriousness of his

erect cock. So large that even my watering mouth struggles to take him inside, choking on his thrusts as his hand rests on the back of my head, fingers gently stroking my hair.

Then he takes my hand and eases me to my feet, my neck craning to keep his face in view. He pushes me against the wall and suddenly he switches. No longer Mr Meek and Mild but the bulldog ready to attack, a menacing tint to his eyes, those thick fingers closing around my neck as he holds me in place, his other hand dipping between my legs, inserting into me while his breath is hot and heavy on my cheek.

His rough gasps as good an indicator of how much he wants me as the throbbing monster between my legs, stretching me like some gigantic novelty dildo.

And the image is too delicious, the hallucinated sounds, the pulsing response to his imaginary touch too great to deny. I clamp my legs over the vibrator, fumbling for the off button when what had been pleasurable becomes overwhelming, my mouth dry and lolling open, dragging in each large breath.

He doesn't even know your name.

Mm. But isn't that half the attraction?

The Trent living in my memory will be a thousand times more pliable than any man in real life could be. A pity I can't conjure his credit card into reality, but a girl can't have everything she wants.

If I had *that* sort of money, I'd never leave bed.

CHAPTER FOUR

TRENT

It must be well into Sunday morning by the time the house empties and I haul myself off to sleep. The house is a shambles but nothing that a baker's dozen of cleaners shouldn't be able to put right by the time my father's private jet touches down at six in the evening.

He'll be most pissed about the missing bottles from his private stash of dark spirits but there's a chance he won't discover those for a few weeks. In the first flushes of a new relationship, he'll be spending time with his new wife and indulging her taste for champagne.

A few weeks, maybe a few months from now, when the shine wears off, he'll be back to drinking alone in the evenings and pretending it's because he's deep and serious instead of a man who mostly hates people and wants to be left alone.

I strip off and slide between the sheets, keeping my discarded tee close by for mopping up duty. When I close my eyes, I see the dark blonde beauty from my dad's study. The grainy images of her from the internal cameras and the far better vision of her in real life.

My phone is handy, cued to the start of the encounter in the library. I have to shake my hand, opening and closing my fingers a few times, before my swollen knuckles can safely grip the device. I should probably have my hands soaking in ice water right now, getting the swelling down before it does more damage.

Instead, I force them to curl around the phone and hold the screen steady.

The replay lacks the excitement of the moment but it's good. Better than good. Great, even fantastic, when compared to what my overseas service providers have managed so far.

Her face is so expressive. The changes from moment to moment exquisitely detailed. The two boys are crowding her now, one with his hands in her hair, the other rolling her dress up her thighs.

The video flutters at the point I cut it, then repeats from the start but I toss it aside, imagining an alternate ending. One without a knife and a standoff. One where I didn't come barrelling through the door, taking out the punishment I deserve on the lads who were following those same inclinations in real life.

In my head, she gets dragged off the stool, the boy twisting her hair to force her over its seat instead, shoving her dress up and her tights down. He barely waits until she's uncovered before jamming his dick deep inside her. When she opens her mouth to scream, the boy in front crams his cock down her throat, gagging her more effectively than any muzzle.

The boy at the door moves across, still stroking himself, waiting until the boy pumping into her gives a last trio of grunts, then pulls out of her, satiated. He shoves him out of the way, using the cum he left behind as lube to thrust his way deep into her arse.

I come with a low groan, catching most of it in my t-shirt, stripping it off to wipe up the rest.

Fuck. I want the real thing. My eyes want to be open, watching her struggle and gag and scream as his hard cock penetrates the soft tissue of her arse. I want to see the fear in her eyes grow dull as she realises there's no way out, not this time, not for her.

I want to watch as the guy face fucking her withdraws and the guy coming in her arse wraps his hands around her throat to put her out of her misery.

I want that, but while still keeping her around to film the whole thing again.

This time, when I close my eyes, I don't see them. I see me. See me touching her and running my hands over her body. Twisting and turning her to maximise my pleasure, taking exquisite satisfaction from her deepening distress.

Anything I want.

Because it's not real.

I sit up, walking across the room to toss my t-shirt into the laundry hamper. A delightful surprise for whoever's tasked with washing my clothes this week. I don't need things to be real. I just need them to look that way.

It really doesn't seem that much to ask.

As I try to fall asleep, the image plays on an internal loop. The caution turning to fear. The dawning realisation that things have gone well beyond her control and the only way back is to comply. To submit.

There's something seriously wrong with you.

No shit, Sherlock.

I roll on my side, curling my knees towards my chest, flexing my fingers to make the injuries burn, the only punishment for the evil tainting my soul.

THE TIGHTHEAD PROP on the opposing team clips my shoulder as I run past, a shit-eating grin in full swing, letting me know it was deliberate. Or, if not deliberate, something he nevertheless enjoyed.

I let him pass, remembering too late that Zach missed kick-off so isn't flanking me, ready to give a physical demonstration of why that shit doesn't fly. Not with us.

The jolt of recall ignites a burn of distemper. He's been late to far more matches than usual, lately. If he doesn't watch out, he'll be off the team, even the reserves.

When the same player next comes within striking distance, still smirking, I take the spark of fury out on him, striking an upper jut to his jaw.

I'm too big to be sneaky. What Zach could get away with through quick footwork and angled shoulders, leaves me exposed.

"Get off the field," the team coach yells when the whistle brings me to a halt. "Now," he adds when I don't immediately move to comply. I edge in the right direction and his face turns thunderous until I pick up some speed.

I land in front of him. Bristling even though I'm in the wrong. "What's the matter?"

"You really don't want to be asking me that question, boy," he replies, turning his back on me as he whistles for the game to recommence, one of the benched players filling my spot with ease.

"Did the other team steal your girl or something?" Price asks with a shit-eating grin as I take a seat next to him. "You know just because you're running doesn't mean coach can't see when you throw a punch."

"He deserved it."

My hands squeeze into fists at the memory, and I loosen them with a wince. The knuckles are still swollen from the fight on Saturday. The damage makes them clumsy, so even when I'm not aiming them at smirking dickheads, I keep knocking them against stuff by accident, reigniting the pain.

I don't mind it. Each time I feel the ache and burn, it reminds me of the recording now stored on my phone and in three different reservoirs in the cloud. Most of yesterday was spent wandering around the house, annoying the cleaners as I tried to help, sporting a boner.

All that, and I didn't even get the name of the girl.

"No doubt. Unfortunately, the rules of the game are working against you there." Price's attention is completely captured by a pass that goes out of bounds. "Hey, ref. Want to grow some eyes?" He ticks his tongue against his teeth with a disgusted groan as the players resume position, no one being called out.

"Where's Zach?" I ask, glancing around the remaining players. "I thought he was just running a few minutes late."

"Probably ducked out of school again. I doubt coach will put him back on the field this season with the number of practices he's missed."

I grunt in agreement, feeling annoyed. Caylon and I both moved schools to keep our group together when Zach got expelled, yet again. Now, long months after the terrible business with Robbie brought us closer together, we're all busting apart.

"Your other buddy's missing, too," Price remarks idly, staring around the field. "Couldn't hack the pace."

Given everything else Caylon's got on his mind, 'the pace' of this tinpot school rugby team probably doesn't rank as highly as Price might think.

The game winds on and I don't get back out there until five minutes shy of the end. Hardly enough time to use my excess energy. When the final whistle goes and we all run to the showers, I still feel as wound up as I did at the start.

"Come in here, Weybourne," coach says when I try to duck out the back. He waits until I take a seat, then asks, "Is there something going on I should know about?"

I shrug. "I'm just on edge."

A nice turn of phrase that roughly translates to 'I'm not sleeping.' Robbie's corpse makes a rude appearance, jolting me awake at least once a night. The growing feeling of abandonment from my friends just makes everything seem worse.

"Well, sort it before you're out in the thick of it, next time. That shot was obviously deliberate. I'll have to show the recordings to the vice principal. We'll let you know by end of day tomorrow if you're still on the team or if that move got you sidelined for the rest of the season."

The frustration from being off the field for most of the game today is already eating at me, ruining the equanimity playing hard usually gifts me. If I get benched, that frustration will be all day, every day.

The fear comes flooding out as anger. "It was just a fucking accident."

Coach's expression barely changes but I know he's taking note. I clench my hand, so the pain focuses me. "Sorry. I didn't mean to shout. I just got wound up during the game, all right? It won't happen again."

"This isn't the first time, Weybourne. Get your shit together. If the vice clears you to play again, try remembering it's the entire school reputation on the line."

I nod, making the right noises, but my internal system is still running at far too high a heat when I walk out of there, heading back to the front of the grounds where my car's parked.

The idea of this piece of shit school having a reputation is a joke. We're only here because it's so low on the decile rankings that a discreet bribe to the right officials got Zach a placement after he'd run through his last chances everywhere else.

Since I've attended, not only have I not learned anything new, but I can also feel my grasp on my former education slipping.

Not that I'm trying to be an academic or anything but the option to go on to tertiary education would be a bonus.

This late in the day, there are few pupils still within the boundary fences of McKenzie High School. Those that are lingering around, look like they're waiting on their slower compatriots. A couple are from the drama department, fitted out with 'ye olde' costumes for the Sweeney Todd update they're staging later in the year.

"Wait up," Caylon calls from behind me. "Missed you at the game."

"Because you weren't there," I mutter, hands on hips. "You want a lift?"

"If you don't mind." He shoots me a sideways glance. "Zach wants to talk to us about something."

"Then he should've come to practice like he's meant to." I still turn the car toward his house, not riled enough to miss out on whatever pearls of wisdom he sees fit to dispense. "Hey, you're good at tracking people, right?"

My frustration needs a new outlet and, as it has done a dozen times since the night of my party, my thoughts drift back to the nameless girl in my dad's study. The one who might be able to produce the video I want, if only I can trace her, proposition her, and offer her so much money she can't refuse.

"Sure," Caylon quips back at me. "I type names into this thing called a search engine—"

"Funny guy. What'd you do if you don't have a name?"

"Reverse image search."

I wait until we're stopped at the next set of lights to toss him my phone. "Can you get anything from that?"

He watches it through, then rewinds, screenshotting a few images and bumping it over to his device. "It's not great quality but maybe. You know anything else about her?"

I wobble my hand in midair. "She's around our age and she might work as a prostitute."

"Right."

"Just to pay for uni." I don't even know why I add the clarification. Pretty sure Caylon doesn't give a flying fuck.

"Yeah. Like you know you can just use the red pages if you're desperate. Or try drinking when you're at Stefan's club and see what you attract."

"I have a hard enough time getting my macros balanced without adding alcohol to the mix." I take the next turn, flipping the bird at the impatient driver who might have had the right of way if he wasn't too slow. "Does that mean you can't do it?"

"Maybe. How'd you come across this unnamed female?"

"She was at my party on Saturday." I hesitate before adding, "She might know Able Comers and Eric Vallance."

Caylon turns his lazy gaze back my way, lips creasing with amusement. "Oh, she might. Might she? Has it occurred to you simply to ask them directly? You're better acquainted with those tools than I am."

I clear my throat and flex my hand, showcasing the array of bruises across my knuckles, as colourful as any autumnal display. "We had a slight difference of opinion."

"Must've been pretty bad to get you riled." He shakes his head, turning to stare blankly out the side window.

His face, the same face I've been around since we were in primary school, loses all expression. It's been doing it more and more often lately.

Or maybe I'm just noticing more since the stuff with

Robbie went down. Noticing, because I'm checking for cracks in my two closest friends to mirror what I'm feeling. Hopeful I'm not the only one whose nights are ruined with a constant play-by-play of the same few seconds of the same night until I want to tear the world apart with my teeth and bare hands.

"I'll ask. When do you need it by?"

"No hurry."

He gives me a strange glance; one I can't decipher. Then I run out of time to interpret it, anyway, pulling up at Zach's gate and punching in the access code.

Inside, the housekeeper Zelda is wiping the counters in the kitchen and jerks her chin upstairs at Caylon's query. I lag behind him, my hands shaking for no good reason. A surfeit of adrenaline that didn't get used up in the game, perhaps. Maybe just someone walking over my grave.

"Lilac Tanner turned up at school today," Zach announces when we're both in his bedroom. "She's agreed to complete five tasks—"

"No," Caylon says in his flattest tone.

"I've already negotiated."

"Then do it again and do it better. She's meant to stay away. That was the arrangement."

"What tasks?" I ask. Tanner is the girl who kicked off the disastrous interaction that led to Robbie being shot. Hardly someone I want on closer acquaintance but Zach knows what I like even if he doesn't realise how desperate I am to get my hands on more.

"Whatever you like," he answers with his eyes narrowed, then relaxing when he sees I'm on board.

Caylon bristles beside me but all I can think about is the relief of getting a new supply. If Zach's back in business, then a couple of new videos will set a course correct on my brain. I might finally get a good night's sleep. I won't need to pursue this new girl and corrupt her with my depravity.

"Nothing illegal," he adds, severely curtailing my ambitions.

"I want videos," I tell him, leaving the rest up to his imagination. "And I get two of those slots since you negotiated without us."

Now Zach's the one bristling but I ignore his annoyance as well. He's the one in the wrong here and he knows it. Going around behind the scenes, making deals with the enemy... What the fuck is he thinking?

If I judge by the strange wistful glint in his eye, it's possible he's not thinking at all.

"Trent," my father says the moment I arrive home. A bad sign. "Can you come in here a minute?"

Even worse.

I saunter into the kitchen, trying not to glower at my new stepmother, all twenty-one years of her. Anyone looking would presume she belonged with me rather than him, apart from her being so perfectly put together that I can't stand to look directly into her face.

"We got a phone call from the school today. Your phys-ed teacher said you punched a kid midway through a game."

I shrug, sitting on a stool and rubbing my palm on the counter. This is about the spot where Augie went to town with his date at the party. I can imagine some of the gleam came from her butt cheeks rubbing all over the marble.

"There's no need to smile," Sashe says in what might count for sternness over at her favourite spa. "It's a serious matter."

"Sure, Mum."

"Trent!"

"It was an accident in the middle of a game. I was swinging my arm forward when he was trying to sidestep and it..." I make the gesture and noise for an explosion.

Judging from their expressions, neither of them are impressed.

"You're off the team," my father tells me. "You told me when you switched schools you'd keep your temper under control and now this."

"Don't be ridiculous. You don't get to decide that."

"I'm not—" He breaks off, getting his temper under control. "I'm passing on what your teacher told me."

"He's not a teacher."

"That's hardly the point!"

My combative side comes out, but I clamp down on it. In a fight with my dad, I'm never going to come out on top. "I'll talk to him tomorrow. Once he's had time to calm down from whatever was bugging him today, I'm sure he'll listen to reason."

"You punched a kid."

My hands clench into fists and I have to force them flat against the marble. "I accidentally hit someone *my* age during a high contact sport."

But my father's stopped listening. My new stepmother stares at my hands, then takes a few steps until she's sheltering behind her husband. The rainbow of bruises doesn't lend a lot of weight to my cause.

I slip upstairs to my room, closing the door and leaning back against it while my eyes scan the familiar space.

My father being antsy is nothing new. He's like this every time he takes on a new girlfriend, a new wife. Like only constant vigilance and outward aggression will stop the world from taking her away again.

But nobody needs to wrestle his partners away. Give it six months and his behaviour will slip into its old patterns. Give it a year or two and she'll move out all by herself. By that time, his affections will already have moved on, so he'll be glad to see her go. To create room for the next. And the next.

Right now, it seems like far too long to wait.

My relationship at home might crumble but at least there's hope my friendship with Zach and Caylon is coming right. Like everything in my life is on a gigantic scale and the balance is tipping.

CHAPTER FIVE

ROSA

Harry—my second and final client of the day—wilts on top of me. His hair is still wet from the shower I made him take, and he smells of my co-worker's mango body wash.

It's Friday and although it's been a month or more since the party, I've got into the strange habit of painting Trent's face overtop all my clients. It's weird—it even feels weird to me and I'm the one doing it—but for some reason it's made my sessions easier.

Not that they're hard exactly but you can tire of fucking and being fucked as easily as you can tire of any other job. Some days I long to swap places with the checkout operator at the supermarket just to switch up the routine.

A little thrill that doesn't hurt anyone is exactly what the doctor ordered.

I wriggle to the side a little so I can grab a full breath. Harry isn't fat, but he's solid, through and through. Built like a pound of butter that someone thoughtfully sculpted muscles on.

Now, he rolls off me, pulling me with him, resting his face in the crook of my neck. Snuggling is part of our contract; one of the few clients who likes to be touched after.

"How's your son doing?" I ask, picking up the threads from our last conversation. "Did he adjust to the new school okay?"

"He's talking more again," he says, playing with my hair. "I thought we were going to lose all the progress we'd made, but he's adjusting. The teacher invited us to sit in class with him, but he didn't like that one bit."

"That's a good sign, isn't it? A kid wanting their space?"

"He probably just hated the change in routine." Harry lets out a long sigh, tinged with worry. "Hopefully, now he's a bit settled, we can keep his placement even though we're out of the district. I can't imagine how stressful it'll be for him if we need to move schools again."

He continues talking and I answer as needed while my mind wanders. I think about the future, getting my degree, finding work. Having a kid of my own someday to worry if they're comfortable at school, making friends or not. If they'll be the quiet girl or boy in the corner or the squirmy kid who can never sit still.

"You remind me of her, a little."

I'm startled, quickly replaying the recent conversation to see what I've missed. "Of Alex?" His ex-wife.

"Yeah. She had the same gentle way about her. Loved to be touched, didn't much like talking."

The comparison concerns me a little. Not because I know the woman, but because it means what he's doing here is slipping out into his real life.

I know Harry's lonely, know he doesn't feel comfortable dating while his son struggles with a learning disorder and the large adjustment to his parents being divorced.

Our arrangement is for simplicity. To get him what he needs

while he can't get it through traditional means. His son is currently going through the diagnostic process, but Harry thinks he's on the spectrum, which might mean a longer period than usual before he's stable enough to consider introducing another woman into his life.

But he's paying me to be a substitute girlfriend not a real one. Affection is fine, friends is fine, anything more and I'll need to cut him loose with a recommendation.

"You didn't like that, huh?"

His eyes are glued to my face, reading my expression with an ease that I'd love to find in a genuine prospect. "It's not that I didn't like it, but it worries me."

"Don't. I'm thinking about trying again with Alex, that's all. I miss her."

"Does she want you to try again?"

His eyes twinkle with laughter. "Well, that's the million-dollar question, isn't it? We're getting on so much better now the divorce is over, but I've probably taken it the wrong way. It's what she accused me of while we were together."

When his allotted time is up, he stirs and I take off and dispose of his condom, getting dressed in a kimono and pants while he uses the bathroom for a quick tidy, striding through to the shared kitchen to put the kettle on for tea or coffee.

"Not for me," Harry says from the doorway. "Gotta scoot off early for a meeting. We're good for next week?"

"Yeah, we're good." I walk him to the door, waving as his car pulls out from the curb.

"Ugh," Ceecee says, wandering in from her room. "Want to swap client lists? My three o'clock just called to cancel."

"You're kidding? It's nearly four." I pull out an extra mug and spoon in the coffee and three sugars for her. "You need to institute a cancellation fee."

"I'm sure that'd go over a hit." She pulls an extra chair close to the one she's sitting on to put her feet up. "You done for the day?"

I nod, settling into a chair opposite and gulping at my coffee.

"Did Rina tell you the new fees?"

I groan, tilting my head back until I'm staring at the ceiling. "Please, no. I'm barely skating by as it is."

With a dozen regulars—some weekly, some fortnightly—filling out my eight appointments a week, I already work four half-days.

From that, once I deduct the rent and utilities for this place, the subsidised rent for my flat and *those* shared utilities, then set aside the weekly provision for my quarterly student fees, then deduct incidentals like textbooks or materials, I'm left with about forty bucks a week to my name.

Not even enough for a daily coffee and muffin from the student café.

"The insurance adjustor decided we're a moral hazard and bumped the rates."

"How much?"

When she supplies the new figure, I wince, instantly recalibrating my income against expenses and forecasting for the rest of the year.

"You could sublease," Ceecee reassures me as my expression tells her exactly where my calculations landed. "There's a girl at the prossie collective who's looking for a new spot but can't afford a full room. A few hours here and there will cover it."

"Nah, you're good. I'll sort something out."

I don't mind the share arrangement we have; God knows I could never afford a place on my own and there's no way I want to work from my flat. But there's a world of difference between renting a room in a shared house and sharing an actual bed.

With another appointment, maybe two, per week, I'll be fine. The problem is finding a regular who fits into my available timetable and passes my screening. The mental energy required for my subs means I'm already at my limit there, and I'm on the pricey end for straight sex, which makes it harder to find repeat business.

"Let me know if you change your mind."

My thoughts are so taken up with the increase, I lose track of time while stripping the bed and putting the sheets in the wash. There's another set ready in the dryer and I use those rather than folding them and taking from the top of the stack in the linen cupboard.

When I check the time on my phone, it's gone past four-thirty. I come back to earth with a start, racing from the door, making my bus with seconds to spare.

The owner-operated brothel is in Sydenham and my flat is all the way over in Papanui, a twenty-minute drive that takes me a change of bus at the exchange and a spare hour ten since I rely on public transport.

It doesn't help that I need to collect my laptop from a tiny repair shop in the central city. By the time I make it to the counter, the assistant pointedly frowns at the clock.

"I know. I'm sorry."

The bespectacled boy gives a grunt and holds out his hand. I stare at it for a moment before my brain clicks into gear, reminding me there was a claim stub.

Thankfully, it's in the third place I look.

He brings the battered computer to the front desk, opening it to display the replaced screen.

"Beautiful. How much?"

"There was a lot of spyware on the hard drive I had to clear."

"Mm-hm." I school my features so the impatience doesn't leak onto my face. Given I'm the one keeping him past closing, it wouldn't be appreciated. "Must be all those porn sites I visit."

He cracks a smile that makes him look about twelve, then his face resumes its blankness. "Not that sort... There was stuff tracking keystrokes and a program to take over the webcam."

My stomach gives a nasty jolt. "The camera? Like... remotely?"

"Yeah. You buy this new?"

I snort. "I got it at a school auction, so it's had about thirty previous users."

His expression clears. "Right. That makes sense. If they're lending them out, they often put tracking programs on the hard drive."

"It's gone now, though?"

"Yeah." He pats it like a lap dog. "Clean as a whistle."

I give him my credit card, head tilting as I add the charges into the mix and come up with another impetus to book a new client. Or two. Or three.

"You've got a thirty-day guarantee," he adds, passing back my card and receipt. "Anything goes wrong in that time, bring it back here and we'll take another look, free of charge."

"Thanks."

Once I leave, I dawdle in town for a bit, checking out the new stores and window shopping for things I can't afford. A few years ago, I would have stayed for hours but now I crave the peace of going home, sitting down, and vegging out for the rest of the night.

Lily's going to her senior dance, which means I get Finley to myself for the evening. A lovely treat. Unless she's going out on the prowl, but even being on my lonesome has a siren call to it.

I snort as I get on the bus, pulling my cardigan close around my shoulders and a keeping a firm grip on my bag. Just call me a nana at eighteen and be done with it.

To take full advantage of uni, I should mingle with the other design students more. Some of my fellow classmates could become future employers. Others could be good for networking, keeping my hat in the ring so personal referrals—the lifeblood of any creative industry—will come my way.

At the very least I should attend a few more parties.

But my experience at the last one has jaded me for a while. Everything worked out okay but there were a dozen other ways it could have ended, none of them good for me.

Deep in thought, I turn the corner, getting halfway to the flat before I notice there's a strange car parked by the curb opposite. The glass is tinted, not darkly but enough to make it difficult to tell if there's someone inside.

It looks far too expensive to be driven around this area. I hope whoever parked it there had the good sense to fit a strident alarm.

Probably joyriders.

I fumble my keys as I get towards the front door, opening it, nearly dropping the newly repaired laptop as I juggle it and my bag. Luckily, the table's just through the door and I heap everything on it, then turn back to retrieve my keys.

And pull up short, heart pounding.

A man stands there, dangling my keys from his fingers.

I react to the blocking-the-door bits of him before my brain puts his hulking form through my internal image recognition software, providing a match.

The blond boy from the party.

The blond boy I *liked* from the party.

A whole raft of new chemicals flood my bloodstream. Remembering his strength and size in a far glossier light. Remember the smashing-the-skulls-of-my-enemies with fondness.

"Hey, Trent, isn't it?"

He nods, adding, "Trent Weybourne."

I hold out my hand for the keys, which he drops into my palm. "And how can I help you, Mr Weybourne?"

Into bed, I add inside my head, though having come from work that's probably not the soundest idea.

"You're Rosa, yeah?"

"Sure." I toss my keys into my bag, wipe my palms on my jeans, then reach out my hand. "Let's try that again. I'm Rosa Fenn, nice to meet you. Thank you for saving my arse at the party the other night. Your bourbon was very much appreciated."

He rolls his eyes, a cautious smile broadening across his lips. "My dad's bourbon and I'll be sure not to pass on your compliments, otherwise, he might realise it's missing."

"Come in," I say, waving him towards a seat and closing the door. "Why are you here?"

Trent pulls out a chair but doesn't sit. His eyes move around the room, like he's looking for something or someone. His gaze shifts to me and his smile deepens. A tingle hits me, right in the belly, spreading out a warm glow until it's like there's a fire banked in there.

I hope he's come to see me. I hope it's for a good reason.

It's been ages since I had a boyfriend. A proper one. So long since my thoughts even travelled in that direction, but a large blond rich boyfriend seems like it would hit a multitude of spots. He's hitting some hard already, and he hasn't even asked me on a date.

"I have a proposition for you," he says slowly, his voice rich and buttery, rich and satisfying, or maybe it's just that it sounds filthy, filthy rich.

"Oh, yeah?" I arch my eyebrow because I know it makes me look playful. Lean forward because I know that even with my relatively modest blouse it makes my breasts look perky especially when I press my elbows closer together as I immediately do.

I lick my lips slowly, biting on the corner, wondering how many more moves I have up my sleeve because he still hasn't asked me anything and the clock's tick tick ticking on the wall behind me.

"Um, yeah. So, someone told me you were a prostitute, and I wondered if you're... I don't know how to word it properly... like, available? To hire." His eyes cautiously examine my face. "For a job."

My smile freezes in place as my stomach drops. As stunned as if he'd slapped me in the face. "Sure, we can talk about that."

I struggle to find the right tone, to keep my voice light so he doesn't know how disappointed I am. So he doesn't know the stupid daydreams I've been playing out inside my head.

"Just hold on a second while I grab a cup of coffee. You want a drink of anything?"

"I'm good," he says, sitting when I wave him towards the seat.

In the kitchen, I pop on the kettle, then grip hold of the bench, pressing as hard as I can, focusing on my clenching muscles instead of the disappointment.

It's okay. You need a new client, anyway. This is good.

Good. Yes, good.

Except I'm in no fit state of mind to take this boy on as a client. Not when I'm hiding in the kitchen, hoping I can drive back my urge to cry before I need to go back in the room and smile.

You don't need a boyfriend. You've already got far too much on your plate.

True. Although, it would have been good to have something nice heaped on one of my plates for a change. Something less like hard work. Something to remind me I'm a teenager and meant to be enjoying myself while I've still got the energy.

The kettle boils and I tip my head back, so any tears reverse trajectory and get sucked back in. I make my coffee and plaster a smile onto my face before walking back through to the table.

"Now, what was this proposition?"

CHAPTER SIX

TRENT

When she walks out of the kitchen, I can't stop staring. There's so much more to her than I remember. So much more than I can see on the tiny screen of my phone.

Over the long weeks since the party, I've revisited her in my memory, time and time again, but the edges had curled, the image faded. Now, here she is, in full colour and bright as a thousand stars. My eyes eat her up like she's a buffet and I've just come off a week-long fast.

Beautiful.

My memory downplayed the shine of her hair, how the soft waves of it bounce against her shoulders. It didn't catch the gleam of brightness in her eyes, how it looks like she's on the verge of tears even though her smile is luminescent.

She's so perfect, I feel a pinch of desperation. I've imagined the end product so many times that if I can't get it—now I've finally worked up my nerve to ask—I'll be devastated.

No one else will do. My mind has inserted her into the role too many times to settle for another.

"Don't worry," she says in a soft voice. "Take your time."

I stare at her when I should be putting her at ease, making her feel comfortable enough that she'll consider my request. The seconds stretch into a minute, longer.

As the pressure to speak builds, I find myself less able to put my request into words, even though I practised at home like an idiot. Talking to myself in the bedroom mirror like I'd never spoken to a girl before.

"Were you waiting outside long?" she asks when I'm completely frozen, and I breathe out a sigh of relief.

"Not too long." I smile at the memory. "I knocked on the door before, but Lily answered, which was a bit of a shock. We know each other from school." Not quite the whole truth but good enough.

"No, you don't," she immediately retorts like she knows something. I meet her eyes, ready to rebut her claim, then she adds, "Lily goes to the shittiest high school in the city. There's no way someone who lives in your ginormous mansion goes to the same place."

My forehead creases. "You've met Zach, haven't you?"

She nods and I pause for a moment, wondering how much of what Zach, Caylon, and I have done with or to Lily has made it through to her ears.

Rosa seems like an easy girl to confide in. She probably knows more about Zach and Lily's short but tumultuous relationship than I do. "He goes to McKenzie, too."

At that, she laughs outright. "Sure, but Zach's a bad boy." Her voice drops an octave, becomes so husky that shivers rock out from my core, making my neck tingle. "Are you a bad boy, Mr Weybourne?"

In that second, that's all I want to be. So bad it would go

down in the history books, melting their pages when future students tried to read.

I clear my throat, pulling at the neck of my shirt. I wish I'd taken her up on the offer of a drink because something to do with my hands would be great right about now. Instead, I cast around for some inane small talk, landing on, "Have you lived here long?"

"You mean in this flat?" She glances around as though searching for reminders. "I moved in here back in February, when I turned eighteen."

"I haven't seen you at school."

"At your shit school?" When I glance over, she's wrinkling her nose with amusement. "Got moved ahead a few years and now I'm at uni. I'm sure if I were still at high school, I'd be stuck at McKenzie, too."

My skin is a size too small, like I spent all day in the sun and it's shrinking. I need to get out my offer before I overthink everything and the words stay trapped inside my mouth. "Those boys at the party..."

Her eyes crinkle at the corners. "The ones you beat up?"

"I—" he breaks off, shaking his head. "I mean, yeah, but... They said you were a prostitute."

"How very nineties of them. Do you want to reword that?"

My eyes widen in panic, sensing a trap. "Sex... worker?"

This time the grin escapes before she can rein it in. "Better. What about it?"

"I wanted to... I wondered if..."

"You said you want to hire me?"

"Yes." I sit back in my chair, relieved at the lack of surprise in her voice. "Are you available?"

She takes a seat opposite me, hitching her feet up on the crossbar so her knees rest above the line of the table. "I don't think you want to hire me, Trent. But I can give you some names—"

"No." I frown at the table, scared to make eye contact in case my mouth-brain connection fails again. "It has to be you."

There's a pause as she takes another sip from her drink, moving the coaster around on the table in small circles before replacing her cup. "What do you think I do?"

The question sounds like a test and, glancing at her, it seems like an exam I'm doomed to fail. I sidestep. "What are you studying at university?"

It's obvious to me she's doing the job for money. The flat screams of poverty in every warped baseboard, threadbare patch of carpet, and peeling floor tile.

I have money. For as long as I stay on the right side of my dad, I have lots of it. Enough to pay her way through university if that's what she's after. Enough to cover every client on her books.

All I need is a way in. An angle to work. A way to find the button to press that means I can get what I need.

"Engineering and design."

"You want to be a designer?"

"I want a straight answer to my question."

"You're a sex worker. We've already covered that."

A grin crosses her face then twists into a smirk. "Because we're all exactly the same and we all provide the same service."

The words sound innocent enough but there's a layer of thickness added to her voice that makes me wary. "I want a recording. Just... I can't stop seeing you on the night of the party, with the boys, before the knife. I want something similar that just goes a little further. Nothing terrible."

"You don't get to decide whether it's terrible. I don't do recordings."

"But you *could*," is my immediate retort. "I'll pay you double whatever you usually charge."

"There's nothing to double because I don't do recordings."

"Name your price, then." The whole negotiation is sliding out of my control. "What do you think is fair?"

"If you want a girl to perform for the camera, it's easy enough to find them. Go online." She drains the last of her drink and moves into the kitchen. I hear her rinsing it in the sink, then she returns to the table. "This isn't in my wheelhouse at all."

"It doesn't need to look professional or anything. I like the—"

"I know what you like, Trent. I helped Lily record some of what you like." Her eyes lock to mine, seeing everything. "It was your request, wasn't it?"

The photos and video I made Lily record for me are far tamer than what I planned to ask Rosa for. Zach's rule—nothing illegal—curtailed my requests.

Don't get me wrong, I adore them, still watch them, but if the pair are truly together as a couple like they seem to be, I won't have even those paltry clips to tide me over. Zach might not ask for them to be erased but it'll be the expectation. Nobody wants their friend jerking off to their girl, no matter how many years of friendship lie behind us.

Then a new, worse thought occurs to me. "There's nothing between us, I swear."

She stares at me, wide-eyed for a second, then bursts into giggles. "Oh my god," she says between spurts of laughter. "That isn't what I thought at all."

I sit back, my tension easing a little as I smile along with her amusement. "Oh, so now you're saying I couldn't get a girl like Lily?"

"Are you naturally competitive or did you have to work at it?"

"I—" My brain fizzles, unable to come up with the right answer. "I'm not competitive," I say finally, already knowing what's coming back my way.

"You'll have a better experience if you choose a worker who aligns with what you want. I'm not that girl. This isn't a challenge or a dare or a tease to make it harder for you. There are things I do and things I don't. The thing you want from me is at the nopest edge of my nope column."

"You're doing this to pay for uni, right?"

She shakes her head. "It doesn't matter what I'm using the money for. You're not listening."

The flat refusal eats away at my brain.

I spend my life agreeing to other people's wishes. I'm going to a crappy school because Zach got kicked out again, and he'd been excluded so many times, it was the only place that would take him.

I work with Stefan because Caylon started doing hacking work with him for the money and the rest of us got roped into it because that's what we do. We stick together and we help our friends.

Even at home, I stay out of the way. I'm sure half the exec team at dad's firm don't know he's got a son, let alone one who lives with him.

All the time, doing things for other people because I thought that's how the world worked. Except now I'm the one who wants something and the person I want it from isn't playing ball.

"How many years do you have left at uni? Two? Three?"

Her shoulders slump a little as she shakes her head and I try to imagine what she's seeing. A clueless boy sitting at her table, trying to get her to do something she patently doesn't want to do.

This shouldn't be a lot to ask.

It doesn't *sound* like a lot to ask.

"It's not a video of us if that's what worries you. It can just be you. Or you and someone else you pick, I don't—"

She holds up her hand, palm out, stop. "Please hear what I'm saying to you. I don't do recordings. I'm really not sure how else to explain it."

"I'll pay you—"

"I. Don't. Do. Recordings."

"—your tuition. For the rest of the year."

She tilts her head, and I plough forward, taking it as a sign of interest, as a chink in her thick armour.

"Whatever you need for school. The cost of your rent here. Textbooks. Groceries. Electricity. Send me a bill for all of it, and I'll pay. I just... I *need* this."

Rosa shifts her weight, her gaze somewhere on the floor. She stands, walking past me to the doorway and stopping there, cupping her elbows, nervous.

There's a vulnerability to her that wasn't in evidence before, and it breaks me to see it because I'm the one who put it there.

"I want you to leave."

I get to my feet. The weight of the rejection is so heavy I'm surprised I can stand. "Why? Why won't you help me?"

"I don't—"

"Do recordings," I finish for her, my voice thick with disappointment.

"Because I need to have an end date." Rosa shifts her weight again, frowning, the cupping elbows turning to a self-hug. "That's why." She drags her eyes up to meet mine, the effort visible. "I don't plan on doing this forever and I need to know that once I stop, it actually stops. It's nothing to do with you. It's me. A recording is forever."

"I'd never—"

She cuts her gaze away, and it's like my words break at the same time. Of course, I'd never, but that means nothing. Pam and Tommy never and I could still buy a copy today and that was before the internet really got going. Before people mastered all those new rabbit holes. Before the dark web.

Her explanation makes sense, but I still reject it. The frantic pulse in my brain insists it must be Rosa. No one else will do.

Lily was good. Lily was beautiful. But Lily never made my heart hum with satisfaction the way it does when I look at Rosa's snippet. To feast on the same sight but with my twisted version of a happy ending has become my obsession. The only bright spot in what has been a very fucking awful month.

No. A very fucking awful *year*.

Deep inside me, something connects with her image. Her diminutive size, her wide-set eyes, her expressive face. The waving hands that do far more talking than her mouth.

It *has* to be her.

Seeing her in person again, memorising the ways her physical reality is different than—*better* than—my grainy footage reignites that obsession until it burns deeper into my brain.

I think of Zach's arrangement with Lily. One last try.

"I'll pay your full tuition, until you've got your degree, even your masters or PhD. Any expenses. You can—" My throat clicks, and I have to clear it before I can finish. "You can do whatever you need to during that time, and I'll pay. Five videos and I'll fund whatever you need. You can stop doing everything else you're doing right now."

She tucks her hair behind her right ear, tugging at the lobe. "Whatever you saw on the night of the party must've looked a lot better on camera than it was in real life."

"You looked fucking incredible." I try to hold her gaze but her eyes drift to the side, escaping me when I most need her to stay focused. When I need her to get in sync with me so I can get what I want.

"Why do you need a recording?"

The question puts me on the back foot. I'm the one paying. Why does it matter?

But that won't fly here, and I know it. My face is a hundred degrees too hot. "A while ago... I had an unpleasant experience, so I don't like touching people for real."

Her voice comes back softer, velvet against my eardrums. "Someone hurt you?"

Red pulses over my vision while my chest combusts into flame. "No, nothing like that."

I rub my arm, seeing the deep scratch marks on my wrist. A second, two seconds, then they're gone.

Everything is fine. *Everything is fine.*

"It's better when there's no one there. Not for real."

"Why go to the trouble of a recording if you can just imagine it?"

The idea makes me smile. "The internet's not covered wall to wall in porn because guys have fantastic imaginations."

Rosa relaxes against the wall, her smile becoming more genuine. "Guess not, but we're left at an impasse."

"You could—"

She holds up her hand. "You could, too, so let's park it there."

I nod, casting my glance towards the door, not really wanting to leave and not because I haven't got what I came for.

Or not *just* that.

"What is it you actually do?"

She rubs her elbow with her hand, then raises it to play with the hairs at the back of her neck, tugging them gently. "Straight sex. Sometimes a bit of control stuff. Like a dominatrix but a lite version."

"No whips and chains?"

Her smile broadens. "If you're a good boy. If not, who knows?"

"Do you get to order them about and make them do your chores for you?"

This time, she wrinkles her nose. "No. What makes you think that?"

"Saw a TikTok or something. A woman who gets men to clean her house while they pay her for the pleasure."

The idea delights her. "You can probably tell with one glance, that's a no, but I need to do some research in case I'm doing it all wrong."

I lean forward to whisper, "Call me if you change your mind and I'll pay enough you can hire those cleaners directly."

She shakes her head but that gentle smile stays in place. The one that says she's enjoying herself, just like I am. Enjoying ourselves even though neither of us will get what we want. "Go home, Trent."

"Yes, mistress."

I leave the flat on the sound of her laughter, feeling lighter. A thousand times happier despite being shot down.

CHAPTER SEVEN

ROSA

FINLEY BURSTS THROUGH THE DOOR JUST AS TRENT GETS
into his car, stopping at the entrance to give a wolf whistle as he
pulls away from the curb. "You're taking clients here now, are
you? That should definitely be against the terms of our lease."

"It was a friend of Zach's. Not a client."

"Did I miss, Zachie? Damn. Did he leave any presents lying
around? I haven't snagged anything good for weeks."

I raise an eyebrow at her. "He's at the dance with Lily. No
presents today."

"Hm. So, is his friend as rich as he is?"

My head gets stuck on his offer again. To pay for everything.
My degree, my rent, every unforeseen expense covered. I could
be like one of those students whose parents are wealthy enough
to pick up their tab, leaving them time free to party, to network,
to forge friendships deep enough that they could support me
during rough times.

All in exchange for an exacerbation of my anxiety. The

worry that every strange look, every second glance I get on the street, is from a voyeur.

I shake my head to clear the temptation away. "Seems like it."

"And does he come in a feminine model so I can have a sugar mummy?"

My tongue pokes out at her before I can stop it. "He's not my sugar daddy. He's nothing to me."

"Right." She waggles her eyebrows. "Nothing. Gotcha."

"It's true." I move through to the kitchen to hunt down something for dinner.

The cupboards are stuffed with dried goods, boxes of easy cook stuff, a lot of ramen noodles. My talent in the kitchen extends to me pouring boiling water on something and microwaving it for a few minutes. Anything outside of that I consider both proper cooking and something I don't know how to do.

"Your new rich boyfriend didn't even buy us a decent meal?"

Nothing we have in stock interests me. "I could go halves on a pizza."

She claps her hands together like I suggested a party. "You're on. Get the anchovies and jalapenos on my side."

After the obligatory retching scene, I put through the order. Half a pizza and half something only Finley and the devil could eat.

"You're working tomorrow?"

"Just the one appointment, then I'm visiting mum. What about you?"

"Geraldine wants me to take apart her carburettor and find out what keeps sticking. If you and Lily are both out, I'll help myself to the lounge. We'll need a lot of room."

"Knock yourself out. If Lily's genuinely together with Zach again, I doubt she'll be bringing him back here."

Finley squints her eyes. "What are you saying? This flat's delightful."

"If you don't have anywhere better to be."

She mock hits me and I move to the couch, slumping at one end, too tired to even think about the assignments I have coming due in my courses. And that's without mentioning the group study project, something that I can't remember if we've even picked a topic for yet.

Without permission, my mind returns to Trent's visit. This time it lingers on my pulse of regret. Why didn't he come to ask me out? I would love to strip that big body bare and find out all the ways it could please me and be pleased in return.

When the delivery guy comes to the door, I volunteer Finley to answer it. "You need to come," she calls out while balancing the chips, garlic bread, and pizza box. "There's something on the top step."

I reluctantly move to the door, stepping around her and bending over, expecting the slip of paper to be a receipt or coupon that fell out of the delivery box.

But it's another white envelope. Hand delivered.

My feet turn to ice as I stare at it, seeing the similarities to the card I received before. Stepping outside, I pick it up and open it, watching the crimson glitter fall and be tugged away by the breeze.

The same watercolour heart.

I pull out the card and open it, feeling my body shudder with each thump of my pulse.

The writing on the inside is also in a shade of red, muddier than the glitter, more reddish brown. The same as last time and, with dawning horror, I understand the ink is probably blood.

Everything winds down to a pinhole; I can barely breathe.

This time, I can't make myself believe it's an innocent coincidence. The card is a memory jolt, a taunt, a threat.

"Say cheese."

THE FOLLOWING DAY, Saturday, I visit my mother in the home. It's hard to find out what I need without alerting her something's wrong. And I don't want her to understand the depths of my fear.

It took years longer for her to forgive herself than it took for me to forgive her. The last thing I want is to dredge up the horror again, leave her revisiting it in her last weeks or months, wasting time worrying about something she can't change.

It won't help anyone.

But I want the name of the person who got told the news about my uncle. With so little else to go on, I need to be sure I'm scared of the right person for the right reason. If the gossip about my uncle is nothing more than conjecture, I must know. That would mean the cards are unconnected.

That leaves me with one worry put to bed and another worry —the *right* worry—left in its place.

A few minutes of cautious questioning gets me nothing. Finally, I ask her outright.

"Mel told me," she answers after struggling with her memory for a few seconds. "She was visiting with her son Martin when she overheard the news."

"Melanie Ossa?"

"That's her."

My heart sinks as I type her name in my phone. She's reliable, not prone to gossip. That means it's likely true and I need to do something about the cards before whatever game this is can escalate further.

Putting it aside for now, I settle in for a proper visit. Mum tells me about a next-door neighbour from back when we lived in an 'alternative' community. He'd taught me how to raise a garden from seeds and had a love affair with compost.

"The worms," I exclaim, remembering how it felt to dig through the piles of mulch and have their bodies squirming among the refuse, turning green waste into plant food.

It brings up some memories I haven't thought of for years, ones that I might have lost if not for her prompting. I luxuriate in the warm glow of connection and linger for hours longer than I mean to, staying next to her even when she falls into a long nap.

"Stay safe, love," Mum rouses long enough to say as I sneak from her room. "Have a good time with your friends tonight."

I told her I was going to a movie, but the reality is I'll probably spend the night curled in a blanket on the couch, mindlessly staring at the tv. The same way I ended last night, except then I had Finley trying to chat me out of my distress. Even when I told her nothing was wrong.

When I catch the bus to the police station, the journey takes far longer than it should because I change my mind as we arrive at the correct stop, then change it again once we're three stops past.

On the walk back, I change my mind another half dozen times, faltering to a halt in the middle of the footpath like a freak.

Each time I convince myself it's stupid, they'll never take me seriously and even if they do, they won't be able to do anything, I bump against the other side of the argument.

I need help and I can't do it myself.

Even when I finally arrive at the local station, I walk past the entrance, dawdling among the adjacent stores, talking myself in and out of it five times over before I wrench open the door.

The internal argument also sets my preparation on fire, so when I get to the front desk, I blurt, "There's someone stalking me," instead of the calm, rational explanation I had planned.

I have the card inside a sealed baggie, the glitter still clinging to the outside despite having been cleaned before I put it into my purse. The eyes of the officer behind the counter widen, then he frowns. "You can save that for the interview. Someone'll be with you shortly."

The wait drives me insane, but it looks like my jiggling legs are also driving my neighbours in the waiting chairs batty. So much that I hear an audible sigh of relief as I stand when a PC calls my name. I follow the female constable through to a small room, hunching my shoulders as I take a seat.

"You've had someone following you?"

"Someone sent me this card," I say, once again offering the plastic bag. "There was another one a few weeks ago, with a slightly different message."

She tips the bag back and forth, then sets it aside. "And the message is?"

"The first card said, 'Smile.' This one reads, 'Say cheese.'"

"And do those phrases hold special meaning to you?"

I put a hand to my throat, rubbing against my skin as I swallow. The words stick there, even when I cough to get them out.

"Take your time. There's no rush."

I nod, closing my eyes and frowning, everything inside my brain getting hectic. Images skate across my inside eye, flashes of men, equipment, lighting.

My so-called uncle sitting on a bed covered in a black sheet, patting the space next to him, the space right in the centre frame of the waiting camera. His body naked except for a small towel draped across his lap.

A sob comes out of my mouth, and I hate how weak it makes me sound. I'm furious at the thought this woman who looks barely older than I am will think I'm an emotional basket case. Incapable of even explaining what she wants, why she's frightened.

I clench my hand into a fist until the nails dig into my palm, dig so deep they draw blood.

"There was an investigation... involving me... years ago."

The tiny phrases tear out of me in fits and starts, like they're being dug out of my flesh in tiny little strips. The first phase in a procedure that will strip me back to the bone.

"It went to trial and everything, so it should be in your records."

"Okay. Can I take your name?"

"Fenn. Rosalie Fenn, no middle name."

She types away at her computer for far longer than it should take to bring up a single file. After tapping in endless keystrokes, she frowns at the screen, slowly rolling the mouse down to read further while my heart tries to thump its way through my ribcage, beating a path to freedom.

The silence grows into a smothering blanket, stealing my air. In a panic, I blurt, "We heard he got out of prison, even though he's got years left on his sentence. Then the first card showed up and now... this one..."

I choke to a stop, moving my hand so it no longer circles my throat but presses against my chest. The heel of my palm digs against my sternum. The pain from that and the trenches I've dug with the fingernails of my opposite hand are the only things keeping me from outright panic.

The pain is soothing. I let my mind float along in its current for a while, drifting but inevitably finding a way back to shore.

"There's a sealed record from your childhood," the officer says with an apologetic smile. "Usually, I'd be able to see more details."

"It went to court," I say, not sure how that information will help but wanting to try. "There's a conviction. Do I have to... I don't know, with name suppression, do I have to fill out paperwork to...?"

I trail off, not sure where I was going. My panic dissolves into a feeling of stupidity.

This is stupid. I'm stupid. No one's going to help. Did I expect the police to park a car outside in case I get a papercut from a silly card?

"Sorry about this," the woman says, standing. "I'll need to phone a colleague. I'm not sure why I don't have access. Can I grab you a cup of tea or coffee? Or a soft drink?"

Coffee but I'm already shaking. Another dose of caffeine will send me into orbit.

"A lemonade? Or water. Water's fine."

"I'll be right back."

The sound of the door closing behind me sends me into another tailspin. I'd rather be sat back in the waiting room with my fidgets drawing glowering eyes than sitting here with just my own company. I stand, pacing the room from side to side, counting out the steps before repeating with the largest stride I can, and again with mincingly small ones.

"Here you go," the officer says, opening the door with her shoulder while she hands me a cup of lemonade soda with her right hand and juggles an overstuffed manila folder with her left. "Sorry for the wait."

"That's fine," I say, taking a sip and letting the bubbles fizz across my tongue. "I'm not in a hurry."

"I spoke to the department of corrections, and they've confirmed your assailant was paroled four months ago."

My throat clutches, the mouthful of lemonade trapped until it releases. By the time I can swallow, my eyes water and I put the cup down. "Why didn't anyone...? Shouldn't there have been a hearing? We weren't even told he was eligible for parole."

"I'm sorry. The woman I spoke to said they didn't have a notification form. There's specific paperwork that victims need to complete to be—"

"I was eight," I state in a flat voice. "Nine at the time of the trial." My throat spasms again, this time so painfully it feels cut open. "Nobody told me about any paperwork."

The officer's expression is apologetic but it's not her fault. There's nothing she can do. Nothing anyone can do unless they get handy with a time machine.

"What about the no-contact order?" I meet her gaze and hold it, eyes blasting out a message too rude to come from my mouth. "Is that still in force or do I need to fill out a new form in triplicate?"

"It still applies." She moves her folder and takes out a clipboard. "If it's okay, I'd like to ask you some questions about your experience."

I nod, answering each one as fully as I can, feeling the burn of injustice that the man could be released so early in his sentence. It doesn't seem fair, not when I don't get a reprieve from my intrusive thoughts, from my hypervigilance.

Finally, we get through the morass of detail to the broader questions. "And you're saying this man is bothering you again?"

"Him or someone working for him. He's not meant to have contact with either of us."

"Has your mother received anything similar?"

"If she has, she hasn't told me." I shift in my seat, increasingly uncomfortable. "My mother has late-stage cancer. She doesn't track things well, and she's in no fit state to make a police complaint even if she had."

"I'm so sorry to hear that." The officer taps her pen on the card. "Can you tell me more about this delivery? Was it inside something else?"

"The envelope's in there but it must have been left at my house by someone. There's no postage or address."

"Okay."

"He used to..." My throat is so dry I don't think I can

continue. Another sip of lemonade doesn't seem to help. "He filmed me. He's not meant to..."

I turn away from her sympathetic gaze and stare at the blank wall until I have myself back under control.

This is awful.

They won't do anything. I should never have come.

"I better go," I say, standing like I dropped in at a neighbour's house on a whim. "It's getting late and I..."

My sentence doesn't resolve itself but that's okay. I don't need a reason to leave. It's a free country and I can just go.

"Anything more you can tell—"

I shake my head, unable to muster the will to continue.

The female officer comes around from behind the desk, escorting me to the door. "I'll forward the card to our testing centre to swab for DNA and perform a fingerprint comparison. Once we have those back, I'll contact you. In the meantime, you might find it preferable to stay with some—"

"I already have flatmates. We'll be careful."

"Good." She hands me her card. "If you think of anything new, please call me and if you see the suspect near your home or workplace, call emergency. They'll have the best response time."

"Okay." I pause for a second. "If they come back as his...?"

"He'll be in breach of your protective order and his parole conditions. I don't want to get ahead of things, but that would make him eligible for recall to prison."

"And if that happens, I can fill out the forms?"

She nods. "I'll refer you to the courts department and they can register you correctly."

My hands shake as I leave the station and head for the bus stop. The reassurance I felt in the station recedes further with each passing minute until the entire visit seems pointless.

The man who abused me, abused my mother, will probably

earn no more than a chat with his probation officer, then he'll be free to torture me some more.

If it's even him doing it. You don't know that. It could be a client with a penchant for glitter.

The idea makes me snort with laughter, and it feels so good to release the tension without crying that I do it again.

The bus arrives shortly afterward, this time heading for home, a destination that fills me with a lot more comfort than the last one.

If Finley's cleared her junk out of the lounge, perhaps it's time I sat down to have a talk with her and Lily about what's been happening. Clue them in since if someone's targeting me, they'll be in the crossfire through no fault of their own.

Or not. Right now, I can't imagine initiating that conversation and it's just a card. Not a knife or a bullet.

Everything's going to be okay.

CHAPTER EIGHT

TRENT

I ARRIVE FOR MY AFTERNOON SHIFT AT STEFAN'S CLUB WITH only a few minutes to spare. My morning was taken up with a rugby game, just a friendly with another school, but I lost my temper a few minutes into the second half and spent the rest of the game trying to keep myself in check rather than looking for opportunities.

Usually, I'd have joined my teammates in the clubrooms after, celebrating with a pint—even if mine's more likely to be water than whatever lager is on tap.

Today I didn't bother. Rather than risk the already straining tensions within the team, I opted to run sprints, wearing myself to the point of exhaustion, hoping that would be enough to cata-pult me back into equilibrium.

It didn't.

At work, it's my turn for the entrance doors, which is the same boredom level as any door inside the venue, but with extra razzamatazz to ensure the wealthy patrons aren't offended when they first rock up to the entrance.

I'd welcome the opportunity to flex my muscles, to give any troublemakers a taste of their own medicine, but it's unlikely.

There hasn't been trouble at this establishment, not for ages. The first few months I was in this job, there'd be a beat down at least once a week. Now, it's close on twelve weeks since the last time I got to throw a punch, longer since the last time I stuck my boot in.

It's not that I'm ignorant of what my key role is—appear tough so anyone looking for trouble gives the place a wide berth or wisely holds their counsel. But when you get used to the fringe benefits, it's hard when they go AWOL.

Maybe it'll pick up again in summer. It could be the warm weather is the tipping point that plunges a bout of aggression into a confrontation. If so, let's hope global warming gets its arse into gear because I could use anything it gives me right now.

I'm looking forward to at least catching up with Lily, but when I'm halfway to the changing rooms, Stefan calls me into his office. "She's off work for a few days. Something to do with being appointed her sister's guardian."

Great news for her.

There's the momentary warmth of something working out for someone close to me, soon lost in another rush of frustration. My friend had something wonderful happen, and I found out through our shared boss.

Just in case I'm aggrieved for no good reason, I check my messages. Perhaps one snuck through and I didn't register?

Nope. Nothing to report.

I'm just as bad, immediately tucking my phone away instead of sending her and Zach a quick note of congratulations.

If I remember, I'll try to do it later. Later when I feel less like a third wheel to everyone in the universe.

After work, I shoot off a text but I'm still out of sorts. If it's this bad now, what'll it be like next year when school's over and we all scatter? I don't even know if I'm going to university or Polytech or trying to find a full-time job elsewhere or increasing the hours I work for Stefan.

Panic seizes me, clenching my chest in a fist that grows tighter and tighter.

I had been heading home but I change course, heading for Rosa's flat. She won't have changed her mind, not given how firm she was, but also... she might. Either way, I want to see her again.

It seems unlikely we could become friends after such a disastrous start but suddenly that's what I want most in the world. Well... second most. I'd still prefer my first request, but I'll happily settle for seeing her, chatting with her, laughing with her.

Something good and bright and clean to end off the day.

Since Lily lives there, too, I can drop in and give my congratulations in person. That'll be so much nicer than the toneless text I've already sent.

After diverting to collect a cake, because it'd be rude to turn up empty-handed, I pull up beside the curb across the street. Then I sit there, staring at the lit windows, shadows moving behind the thin curtains the only sign that's someone's at home. Any sense of urgency immediately dissolves, and I relax, remembering the interaction with Rosa yesterday.

She was so sweet but so adamant. Curtailing me at every turn.

My phone beeps, a reply from Lily saying thanks and informing me they're all staying at Zach's house for the time being.

That puts paid to my flimsy scenario. Even if I was still keen on going inside, I now have absolutely no excuse.

After my shift at work, it's now past nine. Not late-late, but too late to turn up uninvited. Soon those shadows moving behind the curtain will be relaxing for the night, getting tucked up in bed, going to sleep.

I turn the radio on, listening to the news broadcast as I adjust my seat to be comfier, settling in for a long stay.

As the channel switches back to music, I close my eyes, imagining the girl moving around on the other side of the curtain. The lips that are so plump they have a crease in the centre, shaded like the inside of a strawberry and I bet they'd be as sweet under my tongue.

Not that I want to touch her. Not for real.

Except, if I concentrate, I can feel the difference where the neckline of her blouse turns into skin, one rough, one smooth. I rub against the side of my jeans as I imagine how the textural changes would vibrate across the pad of my thumb, how it would spread like a ripple across my body, igniting every sense along the way.

Spit pools in my mouth as I think of how her eyelids look so heavy. How slowly they'd open in the morning, turning over, reaching for me. I'd have the caress of her hands against me long before they pulled apart enough to catch a glimpse. Her tongue would snake out, licking those swollen lips, snagging the edge between her even white teeth, a gentle tease to ease me into the fullness of the day.

The song changes and I startle out of my daydream, my teeth snapping shut with enough force they make a sound.

I rub a hand over my face, wondering where the hell all these ideas came from. My favoured romps involve a screen and at least one free hand. Aside from that, I wouldn't even know where to start.

My eyes sweep across the windows, still lit from within, still with the flickers of movement that means at least two people are awake and moving around inside.

I wonder if one of them is Rosa's boyfriend or if not that, a booty call. The angel on my shoulder insists it will be her flatmate, the devil suggests something far raunchier.

Neither of which should matter because she's not my girl.

Movement catches my eye and I squint, trying to make out a shape at the edge of the house. The congruence of darkness against the pool of light from the streetlamp makes it hard to see anything.

I let my eyes rest on the spot, letting them relax, then see the motion again.

Far bigger than a domestic pet. Something moving at the corner of the house.

I sink farther into my seat, trying to hide myself from view. But that's a wasted effort. I've been parked out here for a good twenty minutes now. If it is a person sneaking alongside the house, they've had chance enough to see me.

Instead, I take care opening the door, trying for silence and nearly getting there. I don't worry about shutting it—the noise will instantly draw attention and if someone wants to steal my car, they're welcome to it. I'd gladly take the new replacement from insurance.

Squatting in the shadows behind the vehicle, I try to pick out the same figure I saw before. Once I separate it from every other dark shape across the road, I keep it in my peripheral, waiting for it to move again so I can give chase or sneak across while it's out of sight.

The figure slowly moves again, this time disappearing through a gate to the side of the property. A second later, I cut across to the front yard, moving on the balls of my feet. I'm a big guy but I can be quiet when I want.

I merge with the shadows, my head tilted for noise and

motion. When I hear the snap of a twig, my heart thumps with anticipation. I flex my fingers, exercising the joints in anticipation of the fight I've been craving.

The confrontation is so welcome, I can taste blood in the back of my throat as I slip through the gate, my back pressed against the wooden slats of the outside wall, picking my path with care until I can peer around the corner.

The shadowy figure is halfway across the yard, fiddling with something at their belt.

Giving up on silence, I bolt straight for them, aiming for a tackle. They turn to run, and I misjudge, hitting them lower than I want, thumping them to the ground.

My chest lands on their boots, the heavy soles knocking the wind out of me. The person gives a rough grunt as they fall, then they rear up and kick back, catching me on the side of the head.

"Stop," I yell, happy to alert the people inside to our presence. "I've called the police."

That earns me a double kick, the force of the second stunning me so I lose track of what my hands are doing, releasing my grip.

The figure is up, running again, too quick for me to catch them. I roll onto my back, the night filled with so many stars they can't all be real. There's warm liquid dripping down the side of my face and I fervently hope it's only blood.

I'm on my knees by the time the back door cracks open and Rosa comes out to investigate.

"It's Trent," I announce loudly, holding my arms in the air. "There was someone sneaking around your house."

"Trent?"

There's a second's pause, then the light snaps on; so bright after the darkness, I throw one arm up to shield my eyes, which instantly water.

"What the fuck are you doing in my back garden at night?"

I give a feeble laugh, still getting my breath back. "That sounds like a fun euphemism."

"Really? Cause that sounds like not an answer."

"Give me a second." I rise from my knees to my feet, wobbling a bit and raising a hand to my head where a steady thump is setting in. "There was someone out here."

"Yes. *You*. I can still see you in case you're—Fuck! You're bleeding. Finley!"

There's a shuffle of movement, then a joyful voice says, "You don't have to yell. I was a metre behind you. Hey, random dude. Not cool sneaking around houses this late at night."

"I'm not... There was an intruder."

"Sure there was," Rosa states in a flat voice. "What are you even doing here?" To Finley, "Could you grab a teatowel or something?"

A minute later, she brings it out, tossing it to Rosa and retreating near the door.

"Put this on your cut."

I grab it with one hand, touching the various places my head is throbbing with the other to work out where the blood is coming from.

"No, don't..." Rosa gives an exasperated sigh. "Here. Let me."

She pushes the towel firmly above my ear, making me yelp at the sudden increase in pain.

"Don't be such a baby," she scolds, moving one hand against the other side of my head so she can exert more force, an idea I'm not on board with *at all*.

Except, the longer she touches me, the less I feel the sick pulse of my injury and the more I feel the smoothness of her palms, the dry, slightly cool rasp of her skin against mine.

"We should take this inside," I suggest, meaning because

there's an intruder running around who might circle around to come back and my head has taken enough punishment for one night. That's not the way she takes it.

"Nice try, buddy, but you're not talking your way into a home with two unprotected females in their prime that easily."

"I can put some more effort in," I offer with a chuckle. "What points would you like me to hit first?"

"Wait!" Finley holds up her hand, pointing her forefinger at me. "Is this the rich one?"

"Everyone's richer than you," Rosa quips back and laughs. "But yeah. Mr I'll-pay-your-tuition-for-three-years is far richer than normal." She hikes up her eyebrows. "Far richer than it's healthy to be."

"I'm plenty healthy."

"Yeah, you are," Finley says, followed by an appreciative trill of laughter. "Don't suppose you've got a sister, do you? I like natural blondes."

"I'm sure they like you plenty in return, but no. Sorry."

"It'll have to be a rich friend, then."

Rosa pulls away a little, releasing pressure on the towel and scrunching her face in dismay before replacing it. "We might need to call an ambulance."

"Can I at least sit on the back step? I'm getting woozy." It's not a complete lie.

"Oh, for goodness' sake, Rosa." Finley jumps forward and takes my arm, pulling both me and her friend along with her. "Let him inside before he dies out here and we all get evicted. I'm too young to spend my life worrying where to couch surf each night."

She leads me through into the bathroom, Rosa peeling off the moment Finley takes over applying pressure. I breathe a sigh of relief when I hear the back door close and lock.

"So, you're trying to hire my flatmate to do unconscionable things, are you?"

I lean in the corner formed by the side of the shower and the vanity unit, peeling the towel away from my head. My stomach flips over, greasy at the sight of all the blood. I can taste it when I breathe in, the air thick with an iron tang.

"You aren't fainting, are you? Only, fair warning. There's no way I could catch you, so I won't try."

"I think I'm okay," I say, the words barely audible through my clenched jaw. When I turn my head to the right, there's a large patch of hair turned sandy with blood. "Hey. I'm a redhead."

"Ugh. Don't." Finley takes the towel from my fingers and rinses it out in the sink, which soon looks like a budget version of the shower scene from Psycho, blood swirling down the drain.

"Do you have a phone handy?" I ask. "Whoever was in the back yard could still be hanging around."

Rosa returns with ice and a container of wet wipes. "Best I can do," she says to Finley's raised eyebrows. "And are you serious? About there being someone out there?"

"Who else d'you think did this?"

"You could've tripped," Finley supplies with glee. "It happens."

"There was a figure."

"A figure," Rosa scoffs while her eyes flick around the room with nervous energy, tongue darting out to moisten her lips. "Excellent observation skills."

"It's dark out, all right? I tackled them but they kicked me in the head until they got away."

"Really?" Finley's mouth hangs open and her eyes cut across to Rosa.

She doesn't return the gaze, though. Her eyes fix to my chest, staring in confusion. She wets her finger and touches it to my shirt, raising it for closer inspection.

"What is it?" Finley asks, sounding more freaked with each passing second.

"Nothing," Rosa says, wiping her hand against her blouse and tipping the icetray into the sink. "Let's get a look at this cut."

CHAPTER NINE

ROSA

TRENT STARES AT ME ACROSS THE DINING ROOM TABLE, then repeats, "You can come home with me. There's plenty of room. It's not safe to stay here alone."

"There are two of us," I retort, thoughts still scrambled. "That's hardly alone."

"What size house is it you're taking us to?" When I glare at her, Finley shrugs, "What? It's an important consideration."

"I can also get a guy down here to instal security cameras—"

"Oh? That'd be about right. I turn down your offer and next thing, you're in my back yard fighting imaginary intruders and wanting to instal cameras for my safety." I shake my head, puffing out a derogatory breath. "Nice try, Weybourne. Next time attempt it on someone who'll fall for your bullshit."

"Rosa!"

I crack my knuckles, folding my arms when the release doesn't give me enough satisfaction. "What? You can't seriously be thinking of going home with him. You only met him tonight."

"Be like that." Finley whips out her phone and starts scrolling through her messages, before composing a new one.

"What're you doing?"

"I'm texting Lily to see if she'll vouch for him. I think you and I both know that she will, and I'll show that to you, and you'll have to come up with a genuine reason for not accepting his offer to take us home and lavish us with presents."

My glare feels hot enough to burn as it leaves my head, but she appears immune.

"You are lavishing us with presents, aren't you?" she belatedly checks with Trent who smiles in agreement. "Then it's settled."

"It's not settled. I'm not going to a practical stranger's house in the middle of the night—"

"Why do I have glitter on my jeans?" Trent asks suddenly, cutting me off, unaware I was even talking. Another black mark.

Except it's not his sudden appearance that's upsetting me. I should be grateful for his interference. How would it feel if instead of Trent on my doorstep, I'd found another card? Worse still if it was delivered to my room while I was fast asleep. The jolt of fear is like falling.

When I'm in panic mode, I need things to be tight, in their place, under my control. This big blond boy isn't any of those things even if he's on my side.

He wants something from you, just like all the rest.

"Where's this glitter?" Finley asks, leaning over until her head is practically in his crotch. If I weren't clear on her sexual preferences, I could mistake the interaction as flirting.

I steal another glance and decide even taking her preferences into account, it still looks that way. An observation that upsets me even more and for even less reason than all the other things that upset me.

"Get a room," I mutter.

"Glad to," Finley shoots back. "In a rich boy's mansion if you get your head out of your arse long enough to accept."

"You can go. I'm staying here."

"Not alone, you're not," Trent says as though he has any vote in the matter.

And why is Finley nodding in agreement when I've known her for months and she only met this boy today?

"Rosa, you had glitter in something the other day, didn't you?"

My stomach pulls tighter still, and I rub against it with the heel of my palm, catching Finley's face too late. She's frowning. She understands I'm upset.

"I had a card in the mail," I murmur. "It was nothing."

"I can get someone around to instal a security system—"

"Sure," I say through clenched teeth. "Cameras in every room. Is that about right?"

"That sounds good," Finley declares, her frown increasing. "Even if Rosa is being weird, you can put them in my room so at least if I get raped and murdered in my bed, you can catch the guy."

"If you get raped and murdered in your bed, it'll probably be a disgruntled ex."

"Says the ho."

I ignore her because knowing how unreasonable I'm being doesn't stop me wanting to put my foot down. The longer I argue, the more entrenched my position becomes. "It's very nice of you to—"

"Oh. I brought a cake."

"You...?" I send a victorious glance Finley's way. "Right. So you just happened to be passing at the time you saw an intruder but you bought cake?"

"It's for Lily. For getting custody of her sister."

Now Finley and I are both confused. "Sorry?"

"She didn't tell you, either?"

The news lights up Trent's face. "She must be really busy, I guess. But it's sitting on the front seat—"

Finley claps her hands and dashes for the door before I can stop her. While she's gone, my head reworks the context. Trent with his innocent mission, coming to Lily's rescue, tackling the would-be intruder *for her.*

Once I frame it in the new light, I relax. My body stops its weird alchemy of turning fear into aggression. I can smile at *Lily's friend,* appreciate the bleeding blond behemoth who came to *her rescue.*

I meet Trent's eye and a smile gradually cracks its way through my icy façade.

"What does the glitter mean?"

When I open my mouth to brush the worry aside, the truth falls out instead. "Someone's sent me a few cards, but I've visited the police. They're going to stop them."

Trent holds up his hands, specks of metallic crimson dotted across them, along with grass stains and dirt from the lawn. "Doesn't seem like they're on top of it."

"Give them a chance," I snap back, my unreasonable temper rising again. "I only reported him today."

"Him who?" Finley asks, arriving with a cake box that she unceremoniously dumps in the middle of the table. "I live here, too," she prompts when I don't immediately answer. "If someone's coming after you, they're a threat to me as well. It's not fair to keep it secret if you're endangering me. I'm too lovely to die."

"Far too lovely," Trent agrees.

I hate this. It's a thousand times worse than the police station and that was bad enough. I place my palms flat on the table, holding me steady, like we're in a monstrous storm at sea instead of calmly sitting inside.

"There's a guy who abused my mother, years ago. He's out

on parole and any contact is against the rules of our protective order."

"And he's sending you cards?"

"I don't know. I don't know if it's the same person."

"Yeah," Finley says, cutting the cake into pieces and helping herself before shoving the box towards me. "Because coincidences happen all the time."

She doesn't hide the sarcasm.

"It could be. If they didn't happen, we wouldn't have a word for them."

"What's inside the cards?"

"Glitter," I say, taking a piece of cake because it looks absolutely delicious and judging from the sounds Finley's making, it tastes good, too. "It's a plain white card with a watercolour love heart and crimson glitter. It could just as easily be a client who caught some feelings."

I haven't said those words aloud before and the moment I do, I think of Harry. Lonely Harry trying to do the right thing by his son and not drag a dozen applicants for wife in front of him until he's ready.

"That doesn't make me feel any safer," Finley says around her mouthful. "This is delicious, Trent. I'm sure Lily would've loved it if she were here."

"Aren't you having any?" I push the cake box towards him, holding a slice with my other hand. "There's plenty."

"Nah, I'm good, thanks."

I put the slice back in the box.

"There's nothing wrong with it," he says with the first note of exasperation creeping into his tone. It makes a change from his passivity but I'm not sure it's an improvement.

"Changed my mind, that's all."

"I'm happy to be the canary," Finley says, helping herself to my discarded piece. "Some things are worth dying over."

"I'm watching my diet," Trent explains, pushing the box back towards me. A new battleground. "Coach gave me an eating plan and I can't afford to break it, mid-season."

I nudge the box back towards him. "One slice won't hurt."

His face sets. "I used to be overweight, and sugar was a big part of that. One slice can definitely hurt."

"You'd look good with a dad bod," Finley comments, unperturbed. She sneaks a hand out to clutch him near the waist. "Get a few inches to grab hold of here, and you'll make some random woman very lucky."

I glare at him, locking gazes and waiting for him to submit first. Instead, his chin juts out, a stubborn streak showing up in equal portion to mine. Typical. I teased him about being competitive last time we met and now we're stuck in the middle of a duel. One I don't want to lose.

Finley flaps a hand like she needs to cool herself. "Wow. You could cut the sexual tension with a knife. Is this what counts for flirting over in hetero land? I'm starting to see the appeal."

"Because you're winning at cake," I comment, nearly dropping my eye contact but luckily catching myself in time. "Once Finley's demolished this, you can leave."

My flatmate chortles. "Guess that means you're staying over because you've overestimated my stomach size. Bags you take Lily's room. I'd offer you Rosa's but you'd both end up dead."

I reach forward and finally help myself to a slice. Enjoying an enormous bite before adding, "He's not staying."

"I am or I'm calling a security guard to come and stand here all night. Would you prefer that?"

"I'd prefer to call the police and report a trespasser."

"Good. That's what I want you to do."

I roll my eyes, chewing rapidly until I can swallow and say, "Not for the supposed intruder. For you. The poor guy was probably some TaskRabbit odd-jobs-man, dropping off an envelope when you tried to kill him."

"You know, I could pick you up and carry you to my car right now. I'm about three times your size."

Finley's eyes grow wider, and she pulls her phone out. "If you're doing that, I want to film it."

"No recording," Trent and I snap in unison, then I have to clamp my lips together to stop from laughing.

He sees.

He's doing the same himself.

"Fine," I graciously concede. "You can sleep on the sofa if you're that enthused about home security. But only because this cake is absolutely divine, and it's far too late to be arguing. As a forfeit, you must eat a slice. It's rude otherwise."

Trent relaxes slightly, putting a hand near his plastered-over cut and suddenly I feel bad. Stubborn and ungrateful and insensitive.

"Does it hurt? We've got painkillers," I murmur, escaping the room and dredging them from the bowels of the bathroom drawer. There's a patch of mould in the lino's join. The edge under the vanity has curled from repeat administration of moisture and heat.

To think, I fought to stay here rather than go back to Trent's enormous mansion. A place Finley and I were both happy to party in only a month or two ago with no encouragement.

I bet every guest bedroom has an en suite. Bet they're all at least twice the size of this bathroom. We could have had hot showers in the morning for as long as we could stand to stay under the water.

You still could if you stopped being so defiant. He's done nothing wrong.

Except ask me to film some dirty videos when what I really wanted was a date.

Well, yeah. Apart from that.

Satisfied that I've won over my internal voice at least, I move back to the dining room and drag my seat nearer Trent's. "Tell us what you know about Lily," I say, deciding a change of topic is called for. "When did she find out about Sierra? Are they staying at Zach's for long?"

I press the over-the-counter packets into Trent's hand, then relax in my seat.

"They're probably staying there forever because she's not stupid enough to refuse him when he asks her to move in."

I'm guessing the glare with which Finley accompanies that statement means she's upset with me, but I don't care. If we were hauling arse halfway across town, my stomach would be tight with worry. Instead, it's full of cake.

"If you're going to scowl, could you do it while also doing something useful like putting the kettle on so Trent can have a healthy cup of hot water? We don't want to upset his delicate digestive system."

"Fucks' sake. I'm watching my diet. It's not a declaration of war."

"No," I say with a smile, picking up a fork and breaking off a bite-sized piece of cake, raising it towards his mouth, ready to tease him further. "This is."

Trent locks eyes with me, his irises darkening to navy. His hand reaches for the fork, not grabbing it from me, but guiding it with my hand still attached, lips parting to close around the treat, his mouth gently tugging it free.

He continues to hold the silverware in place, his fingers near enough to mine to make them buzz with his energy, savouring the one bite for the length of time it takes Finley to eat half a slice. Then he leans forward again, his tongue reaching out to lick the traces of icing from the tines.

I can't look away. My tease nothing compared to the one I

got in return. As his tongue swoops across the fat bud of his upper lip, I mimic the gesture, cheeks flushing as the breath in my lungs heating by ten degrees.

Finley sniggers, sitting back in her chair and staring at me with her eyebrows raised. "Get a room."

Since Trent brought us food again, I volunteer to do the dishes. I'm grateful to slip into the kitchen, getting a tiny break from Finley's nervous chatter and Trent's comical attempts to keep up with her jumps in logic and subject.

"Hey," he calls from the connecting doorway as I shake my hand in the water to encourage the suds. "When you said you were doing dishes, I thought you meant putting them in the dishwasher."

"No such luck." I stare at him in amusement as he turns in a semi-circle, looking for something. "You okay there?"

"I feel like I should offer to dry but you don't have a towel."

"Second drawer to your left," I say, encouraging him with a nod. "But you don't need to. There's only a few."

"If I leave you alone, you might decide against me staying the night on the couch again, then where will we be?"

I bite my lip to stop laughing at his forlorn expression.

He stands behind me, reaching around me to take each plate as I finish. The heat of his large body warms my back and I instinctively lean back into him, gently brushing close before I catch myself and jump away.

"Just pretend I'm not here," he whispers in a teasing note.

"That's a bit hard when you take up half the room."

He touches my shoulder with his knuckle, a perfectly innocent gesture, my blouse and cardigan providing two barriers to keep our skin from connecting. But a shiver runs out from the spot, tingles spreading in widening circles across my skin until I shrug the sensation away, finishing the cutlery before letting the water drain from the sink.

Trent's breath lightly caresses the back of my neck, the hairs standing on end, desperate to get closer.

"Did you call the police?" he asks, and I turn, glad of the chance to break away from the magnetic pull of his body. I'd told him I'd do that, but I don't really want to. The card the constable at the station gave me is in my pocket and I pull it out, feeling weariness sink into my bones.

"Is that the officer that took your complaint?"

I nod and he takes it from my fingers. "Do you want me to call? If she wants answers about the man I saw, I'm better placed to give them."

He makes it so easy to say yes, to agree, to let him take control with his calm strength and his unflappable nature.

An officer attends but since Trent gave most of the details over the phone, the man doesn't stay long. After taking a cursory glance around the back yard, retracing the path Trent described, he leaves to attend another call, spending a grand total of twenty minutes.

Finley shoots me all sorts of suggestive glances as I get Trent set up on the couch. In a late bid at gratitude, I offered him Lily's room, but he was appalled by the idea. Especially when it only took a glance to see her stuff is still in there, her possessions not yet catching up to her physical relocation.

As I settle into bed, a butter knife on the cabinet to give me an illusion of protection, I think of us getting another new flatmate. I barely got the chance to adjust to Lily's arrival and now there'll be another new girl. At least, I hope there'll be another new girl. The turnover so far has been so high, the department might, in its wisdom, give up the scheme as a joke.

I snag my vibrator from the drawer, needing the relaxation before I can even think of falling asleep.

Instead of turning it on, I become intensely aware of the attractive boy on the other side of the wall. My memory draws his features with careful detail, lingering on the intensity of his gaze, drinking in everything he sees, the curve of his mouth when he smiles.

The slope of his chest, the hard muscles rippling across his torso, the deep lines of the v trailing into the waistband of his jeans, a sensuous path my hands are desperate to follow to its end.

I roll onto my side, a pulse beating between my legs. The toy goes back in its drawer; I couldn't with him in the next room. To think he might be listening, charting the aural progression of my orgasm from start to finish is both tantalising and enough to make my cheeks heat to burning.

He doesn't want you that way.

Maybe not, but I have a harder time convincing myself of that than I would yesterday. Not after his tease with the mouthful of cake.

I imagine his tongue spending even half that attention on the same spot currently throbbing between my legs and my back arches, my thighs clenching together. With the shock of his sudden appearance fading farther and farther into the background, I can assess the situation more clearly. Think of him ready to fight, to attack an intruder with no concern for his own welfare.

The hint of danger, the same thing that made my stomach crawl as I waited in the police station earlier today, feels a thousand times different here in my bed, with my thoughts full to bursting with Trent.

I flop onto my back, fists grabbing handfuls of my hair and

pulling, keeping me in the moment. My eyes close but my brain continues to work overtime; alternating between the pull of memories I don't want to relive and the far nicer treat of the boy lying on the couch next door.

CHAPTER TEN

TRENT

THE SOFA IN THE LIVING ROOM IS OLD, THE CUSHIONS FULL of so many unexpected bumps and crevices, I expect to have no problem staying awake all night.

Instead, I give a start when I sense someone in the room with me. According to the position of the moon, I've been asleep for hours. Some guard dog I make.

"Sorry," Rosa whispers. "I didn't mean to wake you. Just needed a glass of water."

"No worries." I sit up, rubbing my face. "What time is it?"

"After three." She hesitates in the doorway. "You want some aspirin or something?"

"Panadol if you have it," I ask, though I'm still so sluggish that if I lay back down, I'd fall straight into slumber again, no pain signals allowed. "Did something wake you?"

"No. I've just been reading."

There's a glint of silver from near her hand and as she turns, I make out the shape of a knife. "I hope that's not for me."

"It's just—" She falters, and I shift my weight on the sofa, stretching.

The half dozen aches and pains that report back are evenly split between my rugby practice earlier and my skirmish with the intruder.

She barks out a short laugh, devoid of humour. "This is my talisman for warding off evil, don't you know."

"What is it?"

"A butter knife." She laughs again, this time warmer. "I couldn't take something sharp into bed with me in case I fell asleep and rolled on top of it."

"Yeah. That'd be a hard story to sell to the police. Woman stabs self."

She passes through to the kitchen, returning a minute later sans knife, with a glass of water in each hand and a packet of paracetamol clutched in her right palm, something she passes to me once she's put the glasses on the coffee table.

"I'm sorry for earlier." Her voice is softer, warmer than before. "When I'm worried, I need everything to be as normal as possible. Otherwise, I get mountains of anxiety, and I..." Her words dissolve and she shakes her head.

"There's no need to explain yourself. You want to sit and talk for a while?"

"You wouldn't rather sleep?"

I swallow the pills and lie down on the sofa again, gesturing her towards me. "Come here and keep me warm. If you bore me enough, I will."

At first, I think she's going to refuse, then she slowly moves into position beside me, awkward like she's trying not to touch. I wrap my arms around her, pinning her against me, to override that urge and instantly think it's a mistake.

But I hug girls all the time, at least once a day at school, and it doesn't mean anything. It doesn't feel dangerous... but this does. This does but I can't make myself let go.

"That's better," I tell her, ignoring a thousand klaxons sounding their strident alarms. "Is the useless knife within reach?"

"No. I'll have to wield you instead."

The thought of her moving me at all makes me chuckle. She's tiny against me, her soft hair tickling my cheek. I stroke it back, nuzzling into the warmth of her neck like my nose is a heat-seeking missile. "Did the guy hurt your mum?" I ask, now I've got her trapped.

"He hurt a lot of people," she says, obfuscating again.

From her tension alone, I understand one of those people was her, but I don't press for clarification. Her muscles are already frozen. The wrong word pressing on the wrong nerve will make her shatter. "And there were loads of different charges. His sentence added up to over twenty-three years. I don't understand what he's doing out already."

Her body stiffens further as she talks, and I loosen my grip so she doesn't feel restrained. "How old is he?"

"Early fifties, I guess. A bit older."

"The guy I tackled was nothing like that. I'm sure he's much younger."

"Yeah. It's probably silly."

"That's not..." I bite my lip and take a deep breath. "I meant he's getting someone else to do his dirty work. Not that you're mistaken."

"But I must be. Why would he...?" She shakes her head. "Never mind. I'm going around and around in circles. It's like my brain has found a groove and I can't shake it free to think about anything else."

"Do you want me to tickle you?"

She snorts out a laugh. "What?"

"Tickle you." I give her a test and she wriggles against me, snuffling. "It's very hard to think when you're doing your best not to laugh."

"No. Thanks for the offer but I'll pass."

"Oh. You don't know what you're missing," I tease, moving my hip out of the dent it's found that is slowly warping my spine. "Should I tell you a story? Something to take your mind off your problems and focus them on an imaginary character."

"Hm. Pass." She half turns, glancing at me from the corner of her eye. "Instead of a story, why don't you tell me something true?"

"Once upon a time there was a disturbingly rich boy—"

"Right. Who had an obscene interest in recording things he shouldn't."

I rest my forehead against the top of her head, loving the silky hair, the warmth, the shape of her. "Who said anything about them being obscene?"

"You're hardly asking a sex worker to record something innocent. The world doesn't work like that."

I pick up her left hand, rubbing it between both of mine because it's freezing. "There's a lot of grey area between those two extremes, you know."

"Why don't you like sex for real?" she asks in a small voice. "You obviously have no problem touching people."

"Do you want me to stop?"

She twists around in my arms until she's facing me, shuffling up the couch a little to eradicate our height difference. "No, I don't want you to stop. It's nice. I enjoy being touched."

I pick up her hand and begin massaging it again, the angle harder now because one arm has to go all around her back.

"Did I make it awkward?" she asks, then giggles.

The lack of light annoys me. I want to see the change in her face as she laughs or frowns. See her lips purse as she huffs out a breath.

But the dark has its advantages. It turns it into an anonymous tryst, unable to make out identities in the dimness. Our touches seem more intimate, liberating, arriving out of nowhere, the unexpectedness increasing the sensory appeal.

All of it increases the seductive call of confession.

"You asked me before if someone hurt me," I say, tentatively moving towards the conversation I want to have. Poised, ready to jump back into safer territory if the path ahead becomes too threatening.

"I remember. You said nothing like that happened."

"Not to me." And the next words cling to my throat, hanging on by their fingernails as I try to dislodge them. "Nobody harmed me but I..." I close my eyes, even the scant light too bright for me. "I hurt a girl."

Everything about Rosa is now cautious, and it breaks my heart a little. But she has the right to be. I'm in the wrong on this one. Sometimes that's the only side I can find.

"Was it... the first time?"

"Yeah, but that wasn't... Like, I know it often hurts girls on their first go but—" I break off, listening to her snuffling laugh and opening my eyes again. "Are you laughing at me?"

"No. I swear I'm not. It's just... I meant was it *your* first time?"

"What difference does that make?"

"The difference of having some context for your experience. If you were both virgins, everything could have gone exactly as it's meant to and neither of you would know."

I press my thumb into the centre of her palm, focusing on the small point of massage rather than the larger threat of what I want to say. "It wasn't normal."

"Why? What happened?"

And now I'm flummoxed, wondering where to start. At the beginning will take too long and at the end will sound too rough and I never, *never*, should have embarked on this stupidity to begin with.

I blame the late hour and the shock and the throbbing wound on the side of my head and the loneliness that I feel and keep trying to pretend I don't. The knowledge that for everyone who means something in my life, I'm an afterthought.

"I didn't mean to hurt her at first, but I liked it. I enjoyed hearing her in pain. I wanted more."

"How did you hurt her?"

The question comes back before she's had time to think things through. That's what I tell myself, anyway. Any second now, she'll connect to what I'm saying, and she'll make her excuses and grab her knife and go back to her bedroom and lie awake, except this time she'll be lying awake, afraid of me.

I shake my head, but she grabs my chin with her free hand. The one I'm not massaging as though I'm trying to rub a genie free of its confines.

"How?"

This time, I shake my head again but to get it free. It annoys me she maintains her hold. Not letting me escape even this tiny cage. "I'm big, all right? I think that's... she was ready but it... It didn't really fit."

"Can I touch you?"

She sounds like she wants to, is eager to, a temptation by itself. The richness of desire sandwiches between the opposites of curiosity and caution.

Or I'm projecting and she's husky voiced because she's getting a cold. "This isn't a sex therapy session," I respond after a long pause. "I'm fine with things the way they are, okay?"

"No, you're not, which isn't a problem, but since you insist on helping me when I don't want you to, this is what you get. My help in return, whether or not you like it."

I'm about to issue an angry retort, when I wrinkle my nose and give a soft chuckle instead. "Never thought I'd be with a beautiful girl on a couch in the dead of night, trying to talk her out of grabbing hold of my willy."

"Ew. Call it that again and no one's grabbing hold of anything."

"Fine. My penis."

The indrawn breath tells me that's on thin ice, too.

"Prick? Dick? Rod? Member? Todger? Junk?"

She's now giggling in earnest, and I don't think I've ever heard a sound as sweet. I wish I could keep spouting out names, but my mind draws a blank.

"Why? What do you call it?"

"A cock. Because that's what it is."

"Ooh. Fancy."

Her hand presses against my chest and even through the fabric of my t-shirt, it's enough to make me catch my breath. I already feel closer to her than I have to a girl in forever. There's never been someone occupy my thoughts so fully, especially when I barely know a thing about her. When our interactions to date have been so strained.

"So, can I?"

I cup the back of her head, closing my eyes and leaning until our foreheads gently press against each other. My heart catches in my chest, releasing with an extra-large thump. Her breath whispers across my cheek, tickling my ear.

The rush of red anger that can twist through my body has never seemed so far away.

"Yes," I say in a voice that's barely audible. Her hand shifts from my chest, fingers gently trailing along the curves and ridges of my abdomen, hitting the sparse hairs that strengthen into a thicket as she follows it down, down, down, unfastening my fly and slipping her slim hands inside to find my erection stretching to meet her, to give her welcome as she bends her delicate fingers around its thickening length.

I thrust my hands deep into her hair, fisting around its long strands and tugging until she moans. The sound triggers an answering call from the meat of my brain, and my cock strains, wanting something I promised it couldn't have again, not after last time, not after the mess, the payoff, the stress, the shame.

But it wants it. Not just *it,* it wants *her.* A girl I couldn't have picked out of a line-up a month ago but who's now tangled her threads so closely with mine that we're forming the same tapestry, weaving together a tale that wouldn't work with another player.

"You are a big boy," she whispers and the tendrils of her voice creep inside my ear, winding through the canal like a sinuous temptation. "It's no wonder it hurt, but it doesn't have to."

"It wasn't that I hurt her accidentally," I say on an indrawn sob, fighting an internal battle to the death between what I want to do and what my common sense tells me I can't. "The problem is when I started, when I heard her whimpering, I kept going."

Her opposite hand, now free of my ministrations, curves around the back of my neck, pressing and relaxing in opposition to the gentle pumps she gives my cock. "How old were you?"

"Fifteen."

"Not an age group known for their self-control."

The lightness in her voice is as enticing as the touch of her hands. It hints of things being forgiven and black marks being washed clean. An indulgent fantasy that pulls me farther into its grip with each passing second.

But she doesn't understand and if I don't take the opportunity to explain it to her properly, I'll end with another soured memory. A cracked black fungus releasing its spores until every adjacent branch is rotting from the inside out, destroying anything good until I won't be able to think of her at all. Not without causing myself harm.

I shove at her, trying to push her away. Her touch lightens further but doesn't disappear.

"Talk to me. Tell me what you need me to know."

"You don't understand."

And her lips press right against my ear, the warm moisture of her breath a siren I don't have the willpower to ignore. "Make me. Make me understand."

I'm still holding her hair and now I use it to roll her on top of me, her weight pressing me farther into the couch, leaving her in control, so much safer than the other way around.

Except now it's not just the touch of her hand around my cock but the press of her pussy against me. No matter that it's buried under layers of clothing, I can still feel it. Feel its warm wet welcome in my brain. Feel it opening, eager to draw me inside.

"She was in pain, she asked me to stop and the more she asked, the more I liked her begging, the less I listened. I kept going, getting rougher so she'd cry out louder, and when I was getting close, I... I started choking her and I couldn't stop."

"You killed her?"

The calmness in her voice makes me half-hysterical. "No! But she... I couldn't... She was *hurt*."

"And are you going to hurt me?"

The darkness is overwhelming. I want an interrogation light to shine across Rosa's face to reveal what she's thinking.

She didn't want me here. Now I'm telling her the worst things about myself and she's not stopping me, she's not drawing away in horror.

If I presented this scenario to my father, I know what he'd

say. She's not just pumping my dick, she's pumping me for information and the only reason a person would do that is to use it to hurt me later, to blackmail me later, to get me to do their bidding because the only other choice would disintegrate my name, my reputation.

My father's reputation.

But I can't stop. Or, if I can, I don't want to.

"I want to say no."

The pace of her hand changes, her grip altering so she no longer encircles me, instead pressing the heel of her palm against me, still moving up and down, the steady rhythm becoming irresistible.

I pull my right hand from her hair, detangling from the long strands, curling my knuckles to drag them across her cheek, drifting lower, spreading across her throat, encircling it with my fingers, pressing against her windpipe with my thumb.

I lick my lips, but it does nothing because my mouth has gone completely dry. I lift Rosa, turning again, but this time I place her on the couch, underneath me, pinning her with my weight, wishing there was light enough to see fear mounting in her eyes.

"Struggle," I whisper to her and the hand on my cock moves faster, presses harder, changing grip again to reach to my base, tugging with a sensation so different from my hand that it makes my mind spin with dizziness. "Let me hear you," I murmur directly into her ear as my thumb digs harder, and harder. "Let me hear you squeal."

"Is this what you did with her?" she says, the words disjointed, breaking with the increasing force of my hand. "Is this how you hurt her?"

My mind flashes back to my first time but I shake it loose, finding my place in the narrative again, in the here and now. "No. I hurt her with my dick."

"Show me."

Her hand moves, squirming into her pocket. She pulls out a condom, having to use all her strength to shift me aside long enough to tear it open, returning to her previous position and unrolling it into place along my hard length.

And that sets off another pulse of desire. Because she must have put it in there knowing she was coming out to wake me. She must have lain in bed, planning this, then come prepared.

I force myself to pull my hand away, trying to move off her but now Rosa's arms are around me. She can't keep me in position if I fight, her tiny frame is no match for my bulk, my size, my strength, but I let her fix me in place, pretending for a minute.

The game needs to end soon or the ravenous beast inside me will wake too fully to be put back to bed, but a few seconds, a few minutes... Please, let that be okay because I don't want to stop.

"Are you okay to continue?" she asks, and I jerk, ready to roll off, stand up, but Rosa clutches me tighter. "I don't want to make you do anything you don't want to do, okay. If you don't want to try, that's fine, just let me know."

Her voice is soft but confident, like she can handle any eventuality. I know she can't, that I haven't explained myself properly, she's stepping into danger, and I shouldn't let her, but I don't tell her that. Even though she's given me the opportunity, I'm scared to tell her that and have it stop.

Instead, I whisper, "Why are you doing this?"

Her arms move higher, wrapping around my shoulders, one leg curling over mine. She says, "Because I've got a thing for massive blond men with massive blond dicks," then chuckles, the vibrations creating an additional source of warmth inside my head.

"I'll hurt you."

"That's okay."

"No, I'll really—" My voice chokes to a halt as she slides her sweatpants down. I have to lift my weight for her to do it and I do, even though there's a dull beat in the back of my brain telling me not to, warning me to stop. "I'll really hurt you and I don't want to. I like you."

"I like you, too."

She takes me in her hand again, guiding me between her legs, the head of my cock nudging against her, nudging inside like a warmth seeking missile. My balls ache at the nearness, my ears ringing with a low tone, my mouth full of cotton wool.

I push forward or she tilts her hips, or *something* happens and I'm slowly sliding into her, the sensation so different from my hand that I gasp, my fingers clenching as I drive them back into her hair, into a safe spot far away from her fragile throat.

A hand lands on my shoulder, pressing lightly, and I stop. I stop even though every nerve in my body wants to continue plunging forward, thrusting deeper.

I stop because she's right and there's a wealth of difference between fifteen and eighteen. An enormous gap and it's enough for now but my control is steadily slipping. It's enough for now but give me a moment, give me a few thrusts until I'm fully encased inside her, and it won't be.

Her breathing is funny now, focused. I try to withdraw and her leg slides farther upward, resting against my arse, an encouragement to stop, to rest, to stay exactly where I am.

"Do you want to know what it feels like? You inside me?"

One arm stays around my shoulder, the other makes its way to my cheek, cupping the side of my face while her thumb strokes along the underside of my chin.

"You're stretching me out, so all the nerve endings crammed in there are excited and keep flooding me with messages." Her voice is calm and dreamy, like she's on the verge of falling asleep.

"It's almost painful, and that means there are more signals than usual. It makes time slow down."

Her thumb traces a lazy spiral against my skin. "You stopped me."

"I paused you. It takes a little while longer to get used to the movement."

"You mean, I'm causing you pain."

"No but if I didn't rest for a second, you might do."

"I should stop."

"If you want to." Her hold on me doesn't lessen. Her thumb continues to make its gentle strokes. "But don't stop because you're second guessing everything."

Now it's my turn to laugh against the curve of her neck. "I haven't had the time to first guess things."

"You feel good," she says. "I think I forgot to mention that."

An odd pride ignites at the words, not fading entirely even when I pour the cold water on top that she's used to saying things like that. She probably compliments every man who passes through her door.

Then I have a twinge at thinking such a thing when I don't know. The one occasion she invited me to ask about her profession, I was too absorbed in what I needed from her to take the opportunity.

She tips her pelvis upwards, and I sink farther inside. This time there's no handbrake on my shoulder, no suggestion she wants me to stop.

All my focus circles down to a single part of my anatomy, where I'm joined to her, the sensation overwhelming.

There's a sound from her, a long sigh that could equally be pain or pleasure. My mind takes it the way it needs it, turning it into a gasp of fear. I draw back, the relief of sinking back inside her worth the effort. The grip of her walls around me is so tight it's like she doesn't want to release me, like she would cling hold of me forever if I let her.

And I want to let her.

But the other urges come screaming out of nowhere. I thought I was holding them back, tempering them, but that's a fairy tale I let myself believe because it's so much easier than facing the truth.

That I can't control them.

That I can't control myself.

One second, two, and it's close to being too late when I pull back, pull out, throw myself halfway across the floor, stumbling, my feet tangling, my jeans slung low where she pushed them when she took me out and it takes all my concentration to hike them back up, cover myself, turn away from the girl I left lying sprawled and open for me on the couch.

The girl who must be confused. The girl who'll hate me for rejecting her because even if she pretends it's okay, I know she'll feel it and if I couldn't explain what was happening before we got this far, then how the fuck am I meant to explain what's going on inside my head right now.

"Trent? Are you okay?"

"Just..." I put my hand to my chest where there's an uncomfortable pressure that grows with every second. "Give me a minute," I whisper, sliding my back down the wall until my arse hits the ground.

I bury my face in my hands, so I don't have to look at her.

"I'm turning on the light, okay?"

A croak that might be a yes, might be a no, comes out of me, unable to give a more coherent answer at this stage. All I am is the snarling warring selves within me, each intent on their opposing demands.

The world brightens, and I hear her closing the gap between us.

Rosa kneels beside me and lays a soothing hand on the top of my head. "Can you tell me what's happening?"

I croak out a broken laugh.

She switches position, sitting companionably beside me, her shoulder touching mine. "I should apologise," she whispers in the tone of a confession. "It's been a week or longer since anyone bothered to vacuum the floor in here, so if you have a wealth of crumbs clinging to you when you stand up, that's why."

I snort, shaking my head, still afraid to peel my hands away from my eyes to see the outside world.

"You want a drink of anything?"

"I'm not much of a drinker." I try to rouse the will to stand but it doesn't take. "Guess I should go."

"You're meant to be defending me and Finley from terrible men," she reminds me with a tiny cackle.

"And you're meant to be insisting you don't need any help. You're fine. Everything's fine."

She grabs hold of my upper arm, turning to press her face against it to stifle her burst of laughter. "Oh, you think you know me, eh?"

I finally work out how to lower my hands. "No. I don't think I'm close to knowing you at all." I wait a breath but don't let myself pause for longer. "I wanted to hurt you. When I—" I wave my hand instead of finishing the sentence, not sure how I'd word it even if I could.

"But you didn't."

"But I wanted to."

"But you didn't." She nudges me with her hip, then scrambles to her feet, holding a hand back towards me. "Come on. If you want to sit, the couch is far more comfortable."

"Why don't you care?"

She crouches, pushing the hands away from my face only to

replace it with one of hers, the fingers cooler than mine. "I do care. This is me caring."

Rosa stands again and helps me to my feet. I adjust my clothing, tidying as much as the situation allows. When she leads me back to the sofa, I follow her, meek as a lamb, still tense with the fear that I'll hurt her.

"Do you want me to go?" she asks, and I know what I should say. Instead, I can't say anything, the lump in my throat too large an obstacle to fight past. When she reaches out to squeeze my hand, I grab hold of her like a lifeline.

She sinks onto the floor, resting her head against my shoulder. Each small point of contact a delight.

While I'm trying to think what to say, how to make everything better, I slip into a deep dark hole of sleep. By the time I fight my way back to the surface, Rosa's long gone, and the moon has slunk away from the night sky, sheltering behind the horizon like a coward.

CHAPTER ELEVEN

ROSA

On Sunday, I take a seat opposite Ceecee and pass her a date scone from the local bakery.

"Ooh, thanks love." She happily opens the butter sachet that came with it and spreads a liberal amount across the first half. "And it's still warm!"

I wait until she takes a bite before opening my mouth to ask a question, but she gets there first.

"Let me guess. You're bribing me for some nefarious purpose." She takes another enormous mouthful, face joyful as she chews. "If you want me to take on a client, the answer's no."

"It's not that," I assure her. "But I wouldn't mind your input on what to do with one."

"Tie them up. Isn't that your speed?"

"He's nothing that straightforward." Even though I want her advice, I find it hard to divulge anything about Trent.

It's not like he asked for my help. He's found his own way of dealing with his problem and just because it's obvious it won't last for long—and might even add to his issue—doesn't mean he needs me wading into the midst.

"When we're... he needs to hurt me. It gets so bad that he stops rather than risk it."

"My advice is to find a new client."

"But there must be—"

She holds up a hand to cut me off. "Honey, you're eighteen. You've got enough on your plate with your work and your studies and your mum to worry about how some guy gets his rocks off. If he needs help, let him see a therapist."

I cock an eyebrow at her. "Aren't you the one who told me that's half the job?"

"To be a friend and a sounding board is the job. Not curing some guy who wants to harm women."

"He doesn't want to. He has the urge to."

"And when you're reliant on him controlling himself to avoid getting hurt, you're in trouble. Because maybe one day he doesn't try to stop." She clocks one look at my face and bursts into laughter. "Don't ask for my advice if you don't want it, hun. If he can afford you, he can afford a shrink."

"I don't think he'd go to one."

"Then he doesn't really want to change, does he? Which leaves you in more danger, doesn't it?"

I nod, the movement creaking with annoyance.

"He doesn't know this address, does he?"

My eyes widen as I glance at her, startled at the thought. "No."

She nods and moves to the sink to rinse out her cup. "Good. We don't need those types hanging around, creating a nuisance."

Her client arrives and I don't linger. I don't have appointments on Sunday, so head to the university library to catch up on my studies. Each time I try to clear my mind and relax into the coursework, all I feel is Trent bolting from me in the darkness, anxiety screaming from every inch of his body.

I can't leave him like that. There'll be some way around his problem, I'm sure.

Because otherwise, I've got a crush on a rich maniac and that's certain not to end well.

———————

I'M on the bus home when I get a phone call from the police. The ink used on the card was blood and they obtained a DNA sample for testing but didn't find a match in the system.

"I know this isn't the result you wanted," the officer calmly explains to me. "But we've put an alert out for all the patrols in the area. If you ever see someone, call emergency and we'll be able to take it from there."

I hang up, getting off at the next stop even though it's four from my closest one, preferring the longer walk to be alone with my thoughts rather than avoiding eye contact on a vehicle packed with strangers.

The good news is whoever is bothering me isn't my uncle. It could still be a complete coincidence that the cards started at the same time my mother told me he was out of jail.

And I don't know how old her information is. The friend of a friend network might be good at gossip but it's less reliable with facts. He might have been out for years, and the news just drifted our way at this moment. Trent indicated the intruder had been younger than I remember my uncle being, and that was ten years ago.

Unrelated. I roll the word around in my head to see where it lands.

A stretch of believability maybe but not impossible. That the taunts are image related could be a preference of whoever's bugging me rather than a specific link to my past.

If the first hadn't arrived before meeting Trent, I might have considered him a culprit.

I need to keep a better watch on my surrounding. Heightened vigilance until the threats stop coming or I'm able to move the hell out and get away.

My observation skills need to be top of their game.

Like that car, parked over the road but three or four houses down. I haven't seen it before outside our neighbour's house, but I noticed it when I left this morning and I'm noticing it twice as hard now.

Before I can second guess myself, I stride along the footpath, pretending for all the world that I'm just continuing my stroll, not a nefarious thought in sight.

There's a man in the front seat of the car, low enough down that he's hard to spot from a distance. The closer I get, the tenser his posture becomes. Someone who doesn't want to be seen.

I draw level and glance inside, catching the food and drink containers that show he's been out here for a while.

My system goes into high alert, pulse jumping in my neck like it's a child desperate for parental attention. I wipe my damp palms against my jeans.

He might be casing someone else's house.

Well, if so, it's their lucky day. I get two steps past his window, far enough that he relaxes, then double back, knocking on the passenger side.

"Excuse me," I say when all it elicits is a startled jump. "Can you give me a hand?"

The man has a three-day scruff coating his chin and cheeks, his eyes red-rimmed from too much coffee and not enough sleep. Unless he's out here smoking pot but I can't smell any.

He eyes me warily but eventually works the control to lower the window. Not that he makes any effort to meet my gaze.

"Hey, you've been out here a while," I say, trying to memorise everything inside the car. A hard job considering the amount of refuse he appears to be collecting in his vehicle.

And what does his rubbish matter? I should've got far enough past the car to note the licence plate number, scribbling it down before searching for further details on my phone.

I take the device out, surreptitiously trying to get to the camera setting so I can snap a picture if he suddenly drives away.

"It's a free country," he snarls back, grimacing as he shifts in his seat. He looks a little aged to be conducting surveillance. Now I'm seeing him close up, it seems much more likely that he's an aggrieved ex, stalking his former partner. Everything about him just gives off that vibe.

"It is. But did you notice anyone around my flat? We had a break-in last night and someone got badly hurt. Any help would really be appreciated."

"I haven't seen anything."

"Right. But you were out here last night, yeah?"

"No. I only just got here."

"And you're visiting...?"

"None of your business. Is that all? I'm trying to have a nap here."

The window on his side is also wound down. I send him my warmest smile. "Yes, that's everything. Thanks for your help."

I step away, moving around the back of the car, looking both ways just like my mother taught me, so it appears I'm about to cross the road.

Then I rush for his door, reach my arm through the window, snatch his keys and dance away.

"What the fuck?"

The man pushes his door open, taking a while to get to his feet after long hours spent sitting. I backtrack, glancing around to see if any curtains are twitching, if any pedestrians are approaching.

But we're in a don't hear, don't see, don't report kind of neighbourhood. If anyone is watching, they're making damn sure no one knows.

I snap a photo of his licence plate, then scroll to my keypad to dial back the officer who just called.

"Who the fuck are you ringing?" he asks, the menacing steps towards me faltering. "Just give me my keys back. There's no need to involve anyone else."

I haven't pressed to dial yet. I dangle the keys and watch his eyes narrow, but he doesn't come any closer. The man obviously has more to lose from the police turning up than I do.

"Tell me what you're really doing here, and I'll let you have your keys back." When he doesn't immediately answer, I saunter close to a storm drain, holding them above the grill and watching as his eyes nearly bug from his head.

"Okay. I'm watching a house. It's my job." He jerks forward and I hold the keys nearer to the grate until he retreats. "I'm just getting my wallet out, okay?"

Like I've got a gun trained on him and might fire at the wrong move. The idea makes me smile. "Sure."

"This is my card," he says, holding the battered slip towards me. "I'm a private investigator and I'm tracking everyone who goes in, out, or near this house over here."

He waves his hand in so broad a gesture that it encompasses the nearest three properties, but I know he means mine.

"Who hired you?" I ask but I already know. "Call Trent and tell him I don't need a babysitter, thanks." I close the keys into my fist, withdrawing it safely to my side. "How much is he paying you?"

"None of your business."

I tuck the keys into my pocket and cancel the call to the police, switching it to a call to Trent instead. "Why the hell is a man parked outside my house, staring at me?"

"To keep you safe since you refused my invitation for you to move into Fort Knox."

"You call it that?" I snigger, holding my hand up in warning when the PI takes my good humour as permission to approach.

"It's large, it's secure, and it's full of my dad's riches. Don't you think it fits?"

I take another look at the weary man in charge of my welfare. "Where's the beefy security guard?" I ask Trent, only partly teasing. "This guy looks like he'd go down in a fight long before I would."

"He's there to record details of anyone acting suspiciously and find out who they are and what they're doing there—not to punch them."

"If you're going to have someone stationed out here all day, I want someone who can punch them, too."

"I'm well aware of what you like, Rosa. That's why you've got the runt of the litter."

The response makes me wrinkle my nose, smiling. Trent got me a protector, but not one who might give him a reason to become jealous. It's kind of adorable.

But I still don't want him out here. "Tell your man he's relieved of duty."

"No."

"Then I'll call the police like I've just threatened to."

Trent sighs down the phone line. "Go ahead. They're just going to tell you the same thing I will. He's not breaking any laws. He's not interfering with you. They can't stop him monitoring your house."

"Well, that's bullshit."

He bursts into laughter. "Sure. But it's also bullshit that keeps an eye on you when I can't be there."

And suddenly I'm swallowing around an enormous lump. "You're coming back?"

"Unless you agree with my original suggestion, yes. Until the police catch whoever's after you, me and Elton aren't letting you out of our sight."

"Elton," I repeat with a chuckle.

"It's something like that," he says. "And even if it's not his real name it fits, doesn't it?"

"You're not even sure of his name?"

Someone shouts for Trent and when he answers again, he's distracted. "Sounds like you can see him from where you are. Why don't you go ask him? I've got to go. See you tonight."

"Wait!"

But he's gone, leaving me with a set of car keys and a rumpled man who looks more like he's coming off a three-day bender than someone who's safeguarding my life.

"You want a cup of tea or coffee?" I offer, returning his keys. "There might even be a gingernut hiding in the cupboard unless my flatmates have eaten them."

His face is still exceedingly wary, but the man nods, locking his car before he follows me inside.

CHAPTER TWELVE

TRENT

"You're not meant to spend the afternoon entertaining him," I complain when I turn up with takeaways and another bottle of good bourbon that I filched from my dad's study.

Rosa, Finley, and the PI who's meant to be stationed outside, monitoring the place, are sitting at the table, playing cards and looking like they're about to come to blows or collapse with raucous laughter.

"His name's Edwin," Rosa announces with glee.

"He's divorced and shares custody of his nine-year-old daughter," Finley adds, scraping the pot towards her. "And you can call him Eddie for short."

"I won't call you at all if this is how you interpret instructions," I grumble directly to the man, my words landing with all the harm of a light dusting of snow.

"Don't get on his case," Rosa scolds me in return. "If you're going to hire men to surround me every moment of the day, I get to decide what to do with them."

"If we're taking requests," Finley adds, relieving me of my burdens with a delighted expression. "I would like a female to take tomorrow's shift. Can't have these two flirting all day long and leave me stranded."

Flirting?

I stare at the man who's old enough to be my father and give a small grunt of disbelief. Surely, he's not her type. He's not anyone's type.

"Stop glaring at us," Rosa says with a cheeky grin. "Come sit and play."

"I don't play cards."

"Then grab some plates and cutlery from the kitchen and serve up whatever you've got in the bag. It smells delicious."

I move into the kitchen, storing the three types of ice cream in the compact freezer, having to take a knife to the worst of the frost before they'll fit. The rest of the food is in containers, and I open them on the table, handing out plates and cutlery before taking a seat.

"Help yourselves. No." I point an accusing finger at the PI. "Now I'm here, you're officially relieved of duty. Come back tomorrow at eight and no playing cards again, okay?"

Despite the loud groans of protest from Finley and Rosa, *Eddie* nods his goodbyes and takes off, leaving me with two accusing faces turned my way.

"We were fleecing the hell out of him," Finley says with a growl. "Give us another hour and we could've earned your entire fee back."

"I don't want a desperate, money-starved investigator doing work for me," I say with far more good cheer than I had a minute ago. "Now, d'you like edamame beans or can I have the lot?"

"You don't live here, you know," Rosa says, her attempt at a glare a complete failure. "You can't bully your way through the door every time you want."

"Who's bullying? I just walked in with armfuls of food. Hardly a bully move."

"It's blatant manipulation," she declares, heaping a plate with food. "And just because it works doesn't mean you can act on any other ideas."

"Unless they're as good as this food," Finley interrupts, beaming. "This is amazing."

Once we've finished eating, I take care of the scraps. Rosa follows me into the kitchen, resting against the opposite bench. "Thanks for all of this, but you don't need to hire someone to keep tabs on me."

"I'm not." At her confused expression, I explain, "I've hired him to keep tabs on any potential intruders. Keeping tabs on you is just a by-product."

"I'm out for the night," Finley announces from the doorway. "Thanks for dinner, Trent, and don't listen to a word she says. You can keep coming back as often as you like. We always appreciate when someone else cooks."

Once she's out the door, Rosa and I walk through to the couch. My cheeks grow warmer, remembering what happened here last night, then feel mortified as she says, "I asked someone about your... situation."

"Mm-hm." I try to keep the anxiety off my face. "And did they tell you to leave well enough alone?" Even with my eyes deliberately averted, my gaze crawls back to her face, desperate to read what she's thinking.

"Something like that. Are you in counselling?"

"I don't need—" My teeth snap together, not wanting to draw the obvious retort out of her. "No. No, I'm not."

"I also read up on paraphilias on the way home. Pain is very common. Hence the popularity of BDSM."

"You think I want to tie you up?"

My voice might sound incredulous, but the idea prompts a thousand images to flood my mind, exciting me more the longer I think on it. I can all too easily imagine her bound and at my mercy. Begging me; to start, to perform a specific request, *to stop.*

The blood leaves my cheeks and heads straight in the other direction.

"No, I was thinking more of the Sadism part of the acronym." She stretches her leg out to poke me with her big toe. "Why? Do you want to be restrained?"

All my ideas flip on their heads, and I can't speak for a minute as a cascade of depravity overfills my brain. Straining against ropes or twisting against the metal grip of cuffs. I imagine the thwarted desire, the frustration of wanting to move, to touch, to hurt, to harm but being completely unable to fulfil the impulse, instead writhing inside my bonds.

I meet Rosa's eye, my instinctive response to deny it, push it away, but she can clearly see the temptation twisting across every inch of my face.

She swings around to sit beside me rather than propped against the opposite arm. Her forefinger touches the fiery flame of my cheek, then turns so her knuckle trails down, winding to my neck, then out along the width of my shoulder. The light touch drives my nerve endings insane.

"You would like that?"

I swallow and my throat clicks with a sudden dryness. Even when I clear it, there's still a crack as I answer, "Yes. I think I'd like that."

"And what would you want me to do while you're restrained?"

Another struggle to get the words free. "Anything you want."

She nods, then frowns, the tiny crease between her brows so cute I have to grip my hands together to stop from caressing the small line. I can't touch her. Not while this turmoil is happening inside me. Not when an alternative path to fulfilment is opening before my eyes.

"Can you show me what you like?" When I return her frown, she nods to my pocket. "The videos you like to watch."

"Oh, I..." My voice halters to a stop as I wipe my palms against my jeans' leg. "They're not meant for other people."

"Will it ruin it for you?"

Her question is genuine and although I haven't tried it before, I understand the answer is no.

It won't ruin anything.

It may make me so unbearably overwhelmed that I can't continue, but that's more of a reason to try than to resist.

I tug my phone out, going to the newest video. The same one that disappointed me on the night I met Rosa. One I haven't watched nearly as much as I usually would, even with its drawbacks.

"They're not... it's not real. The whole thing's scripted."

"Okay." She slides her left hand around my upper arm and cuddles closer, her cheek resting against my shoulder. "Press play."

My thumb hovers over the button for a moment, wondering if this is a disastrous idea.

Probably. But so would telling her no and expecting her to let me get away with it. I click the screen and try not to turn my attention to her face. The last thing I want her to feel is my eyes crawling over her, searching for any hint of a reaction.

The action unfolds onscreen, and I wince at some of it; not seeing it for what I want out of it but through her eyes. Watching it almost like a diagnostic aid to tell her what's wrong with me.

Having viewed it enough to have the timing off by heart, I stare at the blank space at the bottom of the image, catching her small facial movements from the corner of my eye. Even though I don't want to see. Even though I'm suddenly desperate not to know.

"You have a lot like that?"

I shake my head. "There are others along the same lines, but a lot of the scripts get lost in translation. This is closest to what I want."

She raises her eyebrows at me for permission, then takes the phone out of my hands, clicking earlier in the recording, then playing out tiny snippets again, committing them to memory.

Finally, I can't stand another second of silence. "What's the verdict?"

"She's hot and they're very well endowed." She swivels towards me, a smile crinkling her eyes. "Not compared to you maybe but getting up there."

"I'm not looking at them."

Rosa wrinkles her nose, drawing me in with her easy laugh. "Sure, but some of us are more interested than others."

Her giggle relaxes me; letting me know I haven't offended her but reassuring me I'm not the butt of her joke, either.

"Does that mean you're coming around to the idea?"

"Of letting you record me?" She squeezes my arm. "No. Just thinking of other possibilities. Wouldn't you prefer a live show?"

She must feel the tremor that runs through me, because she adds, "Not of you and me. Not like that, anyway."

She stands but only to face me, lowering herself onto my lap, her knees either side and her feet curling back over my legs behind her. Her arms link around my neck and it's hard to think with her this close. My hands find their own way around her waist, and I tilt my head forward, so it rests against her collarbone.

Breathing is hard, but it's easier when I'm not staring directly at her. "How would it work?"

"I would find a paid partner to help with the visual and you would sit and watch." Her fingers curl into the hairs at the back of my neck, softly massaging.

I don't think I've ever been near someone so tactile, it's like her skin against my body is as much of a messenger as the words flowing from her mouth.

"We could tie you up if you prefer that."

The excitement surges within me again as my breath dissipates across her skin, my hands moving to press flat against her back, holding her steady.

I imagine watching a man touching Rosa, right in front of me, acting on my wishes, my commands. A proxy to touch her, taste her. A faceless professional who's only purpose is to make her moan, make her squirm, make her scream. Doing everything that I would do without the fear surging inside me.

Sweat beads on my forehead, my breath rasping in my throat. Still a voyeur but privy to so much more than a screen can provide me.

All that, while straining against my bonds, trying but unable to get free.

"Yes," I finally manage with a gasp. "I think I'd like that." And I would try anything just so she lets me stay near her.

"It probably won't be... Once I find someone, I can check with them, but it mightn't be like that." She dips her head towards my phone. "It might be rough, but I doubt anyone's in the mood to playact quite that way."

I tilt my head back, my eyes feasting on her lush mouth. "You don't do stuff like that?"

She shrugs. "Some people might but there's a big difference between playacting something when you're sharing a private moment and hiring someone to do it. There has to be a lot of trust to perform CNC because we'd both be relying on each other to read the reactions and listen for safe words or safe gestures. If we're not on the same page, we might take it too far or hold back too much."

"What's CNC?"

"Consensual non-consent. Agreeing to a rape fantasy that doesn't stop just because someone says no."

I try to visualise it. Someone forcing her in front of me. As the image forms, my ears rumble like they're blocked with cotton wool, my pulse picks up speed. Even in my head, creating the montage from thin air, I have to stifle my reaction.

The mix of desire, of lust, tempered by the idea of someone touching this beautiful girl, this girl I want to make mine... the confused rush of duelling emotions smothers me until I gasp for breath.

"You'll have a safe word, too," she adds, clocking my swing in temperament. "You'll have just as much control as either of us."

"Okay."

"It will—" She breaks off, looking embarrassed and I grasp the thought.

"I'll pay. Anything you need. Take my card and go wild."

She chuckles softly at the idea. "That sounds dangerous."

The possibilities of what she's offering consume my attention so much it doesn't occur to me until the next morning that her bill is probably going to be part of the service. She's only trying to help me because I forced my help on her.

A strange gratitude but I understand its origins and I don't want to fool myself into thinking it's something it's not.

No matter how my thoughts like to play with the idea that she's my girl, to her I must be just another client.

The idea knocks some shine off my day, but I soon rally.

If this works, if it opens another avenue to release, then it doesn't matter what we label ourselves or how Rosa thinks of me. She'll own a piece of me forever and it doesn't matter the cost because I'd give it to her ten times over.

I'm grateful that when she could have kept telling me no, sending me away, she turned me into her special project instead.

CHAPTER THIRTEEN

ROSA

I'm nervous shuffling through the doorway of the prostitute's collective on Thursday afternoon. Not of the office, I've been here enough times to be familiar with the layout and the array of pamphlets offered from every available surface, but of the mission.

I've never worked with a partner to enact a scene before. I'm not sure how to vet applicants or even how to word the ad.

The noticeboard has a variety of positions available, the website a tonne more. There's a PUMP leaflet—pride and unity for male prostitutes—on the side table and I collect it while I examine the current jobs on offer.

My stomach tightens like it does when I submit an online essay. A weird sensation like I'm about to be judged, but that's ridiculous. If I'm the one placing the recruitment ad, I'm the one in the judge's chair.

"Hey, Rosa," a man calls out to me from the entrance.

I turn, then frown, not placing him, although he's vaguely

familiar. His face is oddly bland, the lack of distinguishing characteristics its only claim to fame. Mid brown hair, mid brown eyes, skin tanned in the sun but not so much that he's instantly placeable as a surfer or a labourer.

"Hey," I say back, then return to scouring the board.

He gives a soft laugh. "That's okay. I wouldn't remember me either. It's Andy. I helped with your coworker Ceecee on an occasion a month back."

"Oh, sure." I still can't place him but at least I know the reference. Ceecee runs threesomes on request, mostly with a female partner but on occasions she'll tag team with a male.

Since his face looks friendly enough, welcoming a chat, I gesture towards the board. "Have you ever placed an ad on one of these? I'm not sure of the etiquette."

"No, but I get most of my work by answering them. What'd you looking for?"

"A male partner for a scene." I shift my weight, figuring out how much to say. "It's like a cuck scene, I guess."

Like that but so much more.

The fear that grips Trent disables him, cutting him off from such a pleasurable part of his life that I could weep to think he'll never experience the simple and oh-so-complicated play of emotions, thoughts, and sensations that feed into a good sexual encounter.

I want to free him from the crippling anxiety but there's more layered beneath. There's as much satisfaction in the idea of Trent being restrained, of watching him watching me, finally seeing me the way I was desperate for him to, back on the day he first knocked on my door.

The pleasure of his eyes on me, the growing intensity of his focus, darkening as his pupils swell, smouldering with carnal desire. His gaze locking to mine while pleasure floods my body, wrists straining at their bonds.

I crave the visual temptation of seeing his cock fatten, straining upward in a decadent display of lust; want to watch the pulse tremble along his length as he comes, as his seed pumps and arches in creamy ropes from his body, as he comes just by watching my display, the centre of his voyeuristic attention, imagining the hands on me his powerful hands, the cock inside me his thick cock.

My eyes break away from the board, seeking refuge from my sizzling thoughts in the safety of the black and white tiled floor.

No matter what other desires stir within me, it's a job. A contract with parameters and rules and safety nets and boundaries.

"Yeah?" Andy says, arching his eyebrows and that sensation of being judged flickers at the edge of my mind again. "Any physical requests?"

"No," I answer but realise I never even bothered to ask Trent. He might have very particular preferences and the query should have been automatic.

My head swims for a second, awash in too many responsibilities, too many options, too many fears. The overwhelm steals my breath, the back of my throat aches with sadness.

I thought I had this. I thought I had everything lined up, each demand relegated to its own wee box.

Now everything's spinning out of my control.

But this. This is something I can do right. Even if someone is judging, I can still make the right call and get at least one part of my life back on track.

"It's not about the male, then?" Andy asks, leaning his shoulder against the wall and finger combing his long hair back from his face.

He must be in his early thirties, old enough for me to feel comfortable that he knows what he's doing. I relax a little, my shoulders loosening enough that my posture slackens.

"No. Except as a proxy, I guess."

"No male-to-male contact?"

I shake my head.

"And when is this happening?"

A smile breaks free, and I laugh. "Whenever I can find someone willing to help. Why?" I arch my eyebrow. "You interested?"

"For sure." His gaze travels back to the board, scanning the notices, most of them warnings or reminders on how to be safe. "What's the pay rate?"

Since it's Trent's money, I can afford to be generous. "Five hundred and it'll be less than an hour from prep to completion."

He whistles softly, eyes scanning me again, then wandering around the small area set up like a lounge so visitors can stay, relax, and chat rather than just wait for appointments then go.

I try not to look needy. A bit late since I've already outlined that I have no idea what I'm doing.

But this would be a godsend. Since Ceecee's already vetted him, all I'll need is a clean test card and we can set the whole thing up right now. One massive strikethrough on my to-do list and I can move onto the next with the radiant glow of achievement.

"At your place in Sydenham or is it a private home visit?"

Private would mean Trent felt more comfortable; the brothel's where I'd feel safest. "Sydenham," I decide. Saves Trent's staff or family from wandering in at the wrong time, too. "Next Saturday afternoon if that suits."

Then I can get the whole thing done and go visit Mum after her nap, so she'll stay awake for longer, chatting.

I can tell her the entire story and let her tell me off, tell me I shouldn't get involved with clients, not like this.

Suddenly, I miss her so much that I'm tempted to cut class and head over to the home to visit with her right this minute. My arms ache to hug her, a proper hug like when I was little and ran into something and got a bump or fell and got a skinned knee. When it seemed there was nothing in the world that couldn't be fixed with the application of her comforting arms and soothing voice. The nonsense words she'd murmur until I was relaxed enough to stop bawling my eyes out and tell her what was wrong.

"Fine by me." He smiles, and it's nice to smile back and not have to worry if he's taking it the wrong way or think it promises something more than it should.

I scrawl my details onto a piece of notepaper and hand it over while he rolls his eyes at me. "What?"

"You're writing a note for me while using your phone as the desk," he says between chuckles. "Couldn't you just use the same energy to send me an email?"

"Hey. Writing notes is an art form, okay?"

"I'll take your word for it." He peers at my handwriting, pulls another face, laughingly enunciates the entire message while typing it into his phone, then screws up the paper to throw it away.

"And now I have to ask for your number as well," he adds. "Because otherwise something is certain to go wrong."

"What's yours?" I type it in and phone it immediately, rolling my eyes back at him. "Happy?"

"Ecstatic. You got any idea of what he'll want us to do?"

One of the meeting rooms to the side of the lounge area is free and I haul him in there, nervous about being overheard. Probably the first big sign that I shouldn't be doing what I'm doing.

"He likes things to get rough. How'd you feel about that?"

"Rough on you, rough on me, or rough on both of us?"

"Rough on me." I pause and he waits, immediately understanding there's more to it. The ease of that connection makes me wonder if I could ask for the whole thing. I'm not usually one to pose a question unless I'm fairly certain the answer will come back yes but I can go out on a limb more easily for someone else than I could for my own needs.

"Have you ever done rape fantasies?"

"Male on male, yeah. I had a client a few years back was into that sort of stuff." He looks sceptical. "But that was after he'd been a client for a while. I'm not sure it would work as a one-off."

"No, of course. Not for this time," I babble, trying to undo the question before I even let him properly answer. "Just something to think about. In the future. If he wants to do it again."

"Sure." His smile grows wider. "And what's your safe word?"

"Sugar. What's yours?"

"Red. Why futz with a classic?"

My smile broadens. "Because people stop hearing it."

"Not the people I hang around with." He checks his phone again. "Thanks for the opportunity, anyway. A few more unexpected gigs and I might hit this cost-of-living crisis right in the nuts."

"Sure." I walk away, then turn back. "What's the name of the client that Ceecee vetted you for?"

"God knows. I haven't done any repeats but there've been a few over the last year or so. The last was three weeks ago. Big, bearded guy. She'll know him."

I think I know him, too. At least by sight.

"Send me whatever you want me to do, and we can go from there," he suggests, checking his phone for the time. "I've got to run."

I wave goodbye, hanging around for a few minutes longer just to kill time until my next lecture. Halfway through class, my laptop gives up the ghost and I grind my teeth to keep from swearing.

Out loud, that is. There's plenty of it going on inside my head.

I just got the damned thing fixed. Even if it's still under their thirty-day warranty like the guy said, it's still a hassle to drop it off and collect it. To do without it for the few days it takes for them to work out what's wrong.

Trent pings my phone as I turn it on, coming out of the lecture hall, offering me a lift. There's a small wriggle of worry about his closeness, what thoughts he might be growing, but I push it away.

He has a fetish, but he's nice, he's sweet. Instead of wrinkling my nose that he's crowding me, I should be grateful while it lasts.

Channelling my inner Finley, I wave to him where he's parked in the student carpark. "Just passing by, were you?"

He shrugs. "Nowhere near but I didn't want you to harangue my investigator again while he's just doing his job."

"Harangue." The word makes me snort.

"What else would you call it when you steal his car keys then take him for everything he owns."

"Finley was the one owning his arse, I just sat back and watched." I stow my laptop in the footwell, giving it a tiny kick. "Would you mind dropping me at a computer repair shop in town? My laptop's on the fritz."

He glances across, then takes out his phone, sending a text to someone. A minute later, there's a buzz as it's returned. "Don't worry about the shop. My friend's coming over to your flat to take a look."

"Right. And he's a computer repairman?"

Trent tosses me an amiable smile. "Something like that."

I sit back, giving up on this fight because it doesn't matter, and I already feel good from hiring someone so easily for the planned event.

It's weird to have a wriggle of excitement about a job. Even when I enjoy the physical aspects of my work, or the slow unwind of interactions after, it's still work. It's still something I'd rather pass on in favour of going home and reading or watching tv while inhaling snacks.

But now... this isn't like my usual jobs. I can hear my mother's voice turning strident as she gets into her lecture. On what I should or shouldn't do. On how I keep myself safe.

The safety part isn't just physical.

It's the mental strain of forming intimate relationships then unhooking them at the end of a scene. The delicate handling required when someone becomes too enthusiastic, wants too much of my time, and I have to pull back before a preference becomes an obsession or worse.

Now, here I am, leaping into this thing with a boy who I feel a growing connection with. The push and pull of a normal relationship based on interest and attraction rather than the transactive nature of my usual job.

I should walk away but even if it weren't for the threat from my mystery card deliverer, I don't know that it would be that easy. Even this early, the first tentative tendrils of a relationship are putting down roots.

It's the same way I felt after a week spent living with Finley. We clicked immediately and I can't see a future without us being in each other's lives, no matter what they might entail.

At home, Trent parks across the road and waves to another vehicle, already waiting at the curb. A lanky boy gets out and I stare for a moment, gobsmacked.

He's remarkable. Like someone pointed to all their favourite bits of their favourite humans and wove them together into the world's tastiest snack. Enough to satisfy any girl's hunger.

Then his blank eyes meet mine and I glance away as a shiver catches hold of me. Trent's warm gaze is the perfect antidote, heating me back to normal.

"This is Caylon," Trent says, putting his arm around my waist. His hand lands on my hip like it's natural, like it belongs there. "He's a tech genius."

"Compared to my friends," the boy says in response, giving a half shrug before turning to stare at the flat. "If you stacked me against an actual genius, I'd fall short. This you?" He gestures across the road and, when I nod, he leads the way, falling into an alpha position with so little fanfare that I hide a smile.

He has to drop back when we get to the door and I unlock it, waving them through before I secure it behind us, putting my useless laptop on the table.

"It froze in the middle of class," I say, the explanation probably falling short on detail, but I don't know enough to add more. "The same thing happened a few weeks ago, and I got it repaired but I guess it didn't stick."

"Sure." He unrolls a mat with a tiny set of tools that make me think I should go have an eye exam soon.

"You want something to eat or drink?"

Caylon barely registers the words, and Trent answers, "No," for him, then drags me over to the couch to keep out of his friend's way.

It doesn't take long. The boy glances over with a confused expression. "You said this had been repaired?"

"Yeah." I recite the name of the shop and he shakes his head. "This laptop is full of spyware. There's a program to allow remote viewing and a—"

"No. He told me he found all of that and wiped it."

Caylon's gaze locks on mine for a few seconds, then he curves his lips into a smile that never reaches his eyes. "Everything on here was installed on the same date." He turns the screen of the monitor he brought with him towards me so I can read it for myself. "Is that the day you took it in?"

"No." My skin crawls, gooseflesh popping out on my upper

arms. "Is there... Could someone have done this over the internet or something?"

"You mean remotely?" When I nod, his eyes defocus completely, then slowly return to their previous level of dead. "Not without having physical access for at least part of the time. The rest..." He shrugs, but it's not the sign of a man confident that's what happened.

"It wouldn't have just reinstalled itself?" I ask, a last grasp at hope.

"No." He reassembles the laptop and rolls away most of his tools, then frowns at Trent who nods back to him. "It's a nice day. Do you want to sit outside for a bit?"

I'm flummoxed but Trent puts a hand on my lower back, not giving me much choice as he pushes me ahead of him. Three steps from the back door, Caylon asks, "Can I check out the rest of the place."

And I twig on why he wanted me out of the house. "You think someone's installed more spying software?"

He scrunches up his nose, briefly returning to the physical perfection of earlier as enjoyment dances in his eyes, then it blinks out like a light. "No, but hardware's not out of the question."

I sit on the concrete step, curling my knees to my chest as Caylon searches through the house. The two blessings are that Trent's comforting arm is around my shoulder the entire time and that the hunt is completed quickly.

While my insides twist like they're caught in a ceiling fan, he tours me through the photos he took of the flat, giving me a completely different perspective of the familiar spaces so they turn alien and unwelcoming.

The images capture the tiny glittering cameras and mics hidden in crevices around the house. One is tucked in a plug outlet, another in the corner of the defunct cooktop fan.

The most invasive microphones are in the bathroom; hidden in the floor drain and the chipped edge of the medicine cabinet. The most distressing cameras are the ones in my room, recording me from the bedside lamp and the wardrobe.

The lamp that I brought with me from my foster home. The one that means whoever did this, did it after I moved into the flat.

A mic and no cameras in Finley's room, the same in Lily's. Two mics and two cameras in mine.

I shudder at the thought of someone watching me while I sleep, while I change, while I fiddle about with the toys from my bedside drawer. Distress fires through me leaving charred wreckage in its wake.

It's outside the realms of coincidence to think a house would randomly be bugged at the same time I'm getting gut-churning mail and my computer found a new affinity for spyware.

"Do these have a way to trace back who put them there?"

Caylon shakes his head, turning on his heel to stare through the window into our lounge, eyes poking and prodding at every nook and cranny in case there's something his gadget missed. "No, they're not relaying a signal we can follow. Even if we tear them all out, we won't pinpoint its owner."

"Come home with me," Trent declares, folding his arms when he sees my lower lip jut out in defiance. "There's no way I'm letting you stay here as a target."

"I'll wait until the police tell me what they do or don't need me to do."

"You've called them?" Caylon asks, his eyes not moving to my face.

"Not yet, but I will. They can add these details to the rest of it."

"There's been someone sending threatening cards," Trent explains. "But this is an escalation."

"It's not an escalation because he's obviously been doing this the whole time." I rub my left arm, feeling the roughness where my goosebumps have set in for the day. "So there's no more danger than there was yesterday."

"But we know about it now, so we—"

"Exactly," I say, cutting off Trent. "We know about it, so I'm actually far safer than I was then because now I know the fuller extent of it. I'm better prepared."

"If you haven't called the police yet," Caylon says, ignoring both of us, "then I've got a counter proposal. The police *might* find who did this and they *might* lock them away for a while."

A huff bursts out of me. "They're better placed than I am."

Caylon exchanges a glance with Trent and the day takes another ominous turn when he nods.

"We could use you as bait to trace him privately and take action to ensure he never bothers you again."

My head spins, spine tingling like it's about to lose all feeling. I'm about to protest, I'm not bait for their private game, I'd rather stick with the police, then Trent takes my hand, squeezing. "We'll make sure he never bothers *anyone* again." His eyes are stormy, rough seas ready to drag under anybody foolish enough to venture from shore. "Do you understand what I'm saying?"

They're talking about killing him.

I wait for the guilt to hit me. For my conscience to rise and declare its preference to remain clean. Instead, a thrill of satisfaction wriggles along my spine.

Yes. They're talking about killing him and I'm glad.

If they find evidence linking back to my uncle, who must surely be behind this, no matter what the police DNA results say, his is another name I'd gratefully add to their list.

"What do I have to do?"

CHAPTER FOURTEEN

I'm not happy about dangling Rosa in front of a malicious stalker like a piece of tasty meat. However, there's no way I'd turn this task over to the police and without another option occurring to me, I grudgingly accept that it's the best thing to do.

We remain outside, out of reach of the mics and cameras, while talking through the logistics.

"Don't do anything out of the ordinary," Caylon tells her. "The idea is that nothing has changed, nothing has been discovered. Don't parade about in front of the cameras and don't hide from them, either. That'll be a dead giveaway."

I see the strain of that last request hitting. Her face is so pale she looks ill, her jaw clenched so hard her gums must be groaning.

I understand her worry. It's the same thing that stops her helping me in the way I need most.

"When we find him, we'll destroy every recording," I

promise her, easing some shadows from under her eyes. "Caylon will trace every account he's ever touched upon and wipe them clean. There'll be nothing left."

Rosa nods but my words are totally inadequate compared to her worry.

"If my dad has to buy every cloud storage facility under the sun just to wipe them clean as a backup, we'll do it."

"Mr Moneybags," she teases, rolling her eyes, but I'm glad to see some of the despair wash away.

"It could be weeks," she tells me outside, while waving goodbye to Caylon. "Or never. Just because it feels imminent after discovering all those devices, doesn't mean it is. Unless they know we've discovered them."

"It better not be," I growl, instantly trying to sort out how to get there sooner. "Maybe we should muck about with a few of the cameras. It could force them to come forward to attempt a repair."

I walk inside, feeling far more positive about my spur-of-the-moment suggestion.

"Or you could just stand there, glaring straight at one," she whispers into my ear with a laugh. "The poor thing's probably wondering what it did wrong."

I don't like anything about the arrangement, but Caylon and Rosa are both a hell of a lot smarter than me, so I defer to their intellect. Once we catch the bastard, I can put myself to better use smashing the fuck out of them until they never terrorise another innocent girl, ever again.

"Oh, good news," Rosa says, her smile fading to one with less certainty. "I found someone happy to join in with a live show." She must see something in my face because she adds, "If you still want to do that."

I reach out to catch hold of her, drawing her into a hug. The scent of her hair is probably cheap shampoo that would smell basic on anyone else but on her, it's delightful. Especially when I'm nuzzling into the curve of her neck, my mouth salivating to bite at her shoulder.

"Is that a yes?"

The rush of desire overwhelms me, and my response is more of a hum than an answer. When I draw back, she's frowning, concerned, and I stroke her cheekbone with my thumb, nodding. "That sounds good. Will it happen here?"

"I'd prefer it at work." She scratches the side of her cheek, hard enough to leave red trails on her skin. "That way I have more control over..." She waves her hand, chewing on her lip as her worry resurfaces.

"I think that's a great idea," I say with far more enthusiasm. "You'll have to give me lots of orders. Otherwise, I won't know what to do."

Her face brightens. "I'm sure I can manage that. And you'll mostly be cuffed to a chair and unable to move."

I pull her back against me for a second, resting my hand on her shoulder, unable to express how much her attention reassures me. "Sorry for being weird. If I'd been normal, I would've swept you off your feet by now, and moved you into my house where you'd be far safer than whatever this plan entails."

Rosa eyes me cautiously. "You wanted to sweep me off my feet, did you?"

The pull in my chest is so painful I can't bear to look at her. "Something like that."

She turns aside, rubbing at her throat like it's sore. "I thought you just wanted to use my services."

My eyes flick to hers, expecting to see the tease playing around her mouth, but there's no sign. Her gaze is steady, her face twisting with confusion.

"Yeah, but... we're friends, too, aren't we?"

More than friends is what I want to say. Would you be my

girlfriend even though I'm a thousand miles from normal is what I *want* to say. I don't have the adequate words to ask for that. She probably deals with sexual freaks all day long. Coming home to another one won't be top of her bucket list.

Such a freak my proposal would be, "I'd like you to be the favourite girl on my phone. The only one I watch. The one I'll jerk off to while not touching you, not the way you deserve, for ever and ever."

The false vow makes me smile even as my chest gives another sharp tug.

And I need to get away, just for a few minutes, just to clear my head because this pull between us is getting stronger and stronger and I'm well aware it's probably one-sided but I don't want it to be. I don't want it to be like that at all.

"I need to go," I abruptly announce. "Got some chores to run. Do you want me to pick up something for tea?"

"Oh, I... You're coming back here, then?"

A jolt runs through me. Touched with a high-voltage wire. "That was my plan."

Her face floods with relief and I inhale my first full breath since Caylon announced his findings. Even if she's just happy I'm shouting her a meal again, I'm glad to see the traces of joy.

"Fried chicken. Pizza. Fish and chips. Burgers. Something like that."

"All four of the major food groups, wow. Someone's working up an appetite."

"Yeah, well. My job is very physical."

I force a laugh but for the first time, I'm troubled. She's allowed to work at any job she likes but I wish she'd taken up my original offer. To let me pay for everything so she didn't need to take another session with another client ever again.

It had been a temptation for her when I made the offer. Now it sounds more like a temptation for me.

You're not even with her like that. Stop being jealous. She's putting herself out to arrange something you might like and that should be enough. More than enough.

Still, as I kiss her goodbye on the temple, I wish circumstances were different.

I wish *I* were different.

ROSA

The countdown until the weekend takes forever. From the moment Trent made his off-the-cuff comment about sweeping me off my feet, I haven't been able to concentrate. Not on my studies, not on my work.

Finally, I pay my mother a visit and the moment I walk through the door she knows something is wrong.

"Come here," she orders, though with the tubes and lines running in and out of her, my getting on the bed beside her must cause considerable pain. But I obey, desperate to feel her arms around me.

Her skin's softer today, smelling of lanolin. I burrow in beside her, placing my arms with care so I don't knock anything important free.

"Can you tell me what's going on?" she says in a whisper. "Has something gone wrong at school?"

"There's a boy," I start, then choke as a sob takes hold.

"Oh, a boy," she says with a chuckle. "They're the worst."

The comment makes me laugh, and I close my eyes, feeling content in a way that's been missing for far too long. "Yeah, they are."

For a long time, we stay like that, her rocking me slightly just like she did when I was five years old and scraped my knee.

Once I'm calm enough to talk, I take the hand cream from the bedside cabinet and massage her fingers, rubbing the moisturiser in with slow, smooth strokes, easing out the knots near her wrists where the cramps strike deepest.

"I thought he was going to ask me out. Instead, he tried to book me for a job."

She winces in sympathy, clutching me with the hand I'm trying to massage. "That sounds hard. You were disappointed?"

I nod, then remember to say it aloud because her eyesight's worse with every visit. "I couldn't even do the thing he wanted and now... he's talking like maybe I got the wrong idea."

"He doesn't sound like the type of client you need," she says softly. "Have you told him to bugger off?"

"Finley would kill me," I say, wrinkling my nose. "He keeps buying us dinner, so she's in love with him."

"Such a slut."

She's joking but the quick retort makes me giggle. "Like either of us can talk."

She laughs, then reaches for the container of water by the bed. I lift it to her lips, wincing at the two-handled plastic sippy cup. I hate how the disease infantilises her. The last time she needed this type of implement, she must have been a toddler. Now she's stuck with it again.

"Did you want him to be more than a client?"

"Yeah." I try to add more but another sob threatens so I concentrate on not crying instead.

"You deserve more than someone who can't tell the difference between a girlfriend and a hooker."

I nod, letting the words soothe my insecurities like an emotional balm. "He's rich," I confess. "Like really, really rich."

"Then you're better off out of it," Mum declares. "The world's already being fucked by billionaires. You don't need one of them fucking you directly."

The pronouncement hits my funny bone so hard that I convulse with laughter, eyes streaming tears, unable to even think about saying another word because I can barely get a breath in, let alone coordinate the rest.

"He offered to pay my expenses through university. Even through to a PhD if I wanted that. Rent, bills, anything."

She rests her hand on my cheek, eyes opening wide so even with her damaged retinas it's like she can clearly see my face. "My girl can't be bought like that," she says, and there's so much pride behind the words that I'm overwhelmed with gratitude that I still have her here, can still come to her for comfort.

I cement the words in my memory, the tone, the fierceness. I write them so deeply that I'll always be able to bring them out if I need to.

She doesn't need to know how Trent looked while he was making the offer. His desperation. The lost expression, like he didn't know how he wound up at this point or how he'd ever make his way back to where he should be.

I need to extricate myself.

I've let my emotions overtake my self-interest. Instead of spending the past week working out the details on how to cater to a client who doesn't feel like a client, I should have spent my time working out how to get away. To sort out my own problems just like I've done for every problem in my past.

That's the way forward. Much as I leapt at Caylon's suggestion of them tracking the culprit and killing him, I should have stuck to common sense. I should go to the police right after my visit and tell them what he discovered in my home.

Once they understand the urgency, I can call off the hit.

The hit.

Even whispering the words inside my head, it feels unreal. That's not the person I am. I've never trawled through the dark web finding out what price people place upon a life.

Go to the police. Tell Trent everything's off. Thank Caylon for his help but insist on taking over from here.

That's the right thing to do.

The responsible thing to do.

Leave it in the hands of the police and get back to worrying about the things I have control over. My work. My studies. My friends. My mother.

I have the booking with Trent for tomorrow, then after that, I'm opting out and calling it quits.

As I wait for the bus home, my mind is calmer than it has been for a long while. That more than anything convinces me I'm now on the right path.

CHAPTER FIFTEEN

TRENT

WHEN I TURN UP AT THE HOUSE IN SYDENHAM, MY NERVES are an absolute mess. I pull to the curb and glance around me, surprised to find the place looks no different from its neighbours. The front berm is just as tidy, the garden beyond the wooden fence just as cared for.

I'm not sure what I was expecting. All I know is this wasn't it.

Once again, my emotions are wobbling out of control. Last night didn't help.

After months of avoiding any retribution on behalf of Robbie's death, Caylon, Zach, Lily, and I had finally been confronted by his distraught mother. The investigator she'd hired to find him—or failing that, find his dead body—had lured and coerced us to an empty warehouse for a final showdown.

It's over now. There won't be any further fallout. A relief except my nerves are still twanging from the overdose of adrenaline. If today's appointment had been for anything else, with *anyone* else, I would have cancelled.

But this is too important.

A pedestrian turns the corner, walking towards the house. Even from this distance, I can tell it's Rosa. Her figure, her clothing style, her gait—it's all cemented into my memory, impossible to shake.

My stomach falls in a slow forward roll, then doesn't stop. I put a wrist to my forehead, beads of sweat popping out despite the cool temperature.

I want this to work so much I'm making myself sick.

Rosa tilts her head as she gets closer, squinting, presumably to see if it's me inside the car. I had offered to drive her, but she insisted on making her own way, saying she needed time to centre herself.

A desire I fully understand.

I get out, opening the door slowly so I don't freak her out, then stepping out of the car as she draws level. "Hey, there."

My hands don't know what to do with themselves. I close and lock the car, store the keys, then shove them in my jacket, even though the pockets are placed ridiculously high, making me look like a bully boy from the romper stomper era.

"Have you been waiting long?"

Her tone is friendly but so distant I experience a pang of fear. Is this where my kink has brought us? Civil but a million miles apart.

What did you expect? You're the one who wanted to be her client.

But that impulse seems so long ago. Belonging to a different boy with different priorities.

Before I felt the rush of protectiveness that swamped me when I understood she was in danger. Before I talked to her, got to know her, learned her quirks and interests, her sense of humour, the way her mind absorbs facts and clicks knowledge together in new and interesting ways.

The way she's here because she wants to help me. Even after I gave her no reason to want to. Even after I warned her why she shouldn't be near me. Why no one should be near me.

"Not long," I say, trying for her same level of calm. "I'd just pulled up when you turned the corner."

I hesitate, turning back towards my car. "Should I come in with you now, or would you prefer I wait until it's all ready?"

A genuine smile breaks through her façade and she grabs my arm. "No way, mister. I'm not leaving you out here to second guess things and make an opportune escape. You're coming inside and you get the pleasure of making small talk with me while I prepare." She leans in closer, getting on tiptoes so her breath caresses the side of my neck. "If you're very good, I might even let you have a biscuit."

"Is that how you coerce all your subs into obeying you?"

She shakes her head with mock sadness. "Unfortunately, I can't tell you that. State secrets and all that jazz."

Inside the house, she leads me through to a dining room with a large table and eight chairs. A woman sits on one, knees to her chest, with a hot drink perched on top of them, scrolling through her phone.

"Hey, Kim," Rosa says in greeting. "Did you get your car sorted?"

The woman glances over, looks back to her phone, then stares at me in surprise. "Yeah," she says, hooking her eyebrows at Rosa, then she shakes her head. "I mean, no. It's still in the garage waiting for spare parts I can't afford. You catch the bus, right?"

"Sure. The stop's just around the corner."

"Mm. I might need to take it if my boyfriend doesn't get his arse into gear and pick me up."

"You want a lift?" I offer. "I can drop you somewhere if you like."

Rosa looks startled. "Ah, no you can't. You're going to be busy for the next hour, remember?"

"Sure. Yeah, sure. But I could—"

I'm saved by a knock at the door. While Rosa goes to answer it, I try not to stare at Kim who's only dressed in a robe over her underwear. "First time? Don't worry. We don't bite unless you pay extra."

My ears burn and my entire face must be glowing red.

Somewhere between the idea and the reality, I've lost all my chill. To be in this space, knowing what comes next, feeling it bear down on me like oncoming traffic, uses all the attention I usually put into remaining calm, appearing staunch.

"Kim! What'd you do to him?" Rosa says with a laugh when she walks back in the room. She reaches out to touch my hand, a tiny buzz of reassurance. "This is Andy." She introduces me to a guy in his late twenties, early thirties, and I can't even meet his eye.

Suddenly, this feels like the worst idea.

"Come on through," Rosa says, touching the back of my hand again. "We'll get the room set up and we can talk." She turns to Andy. "Help yourself to a cup of tea or coffee. I'll come back and get you in a few minutes, okay?"

"Sure." Andy takes a seat next to Kim, eyeing her appreciatively. "Haven't seen you around here before."

A car horn sounds outside.

"And you won't see me this time, either," she says, leaping to her feet and dumping her cup in the sink. "Gotta go."

The moment she leaves, I relax a little. I trail Rosa into the bedroom, large and clumsy. She waves at the bed. "Take a seat.

I'm just going to change." She drops her oversized handbag on the floor and pulls out a few fancy looking pieces of lingerie. I stare at one of them, frowning. I've seen the same piece before but back then it was on Lily and she was pouting at me in a photograph.

Rosa follows my gaze and interprets it correctly. "Yeah, we divvied up a lot of the stuff Zach gave her. You don't mind, do you?"

"No, I don't mind." I pause for a second, then add, "I'm really nervous."

"I know," she says, stripping off her top and laying out the garments on the bed. "There's an en suite if you want a shower. Sometimes, that helps people to relax."

"I can't think of anything more stressful than getting naked and taking a shower."

She bursts into giggles. "Oh, really? Because I know *way* more stressful things than that."

Balancing on one foot, she reaches over to her bag and pulls out some thick twist ties. "Like these, for instance. Do they get your heart pumping or what?"

I take them from her, turning them over in my hands, seeing how they're connected. Although I've seen them on tv before, I've never had occasion to use them in real life. They're solider than I would have thought. Much larger than the miniature versions my dad uses to keep his old paper files tied together.

"There are cuffs if you'd prefer," Rosa says, moving to a cabinet and crouching in front of it, shuffling through items on the inside shelves. "Like these?"

She holds up a pair of fluffy handcuffs that can't be mistaken for anything but a sex toy.

"Maybe not those."

"Sorry," she says with a wink. "Didn't mean to threaten your manhood with the fluffy pink bondage cuffs."

The tease makes me laugh and I relax further. "What other goodies do you have in there?"

"Lots and lots of things," she says, eyes sparkling. "But you have to be very good or very, very bad to get a look at anything else."

The thought of either sends a rush of heat straight to my groin. The old darkness lurks underneath, pacing back and forth, hoping for a break in concentration so it can pour through the gap, taking over, taking control.

"These feel more solid," I say, holding up the ties. "I think I'd prefer them."

She sits back on her heels, leaning on the cabinet door for balance. "We can do it without. I know it's a lot, especially when there's someone else in the room. I've got some wrist protectors so they don't accidentally cut into your skin, but I could use those as the chief restraints. That way, you get to feel bound, but you can break free fairly easily."

The darkness inside me perks up, head tilted, listening.

"No," I say before it can agree in my stead. "I'll feel better with genuine bonds." The only way I can be sure I won't break down midway through and try to hurt her. Or worse, succeed in hurting her. "Do you know Andy well?"

She shrugs. "I've met him a few times, but we've never worked on a job together." She stands and moves to sit beside me on the bed, her slight weight pulling me on a lean towards her. "We can try this without him. Since you're paying him the same either way, he won't mind."

I put a hand on the back of my neck, eyes closed, rubbing my hair the wrong way then smoothing it down again.

What I want is for all of this to be in the palm of my hand; contained, easy. The idea of trying this excites me, even now when my nerves are wound to breaking point, but it also scares me.

It's so big and sprawling and involved. Nothing like pressing play and watching.

But the discomfort might be worth it. That's the tantalising thought propelling me forward when I could have called it quits so much earlier.

We might make a genuine connection, even with all the rigmarole surrounding us. Bigger than the friendship we've already forged. More satisfying than a screen and my hand.

"Could you help do me up?" Rosa asks, turning and lifting her hair so I can fasten the back of her top. It's connected with tiny ribbons and snaps. My fingers feel like rough brutes just getting near something so delicate.

"When you said you were getting changed, I thought you'd duck into the bathroom."

"Mm. Because you're not going to see me in a lot less clothing in a few minutes time."

I touch a finger to the back of her hand. "I did this all wrong."

Rosa tilts her head forward so her loose hair falls like a curtain around her face. "How d'you mean?"

But I can't explain it. I'd have to start with an apology for watching her at my party, watching her get into trouble and not doing anything until she fought back. Explain further, going back so far, I'm not sure my memories are anything but figments of my imagination.

There aren't the words and I'm not sure even I have a good understanding.

"We don't have to do this," she says, putting her hand around the back of my neck, her touch soothing. "I can go out there and tell Andy his services aren't needed. You can leave or we can stay and watch the terrible programmes they schedule on Saturday afternoon tv."

"But you went to all this trouble."

"For which you're still paying me." She wobbles me back and forth, giving a soft laugh. "Usually, I'd be concerned that you'd be out of pocket and not get anything for it, but I really don't think that's as much of a concern for you as it is for my other clients."

I bump the top of my head against her shoulder. "I guess not."

She moves her head until her cheek presses against mine, her fingers curling into the soft hairs on the back of my head, gently massaging. "I wish I were normal."

"Nobody's normal, Trent. Haven't you noticed we're all as fucked up as one another?"

I want to do so much with her. Swing her across my lap and hold her in place while I touch her, kiss her, familiarise myself with her body until every inch is locked in my memory.

But the beast is pacing, swinging its lithe body around as it reaches the extent of its cage, and retracing its path until it hits against the opposite side, then repeats. I can't trust myself to have her, not the way I want, the way I hope she wants, but I'm used to others being my proxy on screens. Her being my proxy in the flesh could reach another level. It could open another world.

"How do I...?" My voice trails into confusion. "Where do I sit? What do I do?"

"Over here." Rosa moves to the larger of two chairs, patting the seat.

There are slats on the back and solid arms. It's heavy enough to need wheels to move but they're locked in place now. It's strong. Even if I pulled with my full strength, there's no way I'd be able to break free.

I take a seat and she reaches for the fastener on my jeans, then drops her hands to her side. "Do you want me to?"

My hands caress the arms of the chair, the head of the bed just a foot away. "Where are you going to be?"

She climbs onto the bed, laying down so I can see her face, her feet the closest thing to me. "Like this?"

"Can you change ends?" I stand and move to the bed, laying my hands on top of the crossbar. "This blocks my view, so if you could be on top, facing me?"

"You'd like that?" She rolls over and knee walks up the bed until her hands rest on the board next to mine. Her face inches away. "I could position myself here and he could be behind me." She turns and looks over her shoulder, picturing the new location. "You won't see him moving inside me."

My smile broadens. "Yeah, I don't want to see that. All I want is to see you. Your reactions."

"Okay." She sits back on her heels, eyes fixed to my face, reading me. "I have a balaclava he could wear."

That jolt of excitement hits me again, stirring my cock until it presses against the thickness of my jeans. "I'd like that."

This is easier. The moving. The talking. Not letting me eat my way inside my head until I can't figure out an escape.

"Could you restrain me before he comes in?" I ask, getting into the role, scripting things the same way I'd tried to do with the foreign cam girls. "Me here. You on the bed, waiting. Then him through the door."

"Like a break-in?"

"Yes." My chest hums at the ease of understanding. I glance down at my clothing, unsure what state I'll be left in after the performance is underway.

"This'll sound weird, but I have condoms. If you wear one, there won't be as much clean-up, but I don't—"

"That sounds good. Can I...?" My face turns red again, the damn traitor. "Are you okay for me to strip? I think that'll work better."

"Take your shirt off," she orders me, sliding off the side of the bed to fetch something from the cabinet. "Then sit in the chair."

I obey her, part amused, part responsive to the new tone of command in her voice. She'd said about being domineering and it hadn't fit in with how she presents but now I get it. A role she slips into just as easily as she slipped into the transparent teddy.

She rolls wrist protectors into place, then loops the ties around the wood, pulling until the first is loosely holding me. "I can take it tighter."

"Okay. Remember, if you're clutching the arm, your muscles will tense against the plastic. The fabric will protect your skin, but you could still bruise or lose sensation if it's too tight."

I clench my hand and test the increase in pressure. After a few goes, I understand how to control it. "You're right. That's perfect."

She nods, moving to secure the other hand. Next, she fetches a belt that she loops around my midriff, hooking it through the slats then fastening it behind the chair. She slides it so the buckle lays against my chest, the cold of the metal just another texture to add to those overloading me already.

Her fingers hover above my thighs as she hesitates. "I should have checked. Are you okay with me arranging your jeans and placing the condom or would you prefer to do that part yourself? I can free you, then tie you again."

The rush of blood makes my head dizzy. "You—" I begin, then have to stop and clear my throat when my voice cracks. "You can do that."

"Do you have a safe word you prefer?" She runs a finger around the inside of each tie, making sure I have room, then kneels in front of me. Her breasts press against the filmy fabric and her eyes look enormous as she peers up at me.

That slight half-smile she always wears looks knowing. Like she's perfectly aware of the effect that position has on me.

With a rush of comprehension, I understand she does. That

whatever I'm paying for her to do here, this is part of it. As carefully scripted and enacted as anything I've ever tried to get done.

"Can I unzip your jeans?"

My eyes almost bug out of my head at the increased pressure as I nod. She leans forward, her slim fingers deftly unbuttoning my fly then slowly dragging down the zipper, so slowly I can hear the individual metal teeth pulling apart.

"Would you like me to pull them all the way off or just leave them open?"

And a minute ago I would have had a very different answer. A minute ago, I was shy, self-conscious, like at any moment I'd cry off and bring this entire scenario to an end. "Take them off."

She runs her hands over the waistband, skimming her fingers over the top and tugging it down a little. Not enough. Raising up farther, she slides her hands down the sides, head bobbing closer to my chest, eyes still fixed to mine until she curves her palms over my arse, grabbing and caressing and rubbing until she whispers, "Raise up," and I do so she can slowly draw them down to my thighs, then my knees, then stopping to take my shoes off so she can pull them all the way off.

I'm scared to glance downwards, my erection straining against my briefs. Once she's folded my jeans to the side and placed it with my t-shirt, Rosa sits back on her heels, just her hand reaching forward to rub the side of her forefinger along my length.

A groan escapes from between my lips, my head tilting back so I can stare at the blank and unerotic tiles on the ceiling. She moves closer, head in my lap, her breath reaching through the fabric of my underwear to warm the side of my cock.

My wrists strain at the ties, wanting to free themselves and plunge deep into her hair, holding her where I want her, controlling her. When I can't, I grip the arms of the chair, squeezing so tightly that the plastic edge of the ties would dig into my flesh if it weren't for the protective bands.

"Just give me the word when you're ready." Rosa sits upright again, breasts touching against my legs, then she cups my kneecaps and pushes them apart, making me spread my legs wide, exposing me. "Do you want me to strip off your briefs, too?"

I can't swallow. My head tips back again, eyes closing. There are too many sensations flooding through me to track.

"I have..." Rosa moves away, and the distance makes me hollow. Even though she's right there, scrabbling through her cabinet of curiosities again, finding something more to make things pleasurable for me. Trying so hard. Wanting so much to please me.

The switch in my brain flips and I struggle against the bonds again. At the movement, she turns, the glance over her shoulder almost enough to make me come on the spot.

"You won't be able to break them," she says, but there's something in her eyes that says she's not telling me everything. I flex my wrists, enjoying the dull chaffing of the plastic. "And the chair's heavy. You shouldn't be able to stand."

I try, not getting far, the muscles straining in my lower back.

"If you truly want to feel bound, I can tie your legs." She moves back towards me, crouching rather than kneeling, eyes glued to my face. "And I have these." She shows me a plug. An internal vibrator, operated by a remote.

Rosa waggles the controller. "I can use this on you while you're watching. It'll help you orgasm if you need the assistance."

While I'm watching. My spirits deflate a little. Yes, I know that's why we're here. No, I'm no longer sure I can stand it. Stand to watch someone else touching her right in front of me.

See him running his fingers over all the parts of her I have yet to touch. That I can't allow myself to touch.

Grief twists me until I struggle to breathe. Rosa lays her fingers on the side of my face, instantly calming.

"Or I could walk out and tell Andy we don't need him," she says as though she reached deep into the meat of my brain and stole the thought.

The last item in her hand is a condom, and she tears the wrapper, pulling it out and resting it on the top of my knee while she slips her hands into the band of my briefs, easing them out so my hard cock juts free.

She smiles at me, a slow, lazy smile full of a thousand promises. She places the condom on her tongue, then bends forward, taking my head into her mouth, tongue moving in rhythmic pulses as she unrolls it using the pressure of her lips.

"Fucking hell."

My head drops back, tears of co-mingled frustration and desire in my eyes. She can't get all the way to the base, nowhere near, but her hand takes over where her mouth stops, rolling the protection down my shaft before gently cupping my balls and giving a squeeze.

"I could dismiss him, then walk back in here and straddle you. Lower myself down on you and work back and forth until I'm finally able to take all of you. Would you prefer that?"

The words don't come out, they're tangled in my head as I imagine the scene, imagine the sensation. No tears. No pain. No fear. Just her expert body giving me what I'd lost hope for.

"You'd be completely under my control," she continues with a dazed look in her eyes and a sing-song quality to her voice. "I'll be careful. I won't let you hurt me, not unless that's what I want. I can just use you for my own pleasure, yeah?"

Her hands wander all over my body. They stroke me, pinch

me, her nails scraping against my sensitive skin until it's hard enough to breathe, let alone listen.

But the words are their own temptation. They insert pictures into my mind that I never would have dreamed up by myself.

She stands, putting on knee on the edge of the seat, right between mine, thrusting it in a lazy rhythm back and forth, back and forth. The same tempo as her voice.

"Do you want me to use you while you're strapped in here, unable to do a single thing to stop me? Ride you until I come, rub you against my clit until I come again. Over and over, as many times as I need, and at the end of it... at the end if you're good, if you're lucky... if you beg me hard enough, I might let you finish."

"Yes," I manage, having to fight my throat to get the sound out. I'm panting, my chest heaving like I've run sprints for twenty minutes straight. "Yes, I'd prefer that."

Rosa touches my face, running her fingers along my jawline, then twisting into my hair, clenching into a fist to tug my head back. "You're sure? You want me to send Andy away and make you my new plaything?"

Her knee inches higher, closer and closer to my throbbing cock, and I would say anything to have her move it further, move until it rubs against me, providing the friction I crave.

Then it touches against me, and I thrust my hips, making the most of it, trying to steal my release before she's ready, the knowledge of how angry she'll be if I get there without her driving me insane with delight.

She leans over until her lips are against my ear. "I don't think so. I think someone might earn themselves a punishment if they're not careful."

And she moves away, all friction, all tantalising warmth and flesh halfway across the room in an instant.

She retreats, still facing me, until her back hits against the door. "Let me take care of my chores and I'll be back."

The words must mean she's popping out to dismiss Andy and she'll be right back. They must. Surely. She wouldn't stay out there, letting me think she'll return at any moment and actually *do chores,* would she?

I let my head rest against the back of the chair, my prick hard enough to ache, desperate for release, waiting.

CHAPTER SIXTEEN

ROSA

It's agonising to leave the room with Trent positioned so perfectly. I know the entwining of work and pleasure will come back to bite me but right now I don't give a shit. All I want is to spend the next few hours taking my pleasure while never letting him get what he craves... until he does.

Until he's grateful enough that he's willing to beg.

I grab a robe from the hooks in the hallway and put it on because I'm a professional and dismissing a paid partner from their expected afternoon pursuits requires a bit more armour than the sheer teddy and scrap of lace I'm wearing.

Never say I don't understand decorum.

"Hey," I say, schooling my features into commiseration as I walk into the dining room. Andy stands at the notice board, scanning the appointments.

Where possible, we try to schedule around each other so the house isn't crowded. There's nothing worse than having trouble with a client while the sound of banging comes from the other rooms in the house. For Kim and Ceecee, who both have school-age children, that means they focus on the nine to three, leaving me free for my afternoons, while Rina mostly works nights.

"Does this mean we have the house to ourselves?" Andy asks, smiling warmly. "Looks like a good system."

"Yeah, it works for us." I cross my arms, using that to hold my robe closed since it doesn't have a belt. "Listen, the client's changed his mind, so we won't need you today. I'm sorry to drag you out of your way for nothing but he'll pay your entire fee."

"You sure?" Andy steps away from the board. His eyes twinkle. "Or is this part of the cuckold rape fantasy and you're just waiting for me to overpower you and drag you into the room?"

I chuckle but it's forced. His teasing makes me uneasy. Usually, someone in the game would have a better idea of exactly why the taunt isn't funny, but I suppose you get all sorts.

"I'm sure. I've just sent through the other half of the money." A deposit went through mid-week to make sure he'd show.

"Mind if I check directly with the client?"

He walks past me, heading straight for the bedroom, and I stall, unsure of the protocol. Then I think of Trent, completely at my mercy and dash after him, putting my hand on the doorknob first and twisting so my body blocks the entrance.

"Yeah, I do mind."

"What's the matter?" Andy asks, his features still playful. "Is he all tied up or something?"

He laughs at his own joke, sweeping me aside and yanking the door open, laughing as he leans against the frame. "Looks like we're all set," he says, turning to look at me over his shoulder. "Come on, now. Don't be all resistant. This is what you booked, after all."

This is disastrous. I grab his wrist and yank him back, getting properly angry. This isn't how you treat clients ever and it's certainly not how you treat *mine*.

"Get the fuck away from there. I told you, you're not required, and you've got your money. Now piss off."

Trent struggles to free himself. The twist ties I used to secure him are scored through. It makes it possible to get free, but it takes a lot of effort.

The cuffs would have been better. They have safety releases on the inside for someone opting out of play.

But he wouldn't have used those. He wouldn't have let me secure him with the twist ties if he'd known he could get out of them. He's too scared of what he might do. If they break now, he'll know. He might never trust me again.

"Get out," I repeat, sliding between the two men and trying to walk Andy out of the room. The fury builds until I have my hands flat on his chest, pushing, leaving him in no doubt that I want him gone.

But he still doesn't go. He catches my wrist, leans back to kick the door shut, his eyes scanning Trent and nodding as he sees the belt around his chest, the ties on his wrists, the heavy build of the chair.

"Nice," he says, making the word slither from his mouth though it barely counts as a sibilant. "Guess you can't rescue your woman even if you want to," he says, the tone mocking. "Guess you'll just have to sit there and watch."

He's still playing the part I told him to. The knowledge socks home with an audible thump of relief.

"Sugar," I state, waiting for him to back off, acknowledge the safe word. He tugs at my robe, easily pulling it free, no sign of understanding on his face. "Red," I try when his grip on my wrist grows stronger. "Red, red, red."

The spare twist ties are on the edge of the bed, ready for if Trent wanted his legs secured. Andy grabs one, drawing it around my wrist and the bedpost while my heart tries to pound through my ribcage. I flail my spare hand, terrified of being fully restrained, but that just gives him an opportunity to grab it.

"Now, now," he says in the same teasing voice which means I don't know if he understands what he's doing or not. "No fighting. You'll just hurt yourself." His voice drops lower, becomes more guttural. "Or you'll force me to hurt you, which amounts to the same thing."

"Don't... Let her go," Trent shouts, struggling harder.

"Don't let her go," Andy summarises with a broad smirk. "Gotcha. Wasn't planning to, mate. Not until I've finished fucking her in front of you. Hope you've got those eyes peeled because it's going to be a lovely sight."

He drags me onto the bed, wrestling me until my other wrist is also secured to the post. Then he picks up another tie, squinting at it and at me before he wraps it around my neck, the press of the plastic sending my heart racing, my blood pressure soaring until my eyes bug out of my head.

"Don't... Please, Andy. This isn't part of the game. Please stop."

Trent yells again, kicking out uselessly, the chair placed too far away to reach the bed. He tries leaning forward, trying to stand and lift the seat onto his back, but the weight is too concentrated in the base and legs.

"Stop making all that noise," Andy barks, pulling the edges of the tie through the top slat in the base board, the circle so tight it only clicks in twice before he lets go. My cheek is flat against the wood, any movement threatening to cut off my air.

He moves to the bedside cabinet, eyes scanning the contents. Then he's out of my limited view but I hear the unmistakable sound of masking tape being wound off the roll. The snap as he cuts it with his teeth. Then Trent's ferocious yells are muffled.

Fuck.

Part of me still clutches the idea that this is a misunderstanding. I curse myself for bringing up the fantasy when I should have known better.

This is what happens when you don't know and trust the other participants. I've got the forced cuck scene that Trent thought he wanted but neither of us is willing any longer.

None of this is what I want. What *we* want.

"Sugar," I try again, though his lack of response to the first utterance hollows out my chest.

"Sugar," he mimics, climbing on the bed behind me so he's out of my field of vision. *"Red."*

I sob, the sound caught in my throat, bumping against the thick edge of the tie, and stopping.

"Such a beautiful scene," Andy says in a croon, the sound invasive as an earworm. "You can't imagine how often I've pictured this exact scenario. Lying in bed at night, watching what my cameras picked up during the day."

A bucket of ice water in the face couldn't be as shocking as those words.

My body freezes in fright, mind racing to connect the dots. Scrabbling for alternative theories because the obvious one is too frightening.

I try to place him. How does he know me?

He looked vaguely familiar or is that just because I saw what he wanted me to see?

Panic freezes me in place. My head is a jumbled, chaotic mess. Questions pile up behind my lips.

Too many. Too late.

"You planted the cameras in the flat?"

My voice should be as filled with hysterics as my thoughts, but it sounds calm. Far calmer than Trent as he struggles and shouts muffled vehemence behind his sealed lips.

"I did," Andy confirms. He reaches between my legs, flicking aside the dental floss of my thong until he can shove a finger inside.

I'm wet from my interactions with Trent but that doesn't stop his brutal invasion from being painful. Another sob catches in my throat and I force it into retreat. I can't afford the luxury of tears when my life is at stake.

"You can't imagine how my heart thumped when I walked into the collective. I heard what you were arranging, I tracked your phone there, but I never in my wildest dreams believed I could pull it off."

His crazed giggle sends shards of metal digging into my brain. That and the knowledge I let this happen. The questions I should have asked, the references I should have demanded, all swept aside because he made it easy to believe him.

I'm a fool and I just got both of us into trouble.

"You're so different now you're all grown up," Andy teases, and my bloodstream crystallises into shards of ice, making my entire body shiver, making everything too cold. "Have you shown him your videos?"

I catch him from the corner of my eye as he turns to Trent, smirking. "They're worth the watch. She made such a pretty little girl. So eager to please. So happy to get her rewards. You wouldn't think such a small girl could fit—"

"Shut up," I scream at him. "You shut your mouth."

Trent struggles harder. The chair legs thump against the ground. His roars of outrage barely contained by the masking tape.

Andy's finger squirms inside me, delighting in my agony, at Trent's stifled cries. "When I saw your videos, I thought nothing could be better."

He slaps me on the arse with his free hand, the fingers of the other still penetrating me, scratching me with his sharp nails.

"But this is a million times better. I get to fuck you while your boyfriend watches, then I get to pull on this twist tie until the light goes out of your eyes. Not exactly what the old man had planned for you, but he can get fucked if he thinks I'm passing up this opportunity."

I buck against him, so flooded with fear that my mind whites out, turning me into a ball of futile instincts, every path to escape already blocked.

When I come back to myself, his lower body grinds against me, the weight pinning me to the mattress. His upper body bends, supported on one hand while he stares straight into my eyes, his glowing with a vicious light.

Trent snuffles around the tape which means he still has an airway. I open my mouth to tell him about the scored ties, order him to struggle harder, that he can get free, then Andy's hand clamps across my mouth.

"I don't think you should talk. You'll put me off my stroke." His giggle is horrendous, cut glass against my ear drums. "You want to take those clothes off, baby? The camera prefers it when you bare your skin."

The old instructions pierce into a part of my memory that's walled off, has been for years. Walled off and bricked up with warning tape crisscrossed over top in case that wasn't enough.

My uncle with his hand on my knee, urging me to strip. *"It's just us here, baby. Ignore the cameraman. Keep your eyes on me."*

Not again.

I kick out, hitting the side of his ankle but that won't do shit. I try to haul myself upwards, get my knees under my chest but all that happens is my arse grinds into his crotch, against his erect dick.

"Fuck yes. Just like that, baby." That giggle again, razor blades across my brain.

He jams his fingers back inside me, curling and twisting and stretching. The invasion so unwelcome that I nearly vomit.

A self-preservation instinct kicks in, driving back the nausea. He might pull his hand away if I throw up, but he might just let me choke on it. Who the fuck knows?

"You got any requests, big man?" Andy turns his attention to Trent. "I aim to please."

I can't get free. My arms are spread the width of the king size bed, my windpipe crushed against the fancy piping that stretches above the baseboard. The best I can do it twist my head to the side so the plastic won't cut into my windpipe as cleanly.

He lets go of my mouth, settling farther down my body, pulling my legs apart before landing between them, curving his hands under my stomach, reaching up to grope my tits.

"Nothing? No suggestions? Guess it's just down to me, then." He growls, pinching my nipple so hard I see flashes of white. "Luckily, I have a long list of interests and according to your chart, we've got nothing but time."

Trent makes a muffled noise that could be a shout. Could be anything.

If I alert Trent about the restraints, it'll tell Andy at the same time. I don't know what he has planned, but in the seconds it takes Trent to respond, he could hurt him, kill him even.

Provoke Trent. That's a better bet.

Get whatever monster he thinks lives under his skin to come to the fore and take care of the problem lying on top of me, sitting back and playing with my hair like the fucking freak he is.

He moves again, clicking his tongue against his teeth. "Almost forgot," Andy says, getting off the bed and taking a phone from his pocket. He moves out of my view but judging from the renewed struggles from Trent, he's propping the device on or near him.

"Can't have all this happening without getting a proper record of it for posterity." He turns back, crouching before my wide eyes. "But you're already the expert at those, aren't you baby?" His grin explodes until it eats up half his face. "Smile, honey. Smile and say cheese."

I twist my wrists, screaming into his face, screaming out my rage and my fear and my pain until my throat is an empty wrapper, containing nothing more.

Andy laughs, standing and unbuttoning his fly close to my face. "Go on," he says, pulling his dick free and shoving it towards me. "You've been a good girl so have a taste."

I close my mouth, biting on the inside of my lips to keep them shut fast. Hating my weakness. Hating the restraints. Hating the way the memories claw at the inside of my brain, working free when I've spent so much time and effort keeping them locked away from view.

"Open wide." One hand is on his prick, the other digging at my lips, trying to prise my mouth open.

My range of motion is so limited I can't even turn aside. The nails draw blood from the thin skin of my lips. Finally, I let my jaw relax, opening, then once his finger is inside my mouth, sickening me, I bite down, hard as I can, feeling the skin split beneath the force, tasting the first hit of blood.

"Fucking cunt." He yanks his hand free, bashing me with the other. "You'll pay for that, sweetie." He drops level, his mouth spitting words straight into my eyes. "Once I'm finished, I'll get a hammer and knock out all those pretty teeth."

There's a scraping sound, the legs of Trent's heavy chair against the floorboards. A snap.

I can't see. If he's free, he'll need to unbuckle the belt.

"Put your dick in my mouth and I'll suck it or are you a fucking chicken?" I taunt Andy, trying to keep his attention on me. "If you're working for my uncle, you must be a fucking idiot so being a coward isn't much of a stretch."

He hits me again, most of the blow landing on my ear which throbs, pulsing with heat.

"You're going to regret that," he says, pressing his lips against my ear, turning my stomach. "Someone just volunteered her arse and the only lube you're getting is your own blood."

The fear levels off. Adrenaline so high it no longer has an effect. I force a laugh. "Do that, and I'll shit all over your dick. Think that'll look good on the camera, do you?"

He aims another punch and Trent's right there, batting his hand out of the way, grabbing his neck and thump, thump, thumping his head on the scroll next to me, blood spatter spraying out like colourful rain.

While Andy sputters, he hauls him back, twisting him and bending his arm against his foreleg like he's snapping a dry branch for the fire. The sinewy tear as it breaks is almost drowned out by Andy's piercing shriek.

I lose sight of them, hearing the thuds as further blows land, hearing a scream abruptly cut off in the dull crunch as bone meets the edge of the heavy chair. Somewhere in there, Andy makes a last whimper. The last punch lands with a wet slurp that makes me shudder with disgust.

Trent moves. There's a new noise.

His bare heel stomping on whatever parts of Andy he finds pleasurable. His breaths are ragged, fast, heavy, and I envy him so much it hurts. Envy him being able to destroy this opponent, tear him apart with nothing more than his hands, his bare feet.

Then Trent returns to my line of sight, collapsing with his back against the bed, resting his head in his battered bloody bruised hands. His harsh inhalations the only sound in the room.

He lets his head fall back, staring into my eyes, and the flood of relief to see he's okay is massive, all-encompassing.

"I'm sorry," I whisper, the sound completely inadequate to what just transpired. "Guess I didn't vet him as well as I thought."

Trent reaches out a hand, cups my cheek, twisting around

and taking my lower lip into his mouth, sucking the blood from it before slowly drawing away.

"Is he...?"

"Dead." The flatness in Trent's voice matches to his eyes. Then something sparks deep inside, flashing out at me, a warning pulse like danger. "He's dead."

"I'm sorry," I repeat because I don't have the words to say anything else. "Could you untie me? There should be scissors in the cabinet."

Instead of moving to get them, he touches my face again, leaning forward to take another kiss, this one rougher, deeper. He turns his body while his lips are still pressed against mine, kneeling to get a better angle, using his tongue to thrust my lips apart, to thrust inside.

When he drags his mouth from mine, I take a quick breath, feeling the panic surging forth again, wanting to get free, get out from under it. "Could you untie me, please?"

And my heart beats faster as he cups the back of my skull, pressing his forehead to mine. "No."

He moves, out of my line of sight. Then his weight is on the bed. So much heavier than Andy. Ten times the muscle. Ten times the man.

His naked body straddles mine, his hard cock digging into my spine as he leans forward, his lips finding my ear, whispering, "No. I don't think I can."

CHAPTER SEVENTEEN

ROSA

"Trent?" I say and I hate how timid my voice sounds. "Trent!" Better but he's not responding. Except for his body. His body tells me many things in the loudest of voices.

He props himself on one hand, the other lightly resting on my shoulder. His cock keeps growing but that must be my imagination. I already know he's big, enough to be painful without force. But the monster curling along my spine feels larger than last time. Like even then he was holding something back.

"Please untie me."

"I don't want to hurt you." His voice is a soft growl, teasing the hairs on the back of my neck, sending a cascade of tingles racing across my skin, tightening the muscles in my pussy until they're pulsing with need. "But I also really, really do."

A soft exhalation keeps growing longer, like I'm trying to escape on my own outward breath, escape to safety, to a place before all of this began.

His hand touches against the plastic tie, already taut around my neck. He takes hold of the end and gives a soft tug, pulling it through one click further.

I want to dissolve into begging. If I thought it would help, I would already have begun.

My mind frantically combs through every encounter, searching for a weapon, a solution, a magic word. Certain there must be some combination to unlock the man who wants to hurt me, kill me, from the boy who I've been growing closer to, the one with whom I think I could fall in love.

But every turn leads me back to the same place.

He was here all along. He warned me. He even showed me this creature once before, tumbling away from me, pushing himself into a corner to save me from his claws, from his bite.

I know it won't work now. Whatever self-control he had was at straining point in the chair. To watch his keenest fantasy play out before him must have been excruciating.

He saved me. Saved me when he could just as easily have watched before making a move.

He saved me but only because he was saving me for himself.

"My uncle," I blurt, needing to say something because if these are my last fucking words then I'm going to make them count. "He raped me in front of the camera and sold the videos. That's why..."

Trent pulls my hair back, dropping a kiss on my shoulder and it feels so tender, so sweet, compared to the menace of the situation that I gasp, losing the thread of what I wanted to say.

"I like you in restraints," he growls, his lips buzzing against my skin. "You don't need to explain why you couldn't—"

"That's not why!" I shout, then swallow, feeling the pressure of the plastic against the edge of my jaw.

Did I just pull it tighter? Will my next movement cut it in further, deeper? Will it cut off my air?

"It's not... I'm telling you because I'm scared. Trent, I'm terrified right now. Could you... could you...?"

But I can't ask. That's my last resort. If I beg him to cut the tie from around my neck—*really* beg him—and he doesn't, I don't have anywhere left to go.

Better to die with my last gamble still up my sleeve than play it now and find out exactly how little it gets me.

"My uncle got released from prison. You heard Andy say he was working with him. Can you find him for me?"

"Shh." Trent scrapes all my hair together, holding it in one hand while the other caresses my cheek. "You don't need to say anything now. It'll all be over soon."

And I want to believe he means the sex. I want to believe that, but his finger rubs against the end of the plastic tie again and I know—*I know*—that he means everything.

When he says it'll soon be over, he means my life.

"You said you'd kill the man responsible for planting the camera and sending the cards and I'm holding you to that. Find him. Kill him. Promise me."

"Your uncle."

"Not my real one... my mother will know more. She's in palliative care so you have to ask her quickly. Ask her, get the police file, track Andy's movements. Find him. Kill him. Promise me."

Trent rests his forehead against the bump at the top of my spine. His breath is warm, playful against my back. The heat spreads across my skin. "Anything for you, my love. I promise."

The relief is immediate. My body sags until it's only the ties that hold my torso semi-upright.

"You can say that he did it..." I offer, my gratitude wanting something more than simple words of thanks. "Whatever you do to me... you can blame it on Andy. Say we were having sex, and he interrupted us, that'll explain your DNA."

Trent chuckles, his hand moving over the flat of my stomach, reaching up to caress the underside of my breasts, taking one into his hand and gently squeezing. "No one's ever going to find Andy."

The claim should add to his menace, but it takes another burden from my shoulders.

Those aren't the words from an innocent, getting his first taste of blood. Someone forced to get themselves dirty against their will.

They're the words of a boy whose hands are steeped in the stuff through choice.

"Tell me about her."

His hands pause in their gentle movements, then resume when he finds his place. "Her who?"

"The girl who you hurt."

"I've already told you."

"Not everything." My throat clicks and I tense, worried the band is tightening, then the muscle relaxes. "Why did you start watching videos?"

"That's..." He shifts, moving to the side, stretching his body out, laying his head on the post next to mine so he's looking into my eyes.

The hair he let go of has fallen across my face and he tenderly moves it, the gesture a sweet one if it weren't for the restraints cutting into my wrists and neck, the position making my shoulder tendons feel like they're tearing loose from the bone.

His fingers move over my neck, brush against my cheek, thumb stroking along my jawline until I shudder, dragging in a deep breath.

"There was something I saw as a kid. My dad's always had security cameras at his properties, always had a bank of monitors where you can see into most rooms at a glance. He..."

Trent's eyes lose focus, their sharp colour muddying.

He sits up, moving out of my sight range. Then he straddles my lower body again. His hands reach out to grip my shoulders, repositioning me.

It's a scene. You've agreed a payment. It's just another contract.

"I like you like this," he says in such a deep voice it sounds like its rumbling from the earth. "Completely at my mercy."

I want to beg him not to hurt me, but I'm scared that will trigger him further. I try to relax but it's not possible.

Keep him talking. Keep him connected.

"What did you see on the monitors?"

"There was a woman," he continues in a faraway voice. Like this is an old story he's told a million times before. "I was looking for my dad and went into the security room. Sometimes he'd just sit in there for hours while I played on the floor. Watching the screens, drinking bourbon. It's what he did to relax."

"He liked to watch, too?"

"My dad enjoys owning things," Trent corrects. "Him sitting in that room and watching every piece of his property is like a dragon sitting on his hoard, admiring its gold."

His hands stroke along my back, following the curve of my spine, my tailbone, then tracing a path between my buttocks, between my legs. A second later, he grabs a thigh in each hand and spreads them apart and I let him. I don't want to fight. If I try hard enough, I can turn this into our first time. Mental gymnastics required but I'm used to that. I've been using those since I was seven years old.

His lips press against the inside of my thigh, the tease rippling out until a wave of desire lodges deep inside. I close my eyes, giving over to the sensations, not the fear. Give over to the tenderness, not the sharp bite of thick plastic.

Submitting to Trent's desires and letting them stir my own.

"There was a woman on the screen. In one of the spare bedrooms. A man was there, holding her down."

As he says the words, Trent moves, taking me by the hips and transferring his weight to them, pinning my lower body in place.

"Your father?" I whisper, scared of the answer but needing to know. Needing to understand if his lineage is working against me.

"A stranger," he says on an outward breath.

I drag in a gulp of air in relief.

"She struggled," he whispers, and I take the command, moving against his hands, kicking my heel up, wriggling my arse. "She fought him like she was fighting for her life."

And my panic bleeds out at those words, breaking free in a toxic rush of movement and screams and deep, mindless fear. My head pulls back, trying to snap the clasp around my neck where it doesn't have a hope. Even if it had been one I'd scored through, my strength isn't anywhere near Trent's.

I'm weak on a good day. Winded running for the bus.

My strength is in my flexibility but being able to perform contortions isn't any help when I'm bound, trapped under the body weight of a boy three times my size. A boy who just proved his strength by beating someone to death.

The panic is slow to ebb. I don't know how long I'm in that state, fighting and gaining no ground.

Long enough for my mouth to go dry. Long enough to taste the zing of a nine-volt battery. Long enough to have a buzz in my ears and tear trails staining my face.

"That was so good," Trent says, grinding himself into me. "You're so perfect. I knew you were special from the moment I set eyes on you. Trapped in my dad's study with those boys."

"What happened to the woman?" I croak, not wanting to hear about me, what he thinks of me. "Who attacked her?"

"I watched as she stopped fighting. She screamed until she wore herself out, just like you." There's a strange sensation on my skin, and I take a moment to understand he's licking me. My hip. His tongue must be pressed flat against my skin, lapping in long slow even strokes, then starting again. "When she couldn't fight any longer, he pulled her legs apart, and he shoved himself inside her. It took a lot of effort. The fear made her bone dry."

His fingers dance around the lips of my pussy, teasing at the edges before exerting enough force to slip inside.

"I don't think that's a problem for you."

"It wasn't..." His finger slips smoothly into me, stroking back to rub at my entrance, then dipping into me again, going up to the first knuckle, the second. A new flash of concern ripples through me. My desperate brain trying to solve the riddle of why Trent is why he is, racing to get to the answer before it's too late. "It wasn't your mother, was it?"

He's gone. Moving his hand out and away, moving his body so the bed shakes as his weight leaves it.

My fear kicks in again and I keep my eyes screwed shut, trying to breathe as slowly as I can, in and out, trying to hold it for a few counts but having to give up the attempt when it feels like I'm strangling.

"Not my mother. She died in a boating accident when I was three. Open your eyes," Trent says in a whisper.

When I do, he's right next to me again, crouching beside the base of the bed. There's something held in his hand that I can't quite see but it sends fear spinning through me. A gag of some type. If he puts that into my mouth, I'll be completely defenceless. I can't do that; my mind can't take any more.

"No more questions."

"Okay," I agree, fear turning my voice shrill. "No questions. I'll be quiet, I promise, just please..." His eyes sharpen again, reacting to the words. A way in. A way to get back a tiny piece of control. I don't mind begging if that's all he responds to. "Please don't hurt me, Trent. You can let me go. It's okay. Just please... *please...*"

He moves, getting onto the bed behind me again, hand between my legs, fingers slipping gently inside me. When they withdraw, I know what's coming next.

A scene in exchange for him killing my uncle. Sex for payment. You know how this goes.

He wants to hurt me, so I need to cry out. I'll struggle. Any chance I see to get free or gain advantage, I'll take it.

A scene.

His fingers disappear and the head of his cock nudges at my entrance. My automatic response is to clench my muscles against him, but the only person that'll hurt is me.

I force my body to relax. When he slowly edges inside, I push back against him. Not obviously. Not enough to upset the fantasy playing out in his head. But enough to control his entry, reduce the friction, in the teeniest, tiniest way.

The stretch begins almost immediately. I was wet from our foreplay, from teasing him as I bound him to the chair, but that arousal is gone now. It's been replaced with fear and anger, neither of them known aids for penetration.

"Stop," I murmur when the stretch becomes a burn. Then louder, struggling against him. "Please stop."

Strong hands grip my hips, pulling me onto him rather than him pushing into me. It helps. A relieved observer in my mind notes he could know that, be helping me even as the rest of his body goes against my wishes.

Then he leans forward, his weight falling onto me, his enormous cock sinking deeper until I'm struggling, trying to find a position where it doesn't hurt.

His head is next to mine, breath hot on my shoulder. "Stop

thinking," he says in his deep rumble. "There's not a single thing you can do to stop this, so just let it go." He licks from the ball of my shoulder to my ear, panting with excitement. "You're completely powerless."

And the thought burrows in, leaving a trail of mayhem behind it.

I twist and turn, yanking at the bindings, knowing I can't get free, knowing the struggle will only make them tighter, in carving lines in my skin, making the tender flesh swell.

The whiteness takes over. When I come back to myself, he's slowly thrusting inside me, getting deeper with each penetration, my muscles accommodating him but running a line between pain and pleasure.

Then it tips over.

There's nothing but pleasure.

I'm fuller than I've been before, the sensory overload from just that overwhelming on its own. But then there are the hands running over me, for the first time in so long not at my direction but moving where he wants them to go, where he wants to feel.

The lack of control transforms, becomes glorious.

Trent touches me everywhere. Stroking and caressing and pinching and sinking his cock farther in until I groan at the exquisite edge of pain. He creates marks on my body that will turn into bruises, badges of ownership, of possession, if only he leaves me alive long enough for them to develop.

And that's the thought I can't afford to have. The one that rattles me to my soul.

The panic makes a renewed claim, but this time doesn't grab me completely. Even in the depths of squirming and shouting and struggling, there's a part of my brain revelling in each sensation. Revelling in the loss of control that means he can do what he wants, and the only power left to me is how I react.

And my body responds like it's been starved of affection so long that it confuses this aggression with care, this possession as adoration, the steady strokes of his cock a brutal declaration of love.

Or it's not confused, and that is exactly what they are. Trent's form of a love sonnet is having me restrained and begging and screaming while he ignores every whimper in the pursuit of finding a warm resting place for his oversized cock.

The waves of pleasure grow stronger. The less control I have, the stronger they grow.

"You feel so good," he moans, an echo vibrating across my shoulder. "You're so wet for me."

He moves his arm underneath me, curving around my waist, holding me steady as his thrusts pick up speed, the increase in motion stretching me wider still, so full it's like his cock is diving deeper than my cunt, driving through into my guts, rearranging my insides to create a new path, a longer tunnel for him to plunge inside.

"I'm going to come so hard inside you that it spills out of your mouth," he growls as his other hand moves higher, to my tits, squeezing and fondling them, my nipples already hard from the chill air, now pulling so tight they're painful. "Clench your pussy around me, draw me so far inside you I never find my way out."

I obey, choking out a cry as Trent grabs handfuls of my flesh, gripping so hard I picture it oozing between his fingers. Clutching at me until the only signals broadcast are excitement, enjoyment, tendrils of rapture that spread out, connecting to the similar messages flooding in from all over.

"You're my dirty little slut." His guttural tones play a sensual beat against my eardrums. He sinks his teeth into my shoulder, the pain sharp and strong and so, so good. "My filthy girl with her cunt so wet for me."

He shifts my hips, hitting inside me at a new angle as his vulgarity hits against my ears, bringing so much pleasure I can't stand it.

I fight again, trying to escape as the crash of each successive wave grows higher, the undertow dragging me deep before thrusting me atop the next, taller crest.

There's too much, too much, too much, then all my nerves short out at once. I know my body is convulsing but I'm so far from being in control that I have no way to negotiate this unfamiliar terrain. Pleasure slams into me, again and again, spreading out in wider ripples each time, each new peak feeling impossible to surmount, yet followed by one higher, and higher.

A whistling sound explodes in my ear. I close my eyes because I'm in sensory overload.

"You want to know how the video I saw ended?"

No. A thousand times no.

His hand moves from my tits up to my throat, touching but not applying pressure. He doesn't need to. The plastic band is there, ready and waiting for him to tighten as he pleases.

"When the man had taken everything he wanted, he put his hands around the woman's neck and squeezed."

I gasp, shuddering, still riding a wave that seems never-ending. His words mean something, but it lies just outside my understanding. Transported too far on the ripples of pleasure to care about what's happening back on shore.

"He squeezed the life out of her just as she was coming so her orgasm went on for ever... and ever..."

Trent makes a long groan, his thrusts going from rhythmic to spasmodic, then the clasp around my neck grow tighter, the plastic clicks loud as gunshots.

My eyes flick open but it's too late. There's a hazy film over my vision. The room darkens, so dark I can't see.

I can't breathe but I'm too warm and fuzzy to care. Soft arms pull me into their embrace, rocking me as the last tingles evaporate from my skin and the world retreats too far for me to grasp hold.

CHAPTER EIGHTEEN

TRENT

Rosa's breathing resumes a second after I slit the zip tie with my penknife. The colour didn't have time to leave her cheeks and I sit on the bed beside her, cradling her against me, terrified I went too far.

The fear is a strident counterpoint to the exultation from a few minutes ago. One glorious experience from start to finish. It's been years since I felt this peaceful, this alive.

Strike that. I've *never* felt this sense of wellbeing, like everything in the world shifted a tiny fraction of a degree and now it all lines up perfectly, every join finally slotting into place.

"Hey," I say as her eyelids flutter. "Stay with me."

She curls towards me, towards my warmth, and I'm flushed with gratitude that after everything I did, she still responds positively.

Whether she'll do that once fully conscious is a different story.

I need to move, to ask questions, to clarify. To make calls, get help, get things moving to clean up the mess lying beside the bed.

So many things being added each second to my mental list, but for this tiny moment, I push it aside, rocking my beloved back and forth, back and forth, willing her to recover, to open her eyes, to reconnect.

To let me know where I stand.

"Trent?"

Her voice is a whisper, opaque with confusion. "Time to wake up," I murmur into her ear, cradling her even closer now she's aware enough to make a noise if I do something wrong. "Your nap's over."

She puts her palm flat against my chest, caressing not pushing, and I get the tight bunching behind my ears I get when there's too much emotion and nowhere to put it.

"Let's stand up." I lift her with me off the bed, supporting her weight until her feet find the floor, holding her waist after so she doesn't stumble. "There are people I need to call. Do you want a shower before they come?"

"People." Her head turns to the side, and I move to block her view because she doesn't need to see what I did to Andy. Doesn't need to see how unrecognisable he's become. "What people?"

I cup her head, thumb stroking just in front of her ear. "Do you remember what happened?"

Rosa's eyes are so large they look like I could fall into them. She clutches onto my wrist, staring straight at me, puzzled. Her voice when it does come is in such a whisper, I have to read the words from her lips, or I wouldn't understand them. "You didn't... I thought I was dead."

"I would never do that." She tilts her head and I lean down to press a soft kiss on her mouth. "I adore you."

Her expression is still lost, befuddled, and I wish I could take the time to go through everything.

What we are now, what this means for her.

How once isn't enough for me and this time I'm not walking away just because everything we want is in opposition. Not now I've experienced what we could be.

"Why don't you sit on the bed?"

I guide her back and press on her shoulders until she obeys me. Her head tips too far forward, nearly unbalancing her, then she shivers and rights herself. I fetch a cloth from the bathroom, running the water on it until it's warm, then bringing it through to wipe the blood gently from her face, her shoulders, her hands.

"Where are my clothes?"

They're on the other side of the corpse and I step delicately around the body, careful not to get any more blood on me than there is already. Once I have the garments, I help her dress and walk her through to the next room, installing her on a dining room chair.

There's too much blood on me for a cloth, so I shower it off before I dress, doing everything as quickly as possible so I can get back to her.

The sheets carry traces of Andy's blood where it smudged from my body. Since they're already stained, I drape them over his corpse, so I don't have to stare at it any longer. Don't have to look at the one eye staring blankly at the ceiling and the other lost in a crushed dent filled with blood.

Then I'm out of there, dialling my phone as I sit next to Rosa, pulling our chairs close together so I can hold her with one arm while I grip my device with the other.

"Zach?" I run down what happened as quickly as possible, then ring off after he promises to call anyone else we need. Rosa has her knees curled to her chest, balancing on the edge of the chair.

Bruises are spotted along her arms where Andy grabbed her

to restrain her, on her hips where I held her, around her neck and wrists where the twist ties bit into her flesh.

My mind shies away from what happened, how it felt to be trapped in the chair as I slowly, far too slowly, worked out that the drama playing out before me wasn't sticking to the script.

I've never experienced such helplessness and such overwhelming fury. The rage growing as he laid out Rosa's past, the terrors forced upon her as a child.

My chest still holds the dull ache of realisation, that what I'd asked of her—the request I thought should be so easy—was a mirror to the worst part of her childhood, dredging those horrendous memories from the murky waters of her past into her present.

I can't stand to see Rosa shaking and lift her, pulling her into my lap, cuddling her close to me. Her scant weight reassuring against my legs.

Much as I hate what Andy put her through, I can't feel the same regret for my actions after. Not when it touched me so deeply, so profoundly that I won't ever be the same again.

"We can go home soon. A few friends will be by to help with cleaning up the bedroom, then we can go." I hesitate. "Nobody's coming in to work here this afternoon, are they?"

She shakes her head, then leans it against me, one hand curled up next to her cheek.

"I'll have a doctor come to the house to check you out. Make sure there's no lasting damage."

"Won't they have to report everything?"

"Not the one I'll call. She won't tell anybody about anything." I wait for a second before adding, "Not unless you want her to."

"He's dead, right?"

I drop a kiss on the top of her head, one arm around her trembling shoulders. "He's dead."

"I should've checked him out better." She sobs, whole body shaking with the effort. "He said he'd worked with a colleague, and he knew our address, knew where to come. When I met him, he greeted me like he'd met me before, and I felt embarrassed because I didn't recognise him." She hits at her knee with a fist. "I'm so stupid. After everything, I can't believe I let him just walk into my work without asking for proof of *anything*."

"You're not stupid just because he fooled you. He's probably studied every inch of your life. Knew everything about you. That's not something you automatically think of when you meet someone."

"But I—"

"And it was before we found the cameras, wasn't it? So, you weren't even on alert. Unless he had craft supplies on him, I don't think you can blame this one on yourself."

"Every time Mum asks, I always tell her I'm being safe. I thought I was smarter than this."

I could reiterate that it's not her intelligence in question, but I'm struck by another part of her speech. "You talk to your mum about this work?" And then another. "I thought you were in foster care."

She curls into an even tighter ball. It's like I have a small child on my lap rather than a grown woman. "My mum's sick. Cancer. She got to a point she couldn't take care of me, so I went into the system for a while." Then she slaps me. About as effective as a moth batting its wings considering she's still weak. "And why shouldn't I tell my mother about my work. Don't you talk to your dad about yours?"

"Fuck, no. I tell him the least amount possible about my life just like any other normal teenager."

She snorts out a laugh and I'm overtaken with relief; I want to roar with happiness. She sounds okay. Moving and talking and laughing and joking.

I didn't destroy her. Haven't ruined our fledgling friendship.

"If you're calling yourself normal, I'm gonna have to write to the dictionary and get them to update their description of the word."

"Harsh."

"But fair."

There's a cautious knock on the door and I replace Rosa in her chair before going to answer it. Stefan waits outside, face impossible to read.

I'm so shocked to see my boss on the doorstep, I freeze.

"Aren't you going to let me in?"

"Sorry." I stand aside, moving as a barrier between him and Rosa, then pointing him towards the bedroom.

Zach turns up a moment later, Caylon in tow.

"You called Stefan?"

"Who the fuck else is going to deal with a body on short notice?" Caylon asks, nodding to Rosa while Zach turns a furious stare on her. God knows why. "Are you going to show us or leave us to stumble over the corpse by ourselves?"

I lead the way through to the bedroom, hanging near the doorway while the other two join Stefan in examining the scene. Caylon raises his eyebrows at our boss, who nods. At the permission, he crosses to the sheet and lifts the edge.

"Any idea where his clothes are?"

"By the bed." I nod in the direction, and he moves around, picking up the jeans to dig into the pockets, withdrawing a slim wallet. "There should be a phone somewhere."

Shit.

I angle my way towards its resting place on the floor. The place it fell when I broke free. I pick it up, swiping, but the screen's locked. I toss it to Caylon.

"Thanks." He retreats to the other room and Stefan follows to make a phone call, leaving me and Zach with the body.

Zach stares at the chair with one tie still hanging from the arm, the other on the floor nearby. Stares at the discarded belt, excess to requirements since mine is fastened around my waist.

His gaze travels from the body to the bed, then back to the body. "Thought I was into some weird shit."

"You are into some weird shit. This was perfectly normal until the hired help turned out to be a gigantic psycho."

Zach nudges one of the snapped ties with his toe. "Perfectly normal," he repeats in a flat voice.

"Maybe I meant, it was consensual."

He nods, pursing his lips. "Got a lot of bindings for something consensual."

The air of judgement burns me. Of all the people in my life, the one with the loosest grip on normality shouldn't be sticking his nose in the air like he's any better.

"Is there a fucking problem?"

"Oh, I don't know." Zach shakes his head, hands on hips, staring at the corpse. "Maybe that we finally cleared up the loose ends from a murder *last night*, and you thought we should get started on another straight away."

"Fuck you." I storm over, poking my finger into his chest with such aggression that he appears taken aback. "That was your perfectly avoidable mess that we all got dragged into. You could've talked Lily down and instead you shot our friend. This guy?" I point to the mess on the floor that used to be human. "He was going to kill us. This was one hundred and ten fucking percent in self-defence so if you want to complain and spout your bullshit, find another place to do it because if you don't want to help me after everything I've done over the years for you, then we're fucking done!"

I back away, breathing heavy, annoyed I'm in here shouting when my girl sits alone and hurt in the other room.

And I might have killed Andy, but I don't feel bad about it.

My emotions aren't in the same maelstrom they were following Robbie, always on edge, panic gripping me at a moment's notice.

Perhaps time will change that, but I don't think so. This man's death means nothing to me because the alternative was Rosa. I could kill a million men every day and never have a speck on my conscience if I were killing them to protect her.

As I stare at Zach, my posture changes.

Maybe this is how he felt, shooting Robbie because it was what Lily needed from him. Taking vengeance to release the girl he loved from her obsessive agenda, even if he didn't know he loved Lily back then.

Or he was just being the loose fucking cannon he specialises in being.

Caylon clears his throat in the doorway, his eyes flicking from one of us to the other, like a bored observer watching tennis. "Don't know why you're all shouting. This is a dead guy that nobody gives a shit about. Cleaning him up will be a piece of piss."

Zach glares at me, more offended by my tone than he was at the dead body on the floor. "Sorry," he finally mumbles, and I'm taken aback. He's never apologised for a single thing in his life.

Shock makes my aggression dissipate. "Me, too. I'm a bit on edge."

"No shit," Stefan says, walking into the room. "A few guys are coming to take care of things. No need for any of you to stay." He aims a pointed glance at Caylon who doesn't appear to take any notice.

We obediently file through to the dining room, Zach heading straight out the door while Caylon lingers, head tilted as he stares at Rosa. "I thought we were all on the same page about keeping everything normal until we'd tracked down the creep."

Rosa coughs, then shakes her head when Caylon sends his fiery glance her way. "This is normal," she says in a small voice, putting a hand to her throat when he focuses on her bruises. "This is my workplace. I'm here three weekdays and for a few hours every weekend. Sorry if it doesn't meet your standards."

To his credit, Caylon frowns, eyes unfocused, then nods. "Point taken. Now I've got his phone and ID, it'll be quick work to track down your dead guy."

"What for?" she asks dully. "As you just pointed out, he's dead."

"To find out what we can about him," I tell her, pulling her to her feet and slipping my arm around her waist. "And we're looking for your uncle now, right?"

Caylon looks vaguely surprised. "We are?"

"Yeah. He's the head of the snake, so the jobs not done until we've tracked him down and dealt with him." I twist Rosa back towards me. "That's my end of the bargain, right?"

She appears relieved and my heart is so full at this moment that I never want it to end. "Right," she whispers.

"Good. And now we need to go collect Finley and move you two into my home."

CHAPTER NINETEEN

ROSA

"Oh, my god," Finley squeals for the eighth time in a row as she walks into the bedroom Trent says she can use.

This time I have to agree with her enthusiasm. The bedroom is beautiful. Something a princess would conjure up in her daydreams.

"Look, there's a bed big enough for both of us *and* all our friends." She immediately toes off her shoes to clamber up and bounce on it like a trampoline. "This is so awesome." She stops long enough to flutter the pink canopy, then starts jumping again. "Why aren't you joining me?"

"This is just your bedroom," Trent clarifies with an amused grin before turning to me. "Say goodbye to your friend and I'll drag you farther into the depths of the house and show you yours."

"We could share." I rub my stomach, the whole day swimming in and out of focus with every intake of breath. There's a small spatter of blood on the back of my hand and I zoom in on it. If I squint at it right, it looks like glitter. A tiny speck of a reminder that a man got killed.

And that he fucking deserved it.

Good riddance, but that doesn't stop me feeling nauseous to my very bones.

"You're sharing with me," Trent whispers against my neck, giving me a friendly shake, his strong arms turning my resolve into mist.

Whatever emotions I held for him this morning, they've become a thousand times deeper, more complicated, more rewarding. I need time to untangle them, to pull them apart and try to gain perspective on what's happened, what could happen next.

It's hard to reconcile this gentle teasing giant with the man who tore apart my would-be assailant.

He could just as easily do that to you.

A shiver takes hold and despite the direction of my thoughts, it's not entirely unpleasant. I let them linger, thinking of the moment when he pulled the plastic tight around my neck. When all the worst things he'd warned me about himself could have come to fruition. He could have torn me apart, made me scream with pain... and instead I screamed with pleasure. I clasp my hands on top of his, holding them tighter against me, my trust in him increasing with each passing second.

I'm privileged to see both sides of him, the terrifying monster, and the gentle giant. One a vicious protector, the other becoming my best, my truest friend. Neither of his personalities causing me harm.

"Move along," Finley says, doing a bottom drop before lying back on the bed. "Go show Rosa where you're keeping her, then you can take us on a tour of the rest of the house."

He doesn't need to be told twice and I'm soon entering his

bedroom, suffused with his essence so much I can't help but smile as I walk inside.

It's not just the scent of his deodorant and aftershave, or the assortment of sporting team jerseys displayed, behind glass, on his walls.

There's just something essentially Trent about the entire space. The neat stacks of books on his desk, next to an untidy bundle of stationery that looks like he was using the individual items to represent players, working out tactics for a match.

A stack of clean laundry on a chair that he's taking stuff from rather than bothering to put it away. The food pyramid on his desk. The gigantic screen hanging from his wall. The computer alternating between naked women and All Black greats.

His bed, made with the precision of a hospital matron.

"The bathroom's through here," he says, walking inside and turning on a light. "Take a shower and I'll sort out something clean for you to wear."

He'd insisted I stay in the car while he collected Finley, having a quick check-in with the private investigator before walking into the flat. He'd exited a minute later, her scurrying across the road to clamber into the back seat, a million questions flying from her mouth before Trent got into the driver's seat.

No time to collect clothing. No time to collect my books or my computer or the few personal items I cherish because it's hard for me to spend money on anything but necessities, so when I do, they instantly hold a special place.

I open my mouth to tell him nothing will fit then shake my head, following his instructions. Thoughts are too hard at the moment. To oppose the only person in my life helping me right now would be dumb.

Once upon a time, I thought I was in control of everything, but I've been screwing up left, right, and centre. Time to let someone else take the reins for a moment.

The relief of letting go is as comforting as the caressing warmth of the shower.

Even though I only stay inside it long enough for a quick scrub, shampooing my hair because I can't stand to think of there being blood caught in it for a moment longer, I appreciate the fanciness of the shower. There are sprays and jets and dozens of controls that I don't dare to touch. It's entirely different from the basic cubicle at the flat.

I bet Finley's in ecstasy right now.

That thought makes me smile as I exit, quickly drying myself with the enormous fluffy white bath towels stacked on an aluminium shelf. Trent knocks on the door after a few minutes, and I answer with one wrapped around my head, the other wrapped around me.

"Hopefully, these fit," he says, handing across a brand-new pair of black jeans with a matching black shirt.

They're definitely women's clothing and I glance at him with curiosity.

He shrugs. "Dad's new wife is about your size. I'll buy her replacements."

"No, I'll buy them," I say, the automatic response not even needing to check-in with my brain before exiting my mouth. "I can afford my own clothing."

His face scrunches. "But you don't need to. I know you can take care of yourself, but you don't have to tackle everything alone, not any longer." He pauses, a cheeky light glinting in his eye. "And you can't."

"I can't?" I frown at the last sentence, not understanding.

He cups me around the back of my neck and draws me closer. "You can't afford to replace them. You have absolutely no idea of the ridiculous prices of the stores my new mummy frequents."

About to rebut him, I see the price slip sticking out of the bag and grab it.

Goddamn but I hate that he's right.

That and what the hell are people doing that they spend this much on clothes?

"Okay," I say and my voice squeaks. "You can get this round."

"I have money, Rosa. Just... let me use it, yeah? This is small change."

I nod, parking the battle for another day. "Don't suppose your new stepmum has some underwear going begging?"

"No." His eyes twinkle as his hand leaves my neck and slowly moves along my shoulder, my upper arm, my forearm, sliding across my fingers with sensual slowness before reluctantly letting go. "Don't suppose she does."

He leaves the room so I can change without an audience, and I busy myself with pulling the clothes on to hide my reddening face. The top is a little tighter and the jeans a little looser than I'd pick, but they're a million times better than anything he might have stored in his wardrobe.

When I emerge, he looks happy, pulling me against him. "I've just had word back from Caylon. He's at Andy's flat, combing through everything he can find. They'll probably know more by tonight or tomorrow."

I nod, swallowing hard to get past the lump. "You don't think... he had family?"

"He was going to kill both of us," Trent reminds me, stroking my hair. "If he has loved ones, I hope they meet again in hell."

"Rosa!" Finley yells from her door along the corridor.

"I'm right here," I say, crossing my eyes and feeling a pinch of happiness sprinkle itself over my day. "You don't need to shout."

"Blame my upbringing." Her smile is mischievous and

uncaring. "Come have a look at my bathroom! The shower has fourteen different nozzles. I counted them."

"She's just been in exactly the same," Trent assures her. "There's no need to look at every copy in the house."

"Aren't you going to tour us through the rest of the facilities?" she asks instead, dancing from foot to foot. "Ooh! Do you have a home theatre, like a real one with armchairs and a massive screen?"

He nods, the two of us drawing level.

"What about an indoor swimming pool?"

"There's a heated lap pool, a hot tub, and a sauna," he says, laughing at her excitement, the energy so rampant I get caught up in the same emotion. "But they're all in the same room. And there's an outdoor pool. Although I'd recommend you stay away from that until summer."

"Summer!" Finley jumps up and down, losing any sense of decorum. "We can stay until summer?"

"You can stay for as long as you like," he reassures her. "Mi casa es su casa and all that."

"Your dad can't be okay with letting strangers live in his house without an end date," I declare.

"Be nice if someone stopped trying to ruin everything all the time," Finley muses. "Don't you agree, Trent?"

"I certainly do."

I grab her by the waist, swinging her in a circle. "Gang up on me, why don't you?"

I trail behind the two of them, trying to absorb Finley's ecstasy at the upgraded living arrangements rather than let my low mood drag her down. I think I'm doing an okay job of it, but when Trent drops back to put his arm around me, halfway through explaining the kitchen and the magical fridges full of replenishing food—Finley's assessment—he murmurs, "Are you okay?"

"Do you have the time?" He nods at the stove clock, and I frown. "I should be visiting my mum right now."

"Oh, shit, honey." Finley comes over and the stream of excessive compliments comes to an abrupt halt. "I never thought."

Trent takes my hand in his, tugging me towards an internal door through to the garage. "We can go right now. It's no problem."

"I don't... She gets overwhelmed with lots of people. Just point me towards the nearest bus stop."

"We'll wait in the car," Finley says, inviting herself along as well. "Trent can explain all the gadgets I'm sure he's hiding in there."

"You're tired," he whispers to me. "And you're overthinking everything. Just let it go for a few hours. Every one of your worries will be waiting right here when we get back, I promise."

The assurance is so ridiculous, my mood lightens. "Fine. In that case, show us to your flashiest vehicle."

"So the wealth is growing on you?" His voice is optimistic.

"No, but the area my mum's home is in is so bad you'll have to stay with the car, otherwise, it'll be stolen."

I squeeze his hand before letting it go to get into the bright yellow sports car, then having to get out again because it's the only way Finley can clamber into the back seat.

"That's what happens when you order me to stop overthinking. I come up with nefarious plans."

My mother is stronger than I've seen in weeks, sitting up in bed when I enter the room and tilting her head to get a better view as I rush into her welcoming hug. "Thank goodness," she exclaims as my embrace lingers longer than usual. "I thought you weren't coming."

"I just had a problem that made work run long." Then hastily add, "Nothing bad. It's all being sorted as we speak," before she can ask.

I stare at her in wonder, absorbing every difference. I love when she's like this, closer to her old self. Love it even though it makes the loss hit more keenly. Especially when my traitorous thoughts start to believe she might recover, even though I know better.

"You're looking much brighter today."

"Yeah. I got the nurse to put a line of coke into my drip." I stare at her, dumbfounded, then watch as her face creases with delight. "Ha. Got you."

"You did. It's just the cut-priced coffee, then?"

"Home brand for the win again."

We go through our usual rotation of subjects, the questions and answers feeling as safe and scripted as the call and replies in church. "I've moved into a new place," I say cautiously as the effort of my visit shows. "My routine might be a bit off for a while, but I promise I'll get here just as often."

"Maybe more often," Trent calls from the doorway, ignoring every one of my explicit instructions as easily as he now ignores the upset expression on my face. "Hey. I'm sure Rosa hasn't mentioned me at all, but I'm Trent."

"Is this the billionaire?" she whispers to me as he approaches. "He smells rich."

"Not quite that level but my dad's working on it."

"And what are your intentions towards my daughter?"

He takes a visitor's chair from under the window and drags it next to the bed, trapping me where I lie beside her. "Only good, I promise you. Did she mention we had a bit of trouble today?"

My mum tilts her head, squinting her eyes though I doubt she can see him even sitting this closely. "At work?"

"Yeah. Some friends of mine are looking into it but anything you can tell us about Rosa's uncle would be helpful." My eyes are shooting death rays at him, but Trent just smiles lazily and bats them aside. "We're trying to track him down."

"Shouldn't you be out keeping your car safe?"

"Finley's taking it on a spin around the block," he says with a shrug. "I can't think of anything safer than that."

"Says someone who obviously hasn't seen her driving."

I take my mum's hand and she squeezes it, then clamps her other around my upper arm. "He's not been in contact, has he?"

"No," I state firmly at the same time Trent says, "Yes."

"He hasn't," I insist. "There were some cards that made me concerned, but the police confirmed he didn't send them."

"Is this why you wanted to know who told me he was out?"

"Yes," Trent says before I can jump in with a softer answer. "I'm anxious for your daughter's safety and although she keeps insisting she's perfectly capable of taking care of herself, I don't think this is a situation she should handle alone."

"No. He... what do you need to know?"

"Whatever details you can give us."

"They'll be a decade out of date," I snap at him, blood boiling with fury. Who the fuck does he think he is, coming in here, asking a dying woman questions? "She knows absolutely nothing since he was locked away, just like me."

"We've got some leads," Trent says, meeting my mother's eyes. "But anything we can add to the larger picture helps. Habits, things he enjoys doing, enjoys eating even. It could all help pinpoint a location."

My mother's lips tremble and a new bolt of rage shoots through me. "Can't you ask the police?"

"It's gone beyond that." Trent reaches for the same hand that my mother's holding, his palm so large it easily encompasses both of ours. "Their rules mean unless we have evidence directly implicating him, they can't do anything."

"Implicating him in what?"

My mother's voice is sharp.

"It's nothing," I tell her.

"A man tried to kill both of us earlier today," Trent explains, ignoring every signal I'm sending his way. "We took care of him, but we need to track him down."

"Took care of him?"

"Don't you fucking dare," I tell Trent when I see the look in his eye. "This isn't your problem," I say, turning back to my mother, but it's too late. She has the hard set to her brow that means trouble.

"Of course, it's my problem. Anything involving you and that man is my problem." She sits up further, struggling for a moment with the change in posture, then looking directly at me. "I know I've been sick for a long time, but that doesn't change the fact that you're my daughter. I'm the one meant to coddle and protect you, not the other way around." She turns her stern gaze on Trent. "Until I draw my last breath, you can ask me anything you want, and I'll answer honestly."

"Thank you." Trent abruptly lets go, moving to the door. "Since you're willing, I've got an investigator waiting outside who'll ask them a lot better than me."

CHAPTER TWENTY

TRENT

"What's she doing in a retirement home, anyway?" I ask as we leave the home, Edwin already enroute to Caylon with the scant information we could get from Rosa's mother. "Shouldn't she be in a hospice?"

"They don't have beds available." Her face is set in lines of displeasure. No guesses needed to work out who she's upset with. "I'm in constant contact with the district health board but they haven't found her a space."

"Please let me drive home," Finley calls from the vehicle, giggling with excitement, her cheeks flushed. "And if anyone sends you a ticket in the mail, it wasn't me."

"Sure," I say, bundling Rosa into the back and trapping her when I get into the passenger seat. "You've got a valid licence, don't you?" I belatedly check.

"Yep," Finley says, not meeting my eyes and I fasten my seat belt just in case.

The drive home doesn't lessen Rosa's irritation and once

there, I send Finley into the entertainment room to find something for us to watch with dinner while I pull Rosa aside, desperate to talk some sense into her.

"Do you really think your mother is better off not knowing?"

"She's not well. Today was a good day for her and now it's ruined. She mightn't get many more of those."

"She won't get any if you wind up dead. Did you ever think of that?"

Her hand goes to her throat, hiding the bruises, and I flush with shame. It's been a long day, a terrible day, and yelling at her won't disable the self-protection mechanisms she has in place.

I pull her into my arms and wait until some of her stiff muscles soften. "Both me and your mother just want to keep you safe. It'll be easier if you stop fighting me at every turn."

"I don't want her worried about things she can't control."

"That describes just about everything." I sway her from side to side, one hand moving from her waist to her cheek, cradling it against me. I close my eyes and let my forehead drop to rest against the top of her head. "Please let me take care of you. I don't want every interaction to be an argument."

"Then you should've picked someone to boss around."

I snort out a laugh, relaxing my grip when she struggles free and gives me a curious stare. "What was that for?"

"I'm amused by the idea that I *picked* you rather than you just hurtled into my life at a million miles an hour."

"I didn't." She folds her arms. "I've been minding my own business all this time."

I put her in a quick head lock, kissing her on the top of her hair a dozen times before setting her free. "Well, now I'm minding your business and as the son of an astute investor, expect to double your returns."

She laughs, immediately becoming more pliable.

"How about we find out what Finley's got in store for us?"

We walk into the entertainment room arm in arm, and I'm shocked to see my father and Sashe in there with her.

"Sorry," Finley mouths at me and I wrinkle my nose at her.

"Anything you want to tell me about?" Dad asks in a jocular tone that sounds a hundred percent forced. "Or don't I warrant an introduction to the people you invite to live in my home."

"This is Rosa," I say, keeping her firmly tucked beside me. "And you've already met Finley, I guess."

"It's lovely to meet you," Sashe gushes, rushing over to Rosa until she tries to back up a step. "I haven't met any of Trent's friends before."

"Because you've only been here five minutes."

"Trent," my dad growls in warning.

"Nice to meet you," Rosa manages, peeling herself away from me. "Sorry we didn't get introduced earlier but my mum's in hospital, sick with cancer, and we had to run there before visiting hours were over."

I stiffen at the excess of information.

The girl won't answer the simplest questions I give her but pop her before my stepmother and she confesses everything? The openness rubs me the wrong way.

Then I see how Sashe gushes, how my dad is taken aback, how neither of them is angry nor glaring any longer. My reaction takes an abrupt U-turn.

Guess someone's had a few lessons in emotional manipulation.

It makes me glad I've been let off lightly.

"She's receiving palliative care, but the health board couldn't find the right bed for her," I inform my father since the floodgates have already opened. "I wondered if we'd be able to do something better. A private hospice, maybe?"

"I'm sure I can sort something," Dad mutters and Sashe beams at him.

"You're so generous. Don't you have that friend in oncology." She turns back to Rosa. "He's a genius and is running research into altering medications according to a person's individual genome. Do you think you could get her onto his patient list?"

I clamp my lips together, thinking that's a step too far, but Sashe mustn't yet have worn out her welcome because he instantly agrees. "I'll ring a few contacts. What's the name of the facility she's in currently?"

Rosa recites all the details, grabbing hold of my hand the moment he and his wife leave the room. "Is he for real?"

"Must be because no one would imagine him into existence." She giggles, and I let her lead me to the couch and try out a dozen different cushion combinations before deciding she's reached peak comfort.

I try not to take it personally that I spent ages trying to get her to accept even the slightest help while she let Dad and Sashe swoop in to solve her biggest concern in one go.

ROSA

Finley ended up choosing a teenage rom com with a delightful lack of solemnity. Halfway through the third episode, there's a buzz at the door. Trent answers, bringing a doctor with him when he returns.

"It looks worse than it is," I insist to the middle-aged woman as she examines me in the privacy of Trent's room. Then, in answer to her query about pain, I insist, "It barely hurts at all."

"If that's true, you must have an excessively high pain tolerance." She packs away her stethoscope and sphygmomanometer, pulling out a prescription pad and scribbling on it. "This is for codeine if your pain increases." When I open my mouth to rebut, she holds up her hand. "If you don't need it, then toss it in a week."

She moves to the door, opening it to reveal Trent hovering far too close. She turns back to me with an arched brow. "You want me to let this man inside?"

I wrinkle my nose, watching him squirm, then nod. "Yeah. He's good."

"You should have those hands in ice," she scolds him. "Or better still, stop thumping people."

"People should stop deserving to be thumped, then."

Trent crosses to me, taking me into his arms. "All good?"

"No," the doctor responds. "Not all good. Very far from good." She casts a concerned eye back to me, then nods as though reaching a decision. "This level of throat trauma is slow healing. If you feel breathless at any time, call an ambulance, and don't fuck around. Any delay could kill you."

I stiffen. It's silly but I've never heard a doctor swear before. It amplifies the warning until I'm nervous. Trent puts a supporting hand on my lower back, stroking gently.

"Repeat trauma is a bad idea." She stares straight into Trent's eyes as she issues the warning. "If you like breath play—"

"He's not the one responsible," I blurt, feeling so embarrassed, so *ashamed*, that I keep my eyes glued to the floor.

"You don't have to lie for me," Trent says in a soothing voice, pulling me closer. He nods to the doctor to continue.

"Breath play works just as well with a hand over the mouth. Maybe pinching nostrils closed. You need to avoid any type of throat compression because that shit's dangerous."

"Okay."

"I'm serious." She moves her gaze to me, holding it steady until I feel about the same size as a bug. "If you're into smothering, a pillow works fine. Shove it over your mouth or have him shove you into it, it all works the same."

Trent shifts, pulling me slightly behind him while he moves a step closer to the doctor. "I said, okay. Anything else you want us to know?"

"Play safe," she says, tipping me a wink. "You have to watch out for yourself, even if he's not the one responsible."

She leaves. When I glance at Trent's expression, her departure comes a few seconds before she would have been escorted out.

"Just so you know," he drawls. "I wasn't planning on a repeat performance. If I never see a plastic tie again, it'll be too soon."

I turn, burying my face against his chest, still feeling that crawl of embarrassment. "Never thought I'd hear a doctor recommend smothering me with a pillow."

He laughs and I join him, finding it hard to stop. Every nerve is taut, waiting for another disaster. When his arms hold me tighter, I try to relax into them but every second that passes I become more tense.

"Would you like to sleep with Finley tonight? Help her settle into her new room?"

The suggestion lets me breathe easier. "You don't mind?"

Trent cups my cheek, tilting my head back so he can stare into my eyes. "Would I rather you spent the night in my bed where I can feel you against me? Yes. But today's been overwhelming." He drops a kiss on my cheek, laying a trail of them until he's whispering into my ear. "You need to relax if you're going to sleep, and you need to sleep to heal. If Finley can do that for you, then no, I don't mind."

I nod.

"And if you need me, I'll be lying down the hall. You don't have to wait for an invitation."

I lay my head against his torso, closing my eyes while I listen to the steady thump of his heart. Grateful for his solidity. It's like hugging the largest Kauri in the forest.

"Thank you."

"Tomorrow night, though." He waits until I pull back to look at him before continuing. "Tomorrow night, I'm all yours... and you're all mine."

I SNUGGLE UNDER THE COVERS, stretching my foot out to touch against Finley's leg, making her snort and jerk away.

"Your feet are freezing," she complains. "You know these guys are rich enough to afford socks, right?"

"This is after they've been in socks," I say with a manufactured sigh. "Does that mean you only love me when I'm warm."

"It means I'll only touch you when you're warm. Unless it's summer, whereupon those freezing toes will be welcome."

I roll onto my back, feeling the bruises around my wrists and neck, the aches and pains from my frenetic bursts of energy, the throbbing in the side of my head where Andy smacked me.

Without other distractions, they hurt worse than I thought. Enough for me to be glad the doctor gave me that script.

"Since you're still awake," Finley says in a tiny voice. "Do you want to tell me what really happened today?"

"What did Trent tell you?" He'd gone in to fetch her on his own, insisting I stay in the car with every lock engaged.

"I'm not going to say. Otherwise, you'll just match your story to his and I want to know the truth." She waits for a beat, then adds, "I deserve to know the truth."

"A man tried to hurt us," I say in a hesitant voice, unsure how much to reveal. I trust her with my secrets but now some of those are shared with Trent and I don't ever want to be in the situation where he has to worry.

"Doesn't look like he tried," she answers, reaching out to

brush hair away from my bruised face. "Looks like he succeeded."

And suddenly my tears rush forth, bursting out of nowhere in a flood until it's too late to hold them back. Too late to do anything but let them pour out in all their misery, washing the worst parts of the day away.

They roll sideways across my face as I lie, facing Finley. They build on the side of my nose before rolling across the bridge, dripping onto my pillow. Waves of them, just as I think they must come to an end, a new burst starts.

My breaths shorten, becoming choppy, painful. It feels like everything bad that happened, every horrible thing that I buried deep, is pouring forth, the horrible memories clambering from their graves, the rotting flesh of long burial doing nothing to diminish their power, their ability to harm.

I press a hand to my chest, the sobs cathartic but painful. Finley reaches a hand towards me, and I grab it, squeezing it so tightly her face twists but I can't ease up, can't let go for fear I'll drift away, floating out of sight.

Finally, the tears abate, my breathing steadies and slows.

I think the tears alarm Finley more than anything else. I'm not a crier, not usually. Tough situations usually bring out my inner sarcasm generator, but right now I'm too spent to find the right angle to laugh at things.

The day was overwhelming. Too many things are shifting around me, leaving me unable to find solid ground.

"Trent took care of him," I finally murmur, "but he's connected to another man. Someone who terrorised me when I was young. That's why we came and got you. He's behind everything and I don't know where he is or how to stop him."

"Hey," Finley says, rubbing her hand along my arm in a soothing motion. "I'm sure with the amount of money he'll throw around, it'll take no time for Trent to sort this out. And we're safe here, right? That's why you tossed me into the back of his car and drove me over here."

"Yeah."

I breathe out slowly, trying to make it last as long as possible. When I inhale, I hold the breath again, then gently release it, my composure returning. "We'd better be all right. Could you imagine spending the amount of money this house must've cost and not being safe?"

"No, I can't." Finley giggles. "I'm sorry for whatever happened to you today, but I'm so glad you finally saw sense." She pokes me in the ribcage. "But now I see what I was missing, I'm doubly angry you turned down Trent's first offer. We could have been swimming in this luxury the whole time."

Her take on things instantly cheers me. And she's right. You'd have to be a madman to think of penetrating these thick walls.

But your uncle is a madman.

I push the thought away, snuggling deeper into the covers. Soon the sound of Finley's breathing is so long and rhythmic, she can only be fast asleep.

Trent killed someone to save me today. I keep that thought front and centre while I gently prod at the other things lurking behind.

He scared me. Never as badly as Andy, even when I thought I might die, but the fear was genuine. Is genuine.

All the time I've spent circling the problem, but Ceecee probably offered the best advice. I shouldn't get mixed up with someone who has problems that could threaten my life. I certainly shouldn't drag Finley into his path.

The flip side of that is Trent's desire to hurt me never eclipsed his desire to keep me safe. Perhaps if I'd fought more, or yelled out words designed to hurt him, things would be different.

But I can't deal in what-ifs. I'm having a hard enough time dealing with facts.

Trent wants the experience of hurting me without the lingering effects of actually doing so. In time, those urges could escalate, or they could decline.

I know which one I want. The question is, can I extricate myself if it turns out to be the former rather than the latter?

And does it matter, either way?

I want him. Even after being warned of the dangers, I want him. Today, even in the deepest part of my fear, I still held onto shreds of trust, and they turned out to be worthwhile.

My overthinking does no good. With each answer, I start off a dozen more questions.

I want him. That's the one simple truth under all of it. I enjoy his company, his strength, his warm smile.

Even with my body aching from use, I crave his touch, would be desperate if I didn't think I'd have it again.

The desires twist and turn within me, playing games, twanging at my emotions, finally exhausting me so much that I fall into a dreamless, depthless sleep.

CHAPTER TWENTY-ONE

ROSA

OVER BREAKFAST THE NEXT MORNING, TRENT'S DAD announces he's found a new bed for my mother. "They can accept her today if you think she's up to the move."

"Today?" The speed frightens me. "It's Sunday."

"Yes," he responds with a quirk of his lips. "Does that matter? Are you involved in a religion that insists there's no moving hospice beds on the sabbath?"

Finley cracks up beside me. "Good one."

The man appears first astounded, then delighted by her laughter. She drains her glass of orange juice and Sashe is there with a replacement before she even needs to ask. When she receives a thank you for her trouble, she blushes a deep crimson, the burst of colour making her look even prettier than before.

I sit back, amused at the spectacle. My gorgeous, bubbly friend, inveigling herself into these complete strangers' affection with her effortless charm.

"Tomorrow is fine," I answer when I remember I'm mid-conversation. "I'm just..." I twirl my hands in the air, unable to find the words to express my amazement. "This is so... thank you. Thank you so much."

Trent's dad also glows with colour. "It's my pleasure," he says, before excusing himself to his study. Sashe follows him soon after and Finley watches them go, then turns her hopeful smile towards Trent.

"I feel rude to even mention it, but the two of us are lacking a few supplies. Do you think it's okay to go back to the flat today and stock up or is that off-limits?"

"Definitely off limits," Trent answers without hesitation. "But once you finish breakfast, we can go shopping for whatever you need. My treat."

The grin she shoots me is so full of delight that it coaxes a matching one from me. Thus begins the quickest scoffing of breakfast foods I've ever witnessed before Finley scoots back to our room to get ready, giving Trent a kiss on the cheek while she scampers past.

"You don't have to do that," I begin, collecting our used dishes and taking them through to the kitchen. He stands and moves behind me, pulling me back against him.

"Yes, I do. If Finley walks around the house naked, she'll cause no end of havoc, don't you agree?"

Given the blushes she's already inspired, I don't doubt it for a second. "I just meant we can easily pick up our things from the flat."

"And spend the whole time wondering who's watching you through the cameras? Recording you on the mics? No thanks."

The idea hadn't occurred to me, but now he's placed it in my mind, the twinges of fear resume.

"Sorry," he mutters against the side of my neck as I stiffen. "I didn't mean to freak you out. But wouldn't you rather have a shopping trip? We can stop at the food court for lunch. See what's playing in the movies after."

The day stretches in front of me without the usual host of commitments stacking up until they squash my free time down to a few minutes. I'll have to do something about my course work but most of it's online; safely stored in the cloud.

"It does sound good," I agree. "And even if I don't like it, Finley will enjoy it enough for all of us and a few others tossed in for good luck." I bite on my bottom lip. "But I want to pay you back. It's not right to take your money."

"My dad's money, really, and don't you think the person who has the money should decide whether it's right for you to take it?" Before I can answer, he ploughs ahead, "And this person has decided you absolutely must spend it on as many ridiculous things as you want."

"Didn't realise clothing was ridiculous."

"Perhaps I didn't word that right," he says with a smile as warm as butter. "What I meant was that with a body as fabulous as yours, it's unnecessary."

"So you don't want Finley walking around naked but it's okay for me?"

His laugh melts against my skin. "Good point. I retract that suggestion with immediate effect. Except for my room. The preference will always be for you to remain naked in my room."

There's a tightening in my belly at the words. I'm used to transactions with hard-set guidelines. A contract covering every item on offer, what is and isn't allowed, what the cost is, how long, how much, how often.

Operating without that surety leaves me lost, floating. But I don't know how to open that discussion. Not with this boy who awakens a thousand different emotions inside of me with every touch. Not this boy who killed a man to save me. Killed him, then took his reward.

I shiver and Trent brushes my hair from my shoulder to plant a kiss there. "Please stop worrying. I won't let any harm come to you; I hope you know that."

I do. And him saying it aloud sands away the sharpest edges of my concern.

He gives me a friendly pat on the bottom. "Now, go get ready or Finley and I are leaving without you and then you really will have to walk around naked."

I've only just walked back into the kitchen before Trent bundles us into the car. At my suggestion, we drop by my mother's new room to help get her settled but don't stay long. The move exhausted her and although she seems happier, she falls down the long rabbit hole into sleep a few minutes after we show and doesn't look to be emerging soon.

The next stop is the mall and Finley is in raptures from the start. She picks up a large milkshake from a booth near the door and uses it to gesticulate wildly at all the things she wants.

When Trent privately discloses his credit card limit to her, she goes a bit crazy. We whirl from store to store, Finley steadily growing giddier with excitement.

Everything looks good on her, something she uses to her full advantage. I'm in hysterics as she carefully explains to a shop assistant that the ball season is only just getting into its swing, so having three choices of gown is essential just to get through the week.

It's so much fun tagging along and watching her exploits that the lingering awfulness of the day before is soon blown away.

"You know, I could get used to this," she announces as Trent becomes weighed down with bags, moving behind us like a personal luggage rack, never uttering the slightest word of protest.

Anyone looking at him would think trailing two teenage girls through a shopping mall was the epitome of his life ambition.

Even when Finley insists on buying him the most outrageous hat with large clapping hands set on the top, 'So we can find you if you get lost in the crowd.'

Perhaps he does finally tire of the situation because his effusive encouragement for Finley to get a haircut, colour, manicure, and pedicure, ties her to the salon for a good two hours. He drops the parcels at the car before escorting me back into the mall.

"Where are we going?"

"So many questions," he mutters, holding my hand and walking backwards in front of me until a near miss with a group of determined mall walkers forces him to reconsider.

He whisks me inside a clothing store, moving to the racks and selecting garment after garment while I stand there, blinking in confusion. "What's this in aid of?"

"You," he says, swinging me close enough to press a soft kiss on my lips. "Or me," he admits with a shrug. "I've been watching you avoid picking anything out for yourself all day long and it won't do."

"That's not true," I protest with a laugh. "At least three of those bags were mine."

"Three of the eighty I just hauled to the car?"

"Don't look at me, mister. You created that monster all on your own."

He laughs, his hand lightly pressing against my hair. "And now I want to create a new monster. So," he hands me a dozen different outfits, "here you go. Now get into those changing rooms and try them on while I dream up the fantastic pieces of lingerie I'm going to make you buy next."

Inside the cubicle, I slip into the first dress, smoothing the dark green fabric over my hips, twisting in the tiny changing room mirror to check the back. When I reach for the zipper, my shoulder sends a warning message. I woke this morning with a dozen new aches and pains, stiffness setting in overnight and never quite shaking out again.

I pop my head out, smiling as I see Trent trying to look inconspicuous and absolutely failing. For a minute, I just stare at him, appreciating the eye candy of his well-built body, then I whistle and watch his face light up.

"Need a little help here," I call out, frowning at the shop assistant who turns, ready to be of service. "A big strong man would be preferable."

He saunters over, resting his arm along the top of the frame, his body filling the space better than any door. His eyes slowly travel down the length of my body, then take their lazy time coming back up to rest on my face, one eyebrow raised. "Problem?"

I turn around. "If you could...?"

His fingers envelop the tiny zipper, and he slowly draws it up, his knuckle tracing a slow burning path of fiery tingles along my spine ahead of it. By the time he reaches the end, my skin is pulsing with a thousand different tingles. If it weren't for the lurking assistant, I'd pull him inside, thrust him in the laughably small chair, and mount him right then and there.

The shopping trip, enjoyable as it has been, suddenly drags at me, sparking my impatience.

"You look beautiful," he whispers into the curve of my neck, and I've never felt sexier, more desirable, on fire with dozens of cravings that only Trent can satisfy.

Fuck the assistant.

I turn around, grabbing at his shirt to tug him near enough to kiss me, the gentle press of his lips both satisfying and awakening a thousand more demands, each needing satisfaction.

When I come up for air, my cheeks are burning, his eyes have never looked so dark, black holes sucking me towards their centre. Trent pulls me hard against him and I can feel how much he wants me, feel him stiffening against me, prodding into my lower belly.

And I smile broadly, feeling spicy, naughty, feeling *in control* for the first time since Andy pushed his way into my room.

"Thank you for your help," I say sweetly, moving past him to look at myself in the full-length mirror at the end of the row of changing rooms, running my hands over my curves, angling my body so when I turn, the reflection shows off my tits and my arse, giving a small wriggle before I pout. "I mean, it's nice but I should really try on all of them, don't you think?"

He looks confused, sweetly baffled. "Or I could just buy them all and we could retire to the car to wait for Finley."

I bite on the corner of my lip, leaning towards him as though considering the proposal. Then I stride past him, swinging the cubicle door closed. "Not without trying them on," I admonish. "You don't want to waste all that money only to discover they don't fit."

By the time I'm wriggling into the third outfit, he seems resigned to my lengthy tease, shirt tugged out to hide his arousal, content to sit on a nearby chair and provide zipping up services as required.

As the pile of dresses in the yes column grow larger, his expression becomes more dazed. When I finally reach the end of his selections, he pulls me across his lap, growling into my ear.

"That was fun," I tell him brightly, meaning every word as we escape the store, him once again bowing under the weight of the packages. "And look." I point to the nearby clock. "We're just in time to collect Finley from her appointment."

Even with him hot and bothered, Trent doesn't protest as we detour back to the salon and I go into raptures over the startling streaks of pink and yellow now adorning Finley's hair, matching to the gel coats of her nails.

"This has been the best day," I tell him as Finley mugs him

for the car keys again and we settle into the backseat, surrounded by all the bags that couldn't fit in the trunk.

He brushes my hair from my face, cupping my swollen cheek gently as his thumb traces the edge of my lips.

"The day's not over yet," he whispers, eyes melting me with their unbridled desire. "I have a few more treats in store for you tonight."

CHAPTER TWENTY-TWO

TRENT

"DON'T DROP ME," ROSA BEGS LATER THAT EVENING, clinging around my neck like she's holding on for dear life when the worst that could happen is a brief fall onto the soft carpet. "I could walk myself, you know. I've got legs."

"Lovely, lovely legs," I agree, using my shoulder to knock open my bedroom door, then kicking it closed behind me while I walk over to lay her on the bed.

After our expedition today, I have a tangle of lust and desire built up within me. The long looks she gave me as we relaxed in the entertainment room and ate dinner across the table have done nothing to dispel the teasing anticipation she lit within me while shopping. A tease I'm only too willing to bring to fruition tonight.

"Legs you don't need to use when you've got a personal carrier at your beck and call."

"I thought I should sleep with Finley again. She gets lonely in new places, especially if she wakes up during the night."

"She's eighteen going on thirty. I'm sure she'll manage."

I open my bedside drawers and pull out something I brought in from the garage earlier, hidden away before she saw. The fabric fasteners are built for securing things to the back of trailers or car roofs, but I figure they'll work just as well to restrain Rosa in my bed.

But she appears nervous enough that I close the drawer again. Her legs are tucked up to her chin, her arms wrapped tightly around them.

"Come here," I order her, pulling her into my arms and cuddling her close until she relaxes. "This isn't where I thought we'd be at the start of the weekend."

She gives a soft laugh, nodding. "Yesterday was, without doubt, the worst day of work I've ever had."

"At least it's the last day."

She spins around in my arms to face me, running her thumb along my lower lip while she frowns. "How d'you mean?"

"I don't want you working any longer. If you still want to earn money, I'll pay you to stay home."

Her teeth seize on her bottom lip, chewing the edge of it and tearing open the thin cuts from earlier. I move in, sucking the fresh blood from the wound until it closes in self-defence.

"It's not that simple. I have contracts with the other girls in the share house. There are clients who rely on me."

"They can learn to rely on someone else, can't they?"

"That's not the point."

"I don't want you working for—"

"You knew what I did. I never kept it a secret from you. You knew about it before you came to me."

And I can't believe she's making me spell it out for her. "It's not because of what you *do*. Things have changed. You can't continue working there when it's unsafe."

There's a helpless expression in her eyes, like she doesn't

understand why she's arguing any more than I do, but she's still determined to win.

So, I exit. "But I guess that's your decision."

If she forces my hand, I can pay the other women in the house to either take on her client list or source another worker. I can buy out her share at such a high cost that they'll never renege on the deal.

And if I say any of those things, I'll scare her a thousand times more than she is right now. The opposite of what I'm intending.

"I don't even know how to explain it to them," she says in a tiny voice. "This isn't how I pictured my retirement going."

The relief is immediate and strong. "Don't worry about a thing. I'll talk to them while you're at uni and make sure everything's organised with no ill feeling."

And the relief isn't just about her safety. I can't bear to think of someone else laying their hands upon her, not when I'm in the process of making her mine.

Rosa leans forward to kiss me and that's all the invitation I need. I take her hands and press them above her head, rolling my weight onto her, pinning her to the bed. From there, I'm more cautious. Unsure if I should even try after what I put her through yesterday.

"Can I undress you?"

She wriggles her feet. "You can take my socks off."

"You're sure?" I drift down the length of her body, pressing kisses against whatever bits of her present in front of me on the way. "I've had complaints in the past about tickling."

"No," she tries to draw her legs up while I restrain them easily, barely exerting any strength. "No tickling."

"Mm. I'll try."

I peel off one sock, throwing it in the general direction of the laundry hamper and missing by a mile. I seize the foot and hold it steady, massaging her instep with my thumb. "Any tickles yet."

"No, you're good to proceed."

The next sock comes off, the foot underneath getting the same treatment. The longer I massage, the less she twitches or tries to jerk away. The behaviour reminiscent of the lady herself.

When I've massaged them bright pink, I leave her feet alone and start the trek up to the waistband of her jeans. Her hands come down, whether to help or hinder me I don't find out. I slip off the edge of the bed, returning to the drawer, and taking the fasteners out in clear view of her curious eyes.

"Isn't it your turn in restraints?" she asks, then winces when I roll up my sleeves and show her my bruised wrists, even more colourful than my swollen knuckles.

"It's your turn until I tell you otherwise," I whisper, expecting her to issue one of her knee jerk contradictions. Instead, she turns on a confused smile.

"Is this part of the deal?" she asks in all seriousness. "Is this... am I still bartering for you to kill my uncle?"

The question hits me like a gut punch. That she's having to ask at all is on me because I didn't explain myself and she's been left, struggling to understand.

While I formulate the right words, I secure her wrists to the headboard, testing the bindings won't hurt her unnecessarily; her wrists are also bruised from twist ties. Once she's restrained, I straddle her, leaning forward so my weight is on my hands, my face level with hers.

"There isn't a deal. You're my girlfriend because I love you and I think you have feelings for me. Your uncle is a dead man because nobody gets to do what he did to you and get away with his life."

She doesn't answer but at least she's not instantly in defence mode—a vast improvement from normal. Her expression is cautious, but I can handle that. I can handle anything except outright rejection, contempt, or disgust.

"You're the only girl I've ever wanted, for real, and I'm sure I've already made a million mistakes but I'm going to try as hard as I can not to make any more."

I lean down for a kiss, and her lips are responsive, firm at first, then yielding a little more with each second. The longest kiss on my record, and I can't stop, opening my mouth and thrusting my tongue into hers, feeling the push and pull of resistance and acceptance, the heat spreading out from where we're touching, the shock of it so good that I abandon myself to it, threading my fingers into her hair to keep her where I need her to be, my mind spiralling out of control as her hips buck up to grind her pussy against me.

When I finally pull away, her lips are swollen, the split from where Andy hurt her red and raw. It hurts me to see that, to see the harm someone else inflicted. Different from the marks where I pulled the tie around her neck so hard she passed out, different from the bruises on her hips where I sank my fingertips deep into her flesh.

"I'll kill anyone who hurts you," I promise her, mumbling the words against her skin as I move down her body, pushing up her shirt to kiss the soft skin of her abdomen, fumbling at her waist to undo her jeans before sliding them down, sliding them off, my kisses marking each new inch of flesh I expose until they're off and thrown on the floor behind me. "Anyone who isn't me."

Her shirt is shoved up to where her wrists are bound, and she wraps her legs around my waist when I try to move away.

"Where are you going?"

"To get condoms and take my clothes off," apparently muttering the magic words to have her release me, eyes trailing my every move until I rejoin her on the bed.

I want to ask her if she's okay to continue but I don't want her to say no, not for real. After three years without touching another person sexually, not the full way, I want to feast on the sensation not take sensible, paced bites.

"Tomorrow, we can do whatever you like," I say instead, laying out the ground rules too clearly to be misunderstood. When I roll my naked body on top of hers, I brush her hair from her eyes. "Tonight, you don't say a word unless it's yes."

"No," she says instantly, and I fall a little more in love with her.

"Spread your legs," I demand, and they clamp together, one short round of applause. "Have it your way," I growl, rubbing my thumb against her windpipe, mindful of the doctor's caution, while I force the other between her clenched thighs, using it and my body weight to wrench them apart. "The only person you're hurting is yourself."

I bite into the side of her neck as she opens wide enough to take me. My pelvis thrusts forward, the head of my cock acting like a battering ram as I force my way into her, the drag even through the condom so exquisite that I lose my mind.

For minutes, all I do is give into my own carnal desires, pounding into her until she cries out—maybe for real, maybe not —a reaction that spurs me to thrust faster and harder, holding a hand over her mouth when she cries out my name.

"Don't you say a word," I rumble into her ear. "You want to speak, earn it."

She strains her arms, trying to use the give in the bindings to get free.

"I wouldn't bother. If you do that, I'll just have to pin you with my hand."

Her leg winds over mine, unleashing a pinch of disappointment, then she jerks it up to kick at my calf muscle, hitting it dead centre, making me grunt.

I reach down, grabbing her flailing foot and bending it up,

slamming into her as her foot waggles near her head. "Want to try that again?" I ask, hoping, *praying* that she will. "You'll be so wide open, I'll get even deeper."

Her cunt muscles clench around me at the words, the rush of ecstasy so strong that I skate right up to the edge, having to cease moving to pull back before I go flying over, bringing an untimely end to my fun.

"Was that another protest?" I chuckle against her skin, licking and nipping and sucking my way from one tit to another.

Her teeth scrape against my palm, and I cup my hand so she can't make even that contact, openly laughing at her struggles, feeling in control, feeling ten feet tall, ninety percent of it rock-hard cock, the rest little more than a reservoir for my cum.

I look into her eyes and they're blazing. Her tongue presses against my hand and I switch positions, sliding my fingers into her mouth and clamping her tongue against the floor so she can't speak, only make gargling sounds of outrage that cause a firestorm of activity to rage across my scalp.

My stroke slows, no longer wanting to punish her sweet cunt, not when it's treating me so kindly. Instead, I take my time, luxuriating in the full range of sensation when I withdraw inch by inch, then alter direction and slide into her waiting pussy, pushing farther than I have before, filling her, then stretching her to breaking point until she fully encapsulates my dick.

"Good girl," I whisper, and she rocks violently against me, trying to snap her jaws together to catch my fingers in her bite.

"What? Don't you like praise you filthy whore? You want me to tell everyone that you're a dirty slut handing out her pussy to the highest bidder? I should put your cunt into an auction and see what the market's like for a battered sex toy. Would you like that, hm? Does that get your juices flowing more than being called my good fucking girl?"

She stamps her free foot into my arse, making me laugh, and

I shake her head from side to side. "Naughty. Now you'll be punished to teach you a lesson. I'd say this hurts me as much as it does you, but that would be a godawful lie because it's going to hurt you a whole, fucking lot."

I ram myself into her, beating her with my cock like I'd beat a man to death for laying a finger on her. Like I'd beat someone into hospital for looking at her the wrong way, for slowing when she walks past and letting their gaze linger a second too long, for turning their head to scope out the glorious sight of her arse moving in tight indignant circles as she strides away.

She bends her arms again, fighting against the bonds, fighting against me. This time when her cunt muscles clench it's not because she's trying to take the upper hand or tease me—it's because she's coming in such a powerful rush that her body moves completely beyond her control.

The flush of sweat on her brow intensifies, the colour high, her jaw clamping so I have to pull away my fingers to stop her from biting them clean through.

The shudder runs through her body, too glorious to fight, and I let her take me with her, pumping my seed into the thin catcher's mitt, sliding my fingers from her mouth as she hauls in a deep breath, coughing it out while she melts, the afterglow sweeping her far upstream.

I release her, taking her into my arms and holding her against me, chest to chest, our hearts beating in unison.

The awful things I said in the heat of the moment linger, and I need to clear them away.

"I love you," I tell her to wipe the board clean and start again. "You're mine and I promise to keep you safe and take care of you. Whatever you need."

And her eyes are stunned when I look into them, dazed. Her lips move but no sounds come out of her mouth.

But that's okay. I didn't say those words to get them parroted back to me. What she feels for me is her own business.

I said them because the sooner she realises the better.

She's mine, she has my heart, and I won't ever let her go.

———

ROSA

Afterwards, with my body tingling with satisfaction, I'm desperate to sleep, to escape from everything that happened yesterday; the things that will happen tomorrow.

I want to carve out a tiny pocket of time for myself, to think about what Trent confessed to me. To turn his words over and examine their sparkle more closely. To see which of my emotions it triggers—his jewelled profession of love.

But there's no sleep, no time. Trent keeps me awake.

He holds me long after I expect him to roll away. Even when he finally stirs, it's not to separate himself but to gather my boneless body into his arms and take me through to the bathroom.

He puts a towel on the vanity counter before setting me down, protection against the bite of cold marble, then runs a bath, pouring in bubbles and scents and lotions until the water resembles a large fluffy cloud.

Then he carefully lowers us both into the enormous tub, holding me against his chest, slowly lathering a cloth and wiping down each inch of my skin while the water laps near the lip of the bath.

"Lie back against me," he whispers when my eyelids grow too heavy to bother lifting. "You can rest here while I list everything I adore about you, starting from your exquisite fingers."

I guess because they're what he's currently soaping and massaging rather than being his absolute favourite bits.

My body is sore, not just from where I've been hit, restrained, choked, and bitten, but also where he's stretched me so far, my muscles complain even after they've snapped back into place.

He was rougher the second time. Harder, faster. I couldn't keep up and then I didn't want to. All I wanted was to have him use me like another expensive toy his dad financed. For me not to have to contribute. To opt out, only coming back to myself when the pain receded, and the pleasure mounted; or maybe they rose together in perfect tandem, creating a better harmony than anything anyone's played on my body before.

"Did I tell you today how beautiful you are?" he murmurs, the low voice soothing me as well as any mother's lullaby. "You're so brave and so strong."

The sounds mean nothing. I might be beautiful through a kink of genetics but I'm not brave and I'm nowhere near to being strong.

Nonsense. Sweet nonsense.

It makes my heart soar, restores the balance from the words he growled in the heat of our coupling. The care, the tenderness, the ability to read what I need before I know myself... if this is what falling in love is like, I don't want to stop. I don't want *him* to stop.

I want us to keep falling forever.

"What sort of designer do you want to be?" he asks when he's reached the end of his adoration list and the hot water needs a refresher we've been in so long. Trent's arms are soft around me, ready to lift me if my chin ever falls below the level of the water. It's been an age since I last felt so treasured, so protected.

"I'm interested in clothing design but that's such a long shot I'll probably lean harder into interiors. There's a woman working at a studio in town who's keen to have me as an intern during the summer break. That might lead into a job."

"And what's that? Choosing wallpaper that matches the carpet?"

I reach my arm up to rest my hand on the back of his neck, curling my fingers into his hair and stroking, sensing the shiver that runs through his body at the touch. "Along those lines. There's a girl in her last year who's selecting artworks for corporate offices. That must be fun."

He snorts with laughter, shaking his head. "Have you been in a corporate office lately? My dad has bland junk on every wall, so it doesn't offend anyone who visits. I'm pretty sure that's the opposite to what art should do."

"There might be a few non-beige offices among all those clients."

"Why don't you think the clothing stuff would work? Aren't there new designers popping up all the time?"

"And failing all the time. New Zealand is too small a market to support many at the level you need to be to generate a good income. I could move overseas but then..." I let my sentence trail into a shrug.

"Then you wouldn't be in control," he whispers, setting alight more than the sensitive nerves near my ear. The thrill of being seen pulses through me. "And we both know how much you like to be in control... until you don't."

Some of the fog clears from my mind. The sense of connection grows stronger, surrounding me like a fluffy blanket. Underneath is the same old fear—what you're given can be taken away —but I push it aside.

"You know," Trent continues in a musing tone. "If you need a financial backer to kick start your business, you now officially have one."

"It might be a bit early to think about that."

His arms come around me stronger, his legs wrap around mine, crushing me in an abundance of Trent. I hear the hitch in his breath, wait for him to reply, but the intensity of his embrace is the only answer.

This time, when the water cools enough to be intolerable, we get out of the bath, Trent towelling me dry before turning attention to himself.

"Do you have a t-shirt or something I could wear to bed?"

He glances over, his gaze lingering for a moment longer on my naked form, then his attention returns to where he's tossing the towel into the hamper. "I'd prefer you wear nothing." He walks over and pulls me against him, his cock stiffening as it touches me, then he flexes and makes me jump, laughing.

"I can't go around naked. What if there's a fire?"

"Then I'll hide you behind me and glare at any firefighter who dares to look."

"Or..."

"Okay. As a special treat for your first night sleeping in my bed, you can wear a t-shirt."

He cups my arse in his hands, pulling me harder against him and I duck my head, so he doesn't see me flinching. His hand twirls in my hair, tugging it back so I have to look up at him.

"Did I hurt you?"

"Not really. Nothing that won't quickly heal."

His shirt hangs most of the way to my knees and if I lean forward, even with the crew neck, he gets an eyeful. In bed, I roll onto my side, and he grabs my waist to tug me closer, encircling me with his far larger frame.

It's been a minute since I tried to fall asleep next to somebody. Never since I tried to do it inside someone's arms.

Despite thinking it will take forever, I've barely had time to adjust to his body heat before I'm out like a light.

CHAPTER TWENTY-THREE

TRENT

THE NEXT DAY, MY PULSE RACES AS I WAIT FOR ROSA outside her lecture. Caylon helpfully collected her class schedule from the university server, synching it to my phone a few weeks ago.

Something I'm glad to have now his attention is focused on combing Andy's phone for additional evidence. If I didn't know where she was every moment, I think the stress would lead my head to explode.

"Hey," I call out the moment I see her walking from the lecture hall, juggling her handbag and a textbook while she fits her computer back into her bag. I jump forward, grabbing the laptop when she startles enough to lose her grip, helping store everything away. "Sorry. Didn't mean to frighten you."

She tilts her head back for a kiss, beaming. "This is not me frightened. This is me being happy to see you. Although, you know the bus stop is right there"—she points to the interchange running alongside the campus—"so it's just as easy for me to come to you."

"Even easier now," I say, dropping the car keys into her hand. "Brought you a present."

"In the car?" She presses the button on the fob, scanning the parking lot for the corresponding vehicle. "You might have to give me a better clue."

"It's in the glove box."

She bounces on the balls of her feet, then takes off for the bright red mini. "This is such a beautiful vehicle. Can I drive home?"

"You can do what you like," I say, squeezing myself into the passenger seat and teasing her as she leans across to rummage for her present. "Sit back and I'll hand it to you if you like."

She sits, eyes shimmering in the low afternoon light. I hand her a velvet box, a pulse ticking in the side of my neck because this gift isn't quite as it seems.

Rosa opens the latch slowly, then her mouth drops open. "Is this real?" She pulls out the tennis bracelet dripping with an excess of diamonds. "Oh, no. This is too much."

I stifle a laugh as she drapes it across her wrist, twisting it to better catch the light. Not exactly in tandem with her protest.

"Let me," I offer, leaning across to fasten the catch, pleased when it locks into place with the bracelet fitting her snugly but not so small it'll cut off her blood supply. "And it's nowhere near enough. That's why I also got you this."

The next present isn't as immediately exciting to look at. She takes out the thick papers from the envelope and spreads them out on her lap, giving me a quizzical glance. "Do you want to give me a shortcut or are you happy to sit there while I read through them?"

"They're ownership papers. I thought this car suited you more than it suits me."

She goes still, her gaze sharpening with caution. "You bought me a car?"

"Not bought. We already had the car. I transferred it into your name since nobody else uses it."

Not true but given her hesitation, I'm comfortable with the small lie. If she's this reluctant to accept when she thinks it's just surplus to requirements, I imagine she'd be horrified to find out that I spent a few hours this morning phoning around dealerships to find the perfect one.

"I can't accept—"

"You can. Honestly, it's really easy." I lean over to tickle her until she squirms in the seat. "All you do is nothing, and the car is yours."

Her attention returns to the bracelet, her fingers brushing across the surface of the gemstones, tipping the one way and another, each movement making them sparkle.

"I'm not buying you," I say, trying to waylay the panic seeding in her eyes. "You're already mine, remember? This is just... I know I'm not the easiest—"

Rosa launches herself at me, arms around my neck, crawling into my lap and planting kisses across my neck, my chest, my face. Anywhere she can find.

"Thank you," she says, panting as she sits back a little, hands resting on my chest where my shirt somehow unbuttoned itself without me noticing. "These are..." She flings her hands into the air. "I don't know. Wonderful. Probably words that are a lot better than that, but I can't think of them just yet."

She hugs me again, my face crushed against her chest until the underwire in her bra is marking my chin.

"And fuck being the easiest. I much prefer the most complicated, red flag waving, difficult, demanding side you have to offer. You don't want me getting bored, do you? Because that's all easy ever gets you."

She gradually untangles herself, clambering back into the driver's seat and pulling across her belt. She checks the controls, touching all the shiny knobs and buttons, caressing the leather padding of the steering wheel, waving at someone she knows when they do a double take and laughing.

On her face is a smile of pure joy that I would gift a dozen cars to see. It sparks the same level of joy in my heart.

"I thought you were going to turn it down," I admit, shy in the face of her enthusiasm.

"Yeah, good one. Could you imagine Finley's face if I told her I turned down a *car?* That girl nearly tore me a new one for not taking you up on your first offer to move in. She'd kill me."

Her expression is close to adoration as she glances across at me. "And no doing your shirt up," she chides, smacking my hand away. "God knows you spent enough time getting your body to look that fabulous. The least you can do is flaunt it every moment we're together."

The unexpected compliment takes me so much by surprise that I burst out laughing.

"Better strap yourself in, buddy." Her smile is beatific. "Let's take her for a proper ride."

She drives us all around the city, then the low-speed restrictions get on her nerves, and she drives away from the centre, into the hills, winding along the two-lane blacktop high above the city, the only pedestrians ready to cast their reprimanding glances our way belonging to the grazing sheep.

We're passing over a cattle grid that seems determined to shake my teeth out of my jaw when she finally slows, pulling into the next rest area and parking with the nose of the car just metres from the edge.

I think she's going to get out to look at the view, but the only thing Rosa has eyes for is me. She unbuckles herself from her seatbelt and clambers over to crawl into my lap.

My arms circle her waist while I stare into her eyes. The joyful smile is worth the cost of a thousand cars, her lingering gaze setting my pulse racing faster than the ride to get here.

"Thank you very much for my presents," she says, plunging her hands into the still-unbuttoned shirt, warming them against my back. "I'm very grateful."

Her lips press against mine, tongue reaching out to tease mine, then retreating.

"You don't have to—"

She clamps her mouth over mine again to stifle the words. When she draws back, she takes my chin in her fingers, holding me steady. "Please don't say the things I think you're about to say. I like you. I like you a *lot* and that's separate from you showering me with presents. The least you can do, is allow me to express my appreciation physically without having you think everything I do is transactional."

A blush crawls up from my neckline, a tiny dusting of shame to rouge my cheeks. "I really didn't mean that. I'm just worried that you'll think you need to do something, and you don't." I rest my head as far back as I can, enjoying the changing colour in her eyes as they catch the last dying rays of sun.

She leans into me, her lower body grinding gently against mine as she moves her hand from my chin, rubbing her thumb over my lower lip instead.

"Okay. Then we understand each other. You can buy me anything you want, and I can fuck you any way I want and neither of those things need to be connected at all, except by our mutual appreciation of each other's assets."

The words capture my attention. "Assets, eh?" I lower my hands from her waist, caressing the sculpted mounds of her arse. "I wouldn't mind exploring your assets."

"Good," she says, leaning forward so her hair forms a curtain around our faces, her breath tickling against my ear. "Because I want you to. I also have a little surprise of my own, but I need you to pause your judgement."

"You'll get no judgement from me," I assure her, then wonder if I've said the wrong thing as she bends away.

But it's just to grab something from her bag.

"Now, I know you thought this type of bond wasn't fitting to your masculinity or some such thing, but this is my turn to direct operations, so what I say, goes." With a flourish, she produces a set of fluffy cuffs much like the ones I'd seen in her bedside cabinet.

For a moment, my mind goes somewhere it shouldn't and I jerk it back. Not a task that takes a lot of willpower, considering the temptations on offer.

"Now, just relax," she says, threading the cuffs through the gap in my headrest, securing one wrist in front and one behind.

To reach the second, she pitches her weight forward and her breasts hang tantalisingly close to my mouth. I stretch my tongue out, like I can lick her closer. When she finishes securing the cuff, she stays in place, tugging down the edge of her bra so her nipple slides into my waiting mouth.

"Oh, you're already being such a good boy," she whispers, her voice becoming husky so quickly I can hear her vocal cords thickening with lust.

The praise does something complicated and uniquely pleasurable inside my head. All I want to do is chase that feeling, earn myself another reward. My mouth sucks at her, rubbing my tongue roughly against her to tease at her hardening peak, then letting it rest, warming inside my mouth, before I begin the hugely satisfying process over again.

I hear a buzz and at first think it's coming from inside my head, a rampant train of sexual desire firing my nerve endings until they're excited enough to form an auditory hallucination. But when I feel my body tip, I understand it's the noise of the seat adjustment lever. Soon, I'm three-quarters reclined, my arms still stretching over my head.

"This shirt needs to go," Rosa says in a lilting voice, tugging at the offending fabric and making a growling sound when my restraints stop her from tugging the whole thing loose.

She settles for bunching it up near my bound hands, then strokes my naked torso, alternating between the smooth caresses of her palms and the maddening tease of her fingernails, lightly scratching against my skin.

Her head lowers, taking my right nipple into her mouth, first working at it with her tongue, then holding it between her teeth, the threat of danger making another surge of blood rush straight to my cock.

I tip my hips up towards her, but she closes her teeth a little harder and I retreat, falling into instant obedience. I shut my eyes, letting my body relax into the seat, letting her do what she likes with me, happy to see where it leads.

Her hands curve over my body, initiating a flush of self-consciousness still overhanging from my tubby phase. It's soon lost in the appreciative noises she makes as she discovers each new delight.

She moves lower, at first bending her body in a way I can't even imagine mine doing, then slipping down into the footwell as her hands fumble at my belt.

Once unfastened, she pulls the thick leather strap out of the loops, bending it double and snapping it near my waist.

I flinch back, laughing, then frowning with concern as she smacks it against her palm. "What?" she asks, a devilish smile playing across her lips. "Good boys don't need to worry about getting the belt."

She sits back on her heels, arching her eyebrows. "Unless you'd like that, Mr Weybourne. Would you like me to give you a nice, stinging slap?"

The belt hits lightly against the side of my knee on the last word, making me jump, making me giddy. While she eagerly eats up my expressions, I try to think of butterflies and rainbows and kittens. Anything to ward back the rampant need that's bringing me close to the edge.

"Or would you rather I give you a present?" she teases, her hand creeping towards my waistband again, this time unbuttoning my jeans and slowly, slowly, slowly rolling the zipper down then dragging at my briefs until my cock springs free.

"Such a big boy," she murmurs and the sound echoes in a shiver down my spine. "You make such a good toy."

Rosa mounts me again, pulling aside the scrap of fabric masquerading as underwear, and rubbing herself against me, already wet, the satin kiss a temptation that has me tensing my arms, clinging to the headrest as I try not to buck against her, not wanting another reprimand, wanting only to be whatever she needs me to be.

Her lips seek mine again, mouth gasping as she flexes her hips and grinds hard against me, then eases the pressure, finding a rhythm that makes me shudder and squirm against the moulded seat.

Then she reaches into her bag again, this time bringing out a condom, unrolling it along my length with her warm hands, pausing to squeeze and caress and pump as she makes sure it's covering me from head to base.

She guides me to her entrance, hovering above me, the tease nearly enough to make me black out from need, finally sliding down onto me, encasing me inside her delicious, dripping cunt.

Her movements are sensuous, beguiling, riding me with long, tender motions, taking me deeper each time she slides along my length, so deep that I feel that same old pinch of worry —I'm hurting her, I'm causing pain, I'm too big, too clumsy, too brutal—then a cry catches in her throat, a call of such pure pleasure that pride and gratitude and happiness burst inside my chest, warming me until it singes my flesh.

"You feel so good," she moans, wrapping her hand around my neck and pulling me forward, dragging so hard that the seat rises back into an upright position, all so she can feast on my mouth again. "Is it okay for you?"

A laugh escapes my mouth, transforming halfway through into a groan. "No, it's a thousand times better than okay," I murmur, chuckling again as she bites onto my shoulder, the quick flash of pain a counterpoint to the pleasure that intensifies both.

"You want to come inside my cunt or my mouth?"

"I want to come wherever you want me to come," I tell her, not even having to act the role. It's the truth. Like all my interactions with her now seem to be the truth. Everything so real it hurts. Everything beyond my expectations, beyond anything I deserve.

She quickens her pace, using me like a mounted dildo, taking what she wants, using her fingers when my cock doesn't provide the right friction in the right place and God how I wish my hands were free to take that task from her plate.

Then her breathing hitches, changes, an exhalation that elongates into a sigh. Her muscles clench me harder, shuddering in convulsions as she comes.

I expect her to lift off me, to take that beautiful pussy away, but she stays, rocking slightly, wringing out every drop of her finish until she collapses against my chest in a spent heap.

The loss of movement sucks me back from the edge. I reconcile myself to missing out, cue a self-scolding lesson on how next time I need to read her signs better, reach that same climax with her.

Her hand reaches down behind her, teasing my balls, then cupping them. My interest perks right up and she snuffles out a soft laugh as I tense inside her, creating my own pulse, and then I don't have to because she's moving again, this time at a luxurious pace.

Damp hair clings to the sides of her face, framing her, making her look so gorgeous, so sexy, so tantalising that I'm right back where I was, cresting my wave while she bends to take my lip between her teeth, biting enough to make it bruise, make it swell.

Biting until the blood rushes to the surface, pushing, shoving, jostling for position, waiting for the teeniest, tiniest break.

Then she's sucking, soothing away the pulsing ache.

"I want you to come in my mouth," she whispers, trailing languorous fingers across my torso.

Slowly, she eases herself off me and sinks low, sliding back onto her knees in the footwell, sucking one ball into her mouth, creating a sensation I didn't even know was possible. One that heightens when she moves to its neighbour, carefully disengaging before she runs her tongue along my shaft.

She rolls off the condom, staring into my eyes as she does so. The level of trust from her swells my heart just as much as it stirs my cock.

Then her mouth closes over my tip, sliding me deeper, deeper, until I must be ramming into her throat, choking her airways, just the thought sending me into the beginning of my orgasm, as she pumps her head, increasing the speed as she feels me coming, feels the pulse of my release jolt along my length.

She sits back, licking her lips and pumping me to produce another spurt of cum that she sucks off me, every drop, eyeing my cock like it's something beautiful that she's privileged to touch.

I close my eyes, body relaxing so deeply that I think I fall asleep for the few moments she takes to climb back on top of my body, straddling me, head resting against my chest as she releases my hands from their restraints and I can finally touch her, stroke her, caress her. Wrap my arms around her and hold her close.

"You know anyone could come up here," I tell her, chuckling softly at the thought of someone pulling into the rest stop to look at the view and finding us instead.

My cock also stirs, something she notes, suggesting, "If you're into a spot of dogging, I'm sure we can research an appropriate parking spot online."

"Fuck that. I don't want anyone staring at you while we're having sex. Except me," I add a second later, making her giggle.

"This is a far better afternoon than the one I had planned," she says, sliding off me and into the driver's seat, then reaching back to clasp my hand. "Now, you want to pick another spot where we can tempt fate with a public viewing or go back home where you can teach me all the delights of your shower. There must be some reason the designer put so many moveable pieces in there."

"Home," I immediately vote. "I need to get clean again before I get dirty."

CHAPTER TWENTY-FOUR

ROSA

On Tuesday morning, I'm in the library, only paying half my attention towards the study group discussion. I got lost somewhere in the fair distribution of duties discussion and am just waiting now to find out what I'm expected to do.

I would take charge to speed things along, but three of the other four students are already jostling for that role—part of why we're not getting anywhere with the assignment.

When my phone beeps I don't even check the screen before excusing myself. Once outside, I exhale a frustrated breath and drag the device from my pocket. A worried text lights up the screen and my stomach pinches.

A message from Harry. "*I'm at my appointment but nobody knows where you are.*"

I stare at the message until the text is burned on my retinas, then pocket my phone and head for my car, beeping it open before I'm halfway across the parking lot.

If this is Trent's idea of cancelling my work contracts and

arranging for someone to take on my client load, he's missed the mark. I utter a few choice curse words at him, then at myself for not double checking.

A lot of my list won't be bothered; they didn't care when I slotted in from the last girl and they won't care about another change.

Harry's different. He's already lonely. Even if I wanted to ease away from him, worried about the possibility he'd become too attached, to leave him hanging in the wind like this is brutal.

I feel cruel, thoughtless. I didn't want to interfere, go against Trent's wishes, but I should've got hold of Ceecee to let her know what was happening since we overlap appointments.

Now, I'll have to go there to explain to him and not have an alternative for him to move ahead with.

When I'm stopped at the next set of lights, I pick up my phone to send a strongly worded message to Trent, then stop myself.

Not only is the next driver over staring at me like they're itching to turn me in for texting while driving, but I also don't want to send a text in anger, then have to apologise later when my head clears.

Instead, I do the decent thing and tuck my phone into my pocket, sticking my tongue out at the next driver like I'm eight rather than eighteen, and gunning the engine the moment the light changes, pulling ahead of them as we merge lanes, the slight advantage cheering me far more than it should.

I park the car two houses down, securing the wheel lock and hoping the alarm is loud enough to hear from inside because I'd hate to lose the best present anyone's ever given me. Especially since it's only been a day.

Harry's car is parked in the driveway, and I take a deep breath, putting my hand on my abdomen to steady it.

This won't be comfortable but better the news comes from me.

I open the door, shaking despite my best efforts. Images crowd my brain until it feels full to bursting, crowding each other, trying to win pride of place, a competition to see which one can scare me most.

Andy's face when it changes. The spatter of blood that was all I saw of the end of him. The confusion and shock when he zip-tied me to the bedpost. The dawning realisation that I might not make it out alive.

Enough.

I open my eyes, forcing myself to focus on the room, my movement through it, everything that's happening right here and now, not the horrors stuffed in my memory.

The kitchen is empty, and I touch the side of the kettle out of habit. Still hot and there are mugs missing from their hooks. I tiptoe over to the connecting door through to the dining room and inhale the deepest breath I can; like I'm diving and need enough to plunge down to the ocean floor.

When the door swings open, I expect to see at least one, more probably two people around the table. To find it empty jolts me and I walk straight to the table, then peer at the notice-board to see who's on.

Ceecee and me. The latter out of date.

I move into the lounge, still not finding anyone. Then I pause outside Ceecee's bedroom door.

If she's in there with a client—which she should be—then she'll happily gut me like a fish for interrupting.

I back away, retreating to the dining room and checking my message. Harry's car is outside, so he hasn't left. Could he be hiding inside, out of view, waiting?

I mean, he could. He could do a lot of things.

Why would he, is the crucial question? Why would he not

have approached me outside the house if that's where he was waiting? Why isn't he at the dining table with a mug of coffee, milk, no sugar, rather than nowhere to be seen?

Ceecee should be in her room with her own client. Even if he'd cancelled again like he did weeks ago, and she offered Harry the spot, he's not the type to make that change without thinking it through.

None of it makes sense.

My eye snags on the noticeboard again and I move to read it more thoroughly. My name is still on there, but so is a new girl. Liz.

If Trent did what he said he was going to, and came to tell everyone I'd retired, then she could be my replacement. Considering Ceecee had already mentioned she knew a working girl who was ready to take some hours, I'm sure someone slotted in straight away.

But if she was here, why did Harry text me? He would have complained about the new girl rather than making it sound like I left him high and dry.

I call Trent, worried now and not in the mood to leave that to fester. It goes straight to voicemail, and I leave a message. "Can you call me? I'm at the Sydenham house and there's something wrong."

When I disconnect the call, I try Harry's mobile, praying I'll hear the ring in Ceecee's room and the worst thing that happens today is I'll have put him off his stroke.

It goes straight to voicemail, too. No sound of ringing or buzzing anywhere within these walls.

Don't be such a coward.

I think of Trent's misplaced praise. That I'm brave. That I'm strong.

If he saw me cowering in the dining room, afraid to even knock, he might form a different opinion. I'm upsetting myself with a thousand different scenarios, each one worse than the other, instead of just going down the hallway to tap my knuckles on her door.

The self-scolding breaks through my paralysis. I storm along the corridor and hammer at the door, determined that if I'm ruining their tryst, I'm going to ruin it as badly as possible.

There's no answer. No grunt of annoyance or sharp call back, "What?"

I hesitate, then wrench open the door, pushing so hard that I stumble inside a few steps.

Nothing. No one. Not a stitch out of place.

See?

Before the self-congratulations start, I abort them. I'm no further ahead. With my adrenaline propelling me forward, I walk the few short steps to my room and fling that door open, far more confident.

My stomach plunges to my feet.

Crimson drips off the ceiling. Long arterial streaks are sprayed across the walls, blearing the windows, staining the bedclothes.

My throat seizes before I can scream, cut off by the horror of what's in front of me.

I take a step but my feet tangle, spilling me forward to land heavily on one knee.

A wail slips out of my mouth, scaring me further. I gulp it back, reaching for the chair in front of me, reaching for Ceecee's limp, lifeless hand.

My brain shutters itself from the horror; only letting in one snapshot at a time. The slash across her neck, the river of blood soaked into her transparent blouse. The red fingertips, which is weird because I could have sworn she'd just gelled them blue.

Then I see properly. They're red and raw because some

monster, some animal, some callous fuck pulled out her fingernails.

I cry, large silent tears that drip uselessly down my face. When I shift position, my knee shrieks in pain. I brush a hand over it and knock a small hard object free. It rolls back onto the cheap floor tiles, and I pick it up, lifting it to eye level and blinking my eyes to clear them.

It's a tooth.

My brain is dull, too blunt to think. I lever myself to my feet and stumble past Ceecee, stumble across to the next horror.

Another girl. This one I don't recognise.

Liz. The new name on the board.

On the other side of the bed is Harry. One eye is gouged out. His fingertips are in an even worse state than Ceecee's. His right thumb is missing, and the room grows darker by the second as I understand what that means.

The person who did this used it to unlock his phone.

The person responsible for this atrocity sent the text.

This is my fault. Whoever sent Andy must know now that he's dead, that we killed him.

My uncle. It's the only thing that makes any sense.

He's killed my colleagues, my clients, and now he's going to kill me.

Far too late, I whirl and head for the door. My feet skid in the blood, slip across the tiles. One foot slips and I fall to the left. My arm shoots out, grabs the bed, stopping my fall.

When I lift my hand away, it's stained red.

I move again but the door retreats two steps for each one I take forward. A sob tears out of my throat.

The fear is more immediate, more visceral, than any I've felt before. Whoever tortured these people was *just here*.

The kettle wasn't warm, it was hot.

When I check my phone, I see the message from Harry is still only fifteen minutes old.

My spine tingles, like eyes are crawling over me. The same as when I'm walking along the street and someone catches my eye, gives me a second glance for no reason, sending me on a spiral thinking they've seen me, seen my videos, recognised me from the old films even if I look nothing like I did as a child, even though the chances a random person on the street has seen them are minimal to nil.

I try to swallow and choke instead. Like hands are wrapped around my neck, squeezing.

My hand creeps up, having to check, to make sure.

Nothing there but my bruises and a bite mark, a sign of ownership. Except my owner didn't answer his damn phone and now I'm scared, I'm terrified, I'm riveted to the spot when all I want to do, what I *need* to do, is run.

I try Trent again, stabbing and missing the connect call button three times before I get it right. I hold it in front of me, scared to put it to my ear in case my shaking hands drop it, or I disconnect the call.

Voicemail.

For fucks sake. "Trent, pick up. If you're there, pick up. They're dead." A sob cuts my voice for a second, then frees it. "They're all dead."

I should call the police. My thumb hits the key three times, then I stop. I exit to the home screen.

There was another murder in the same room on Saturday. If the police come, they might find evidence from that and pin the crime on the wrong person. Or persons.

They might lock me and Trent up and never find the man who did this.

Caylon. I flick through to my address book and check it. He answers on the first ring, "It's Rosa. Can you come to the same house as Saturday? There's—" My throat closes, nausea rising. Spit floods my mouth, gagging me. "People are dead and I'm scared."

"Rosa? I'm coming. Is there somewhere safe you can wait? A cupboard? A wardrobe?"

"There's... I..." I spin on my heel, glancing back at the corridor with the open doors. There are two more branching off in the other direction, but I don't think I can. Don't think I can summon the courage to open them, knowing something just as bad as I've already seen could be on the other side.

"My car's outside."

"Good. Lock the doors. Sit low down so no one can see you through the windows. I'll be there as soon as I can."

After choking out a thank you, I ring off, making myself move while the impetus is still there. Through the lounge, through the dining room. My hand clasps the kitchen doorknob, and it twists under my hand.

I snatch my hand back, retreating. I turn to run but too slowly, the door opens, someone steps through, grabs me around the waist.

I open my mouth to scream, and a hand closes over it.

CHAPTER TWENTY-FIVE

TRENT

"Sorry," I mutter, taking my hand away as Rosa trembles in my arms. "Please don't scream. Sorry."

I release her, backing away as she convulses, crying, coughing, catching her breath. When she opens her mouth again, I put a finger to my lips. "Where are the bodies?"

"In my room." She pauses, gasping in another lungful of air. "Three. He tortured them. He c-cut off H-Harry's thumb to access his phone and trick me into coming here."

"But he's not here? He hasn't hurt you?" I step forward, running my hands over her, soothing the terror I felt on the way here, the fear I'd walk in and find something worse than the heights of her distress.

She shakes her head and shrugs. "I don't know."

Adrenaline shakes my body, tightening my muscles, wanting to punch, wanting to fight. I grip my anger in both hands, wrestling it to the ground, pinning it until it's needed.

The priority is to get her out of there. Get her to safety.

"Caylon's coming," she adds. "When I couldn't get hold of you, I called him. He's on his way here right now."

"Good. We're going outside to wait for him. He can take you home and wait there with you while I stay."

She stares at me, appalled. "I'm not leaving you here alone."

I grab her, holding her close, a fierce wave of love coursing over me. "Whoever did this isn't after me."

"He wasn't after Ceecee or Harry either and that didn't stop him." She stops, heaving in a breath, then another. She's hyperventilating.

"I won't let anyone hurt you. We'll find him. We'll stop him. I promise."

"Why did he want me here?"

I don't know. I don't know and it eats away at me.

If he were going to attack, he would have done it by now. Rosa was on her own here for long enough to hurt her, to kill her, to abduct her. The man must want something else, something I can't guess at, and that scares me more than anything.

The television in the lounge suddenly bursts into life. I whip around, ready to fight a dozen attackers but there's nobody there. The picture flickers with a grainy image, an old 4:3 aspect picture that barely fills half the widescreen.

Rosa stares for a split second, then lunges for the remote on the sofa, clicking it over and over, jamming her thumb on the off button, then throwing it at the tv.

It takes longer for me. I stare at the images, watching a young girl and a middle-aged man sitting on the edge of a bed. The hand-held camera means the footage wobbles, dipping enough to make me instantly queasy.

Then the girl turns to face the camera full on and I dive behind the television, yanking the plug from the wall, shaking.

"Where's it coming from?" Rosa asks in a wavering voice. "There's nothing hooked up to it."

I pick up the remote and slide the battery compartment open. Empty.

A rush of anger sweeps through me. Somebody's fucking with her just because they can. Because it amuses them to wreck the life she made for herself, after everything she went through. To claw her back down into the muck.

"We're going," I tell her, deciding that whatever I can do for her I can't do it from here. Not with some unknown player pulling her strings.

"No. Turn it back on."

Her face is scrunched in concentration and when I don't move quick enough for her liking, she dives past me, shoving the plug back in the wall socket.

The television bursts back into life and I have to look away. Sick knowing that this was in her past when I asked her to record a video for me. Like rubbing her face in the worst thing she'd ever been through.

"There," she shouts, jumping forward to point at the screen.

I force myself to look, focusing on where her finger directs me.

The camera angle is low, the device must be resting on a chair. A man in his late teens or early twenties walks in and out of the shot, presumably the cameraman. He adjusts the straps on Rosa's sundress, gets the man—her 'uncle'—to move an inch to the side.

He disappears and a moment later, the footage wavers all over as he picks up the camera, hosting it to shoulder-height.

"What am I meant to be looking at?" I ask, looking away from the gigantic screen as she turns to face me.

"I think it's Andy." She drops to her knees, searching behind the television for something plugged in the back. "He must be streaming it somehow," she mutters, drawing back and staring at the images with renewed frustration.

The picture stops, looping back to start from the beginning again.

"What do you mean?" I ask, confusion warring with panic. "Andy's dead."

"Him," she shouts, pointing to the cameraman. "It's why he looked vaguely familiar. It's..." She turns to me, eyes wide, seeking confirmation, seeking reassurance.

"We need to get out of here." I grab her arm and tug when she doesn't immediately respond. "We're right where he wants us."

"But if it's him—"

"Caylon can look into it. We need to go."

I pick her up when she tries to protest, tearing through the house and out the door, sprinting along the side path until we're out on the street. In full view of anybody who cares to look. More exposed and safer at the same time.

Caylon pulls to the curb while I'm seating her in my car, and I wave him over. "There's a video playing inside. Rosa thinks Andy is on it."

"The dead guy?"

The door opens as Rosa tries to scramble out and I give her a warning look before slamming it shut again. "I'm taking her home. Once she's safe, I'll come back here or anywhere you want to meet me. If you can track Andy's connections, we might find the guy we're looking for."

He gives me a dull stare that I feel to my soul. "Like I haven't been doing that already?"

"There's three bodies in there," I add like they're an afterthought.

Rosa rolls down the window, holding out her phone. "This is the number he called me from," she explains. "Can you trace that back somehow? It belongs to..." She struggles to swallow before trying again. "It's Harry's phone but if you can trace—"

Caylon takes a shot of the number. "I'll see what I can do." He turns to look at the house. "Gonna be straight with you, man. I'm not keen on going in there alone."

"Don't," Rosa says before I can answer. "He's still around here, I know it. The kettle was hot, he's rigged something with the tv, he's using Harry's *thumb* to..."

But she can't finish the thought.

"It's bad," I summarise. "Get some of Stefan's heavies over here or follow me home and—"

"He's on his way here already." Caylon glances over his shoulder at the nondescript house. Nothing visible from the street to suggest the carnage inside. "Believe me, I'm happy to wait outside. I'm too pretty to be a hero."

Rosa stares at him, open-mouthed for a second, then bursts into semi-hysterical laughter.

Caylon rolls his eyes at me. "Get going. I don't need your girlfriend making fun of me. The only reason I'm here is the alternative was watching repeats of terrible movies with my mum."

Right now, I'd swap in a heartbeat.

On the drive home, all the other drivers annoy me. I lay on the horn more than I ever have in my life before, breathing a sigh of relief when I finally pull up to the gate and type in the code to enter.

"Stay with me," Rosa begs when I escort her to the door and inside. "Please let your friends deal with whatever it is. I don't want you putting yourself in danger."

"I'm already in danger." The words were meant as a reassurance, but they miss the mark.

"You can stay here. You should stay here. This whole thing is like a horror movie and the first rule is, never split up."

"The first rule is never have sex because you'll be the first victim."

"Damn," she mutters, still clinging to my arm. "Guess we're both goners, then. We should go upstairs for another quickie since we've already signed our death warrant."

I pull her into my arms, hugging her like it's an Olympic Sport. "We'll find him. I promise. We'll find him and put him so far in the ground even the devil won't know where he's gone."

"Can't we just call the police?"

"And tell them we're also killers, but their side's worse?"

"Something like that."

"Stefan employs a lot of heavies for protection. I'll see if he can rustle up half a dozen to come here as an added layer of protection."

"Is that their official job title?"

A laugh escapes against her hair before I press a half dozen kisses on the top of her head. "My job title's bouncer if that sounds better."

I take her chin and tip it back, claiming her lips with a soft kiss that soon grows deeper. I'm like an old knight riding off to battle, staking a claim so he has someone to fight for, someone to return to.

When I release her lips, I keep my forehead resting against hers for a few seconds longer. "Don't open the door to anyone unless they identify themselves. It's okay to turn people away. If they're working for our side, they'll still protect you, even if they're locked outside the gates."

"Okay."

The way she falls into line deepens my unease. I'd prefer her obstinance, her opposition, because that would mean she still thinks she can win the fight.

Her voice sounds incredibly young as she whispers, "No matter what happens, come back to me, okay?"

She pulls back, staring into my face, reading my tiniest

change in expression. So, I haul a reassuring grin out of some-where. "I promise. None of us are going to take any chances."

And then I have to tear myself away from her and go, because to stay another minute would mean I never go at all, and the danger to her is too great to leave it in someone else's hands.

I leave and when I turn to close the door, I take a snapshot of her for the road ahead. Even her worried expression, the way she nibbles at her thumbnail, the pinched concern etched across her features, aren't enough to dim her beauty.

WHEN I ARRIVE BACK at the house, Stefan stands at the front door, Caylon a mini-me version beside him. His glance of concern is enough to stop me in my tracks. My boss is many things, but I've never seen him anything but calm, composed, capable of doing anything that needs to be done.

Now there are lines scored around his mouth, dragging down the corners of his eyes.

"You saw?"

He nods and Caylon can't meet my eyes. My stomach twinges at putting him through this, especially after Robbie. It's obvious to me he's already on the cusp of falling apart and I don't want to be the straw that breaks him.

"It's okay if you want to leave," I whisper to him, hopefully out of Stefan's earshot. "You'll be better off working your magic in trying to track down the mobile number or find where the cameras were feeding their images to."

He stares at me expressionlessly for so long it's like someone accidentally pressed his pause button. Then he breaks into an enormous smile. One that actually reaches his eyes. "How about you don't tell me what I'm better off doing and I won't tell you *who* you're better off doing?"

I strain for a second, then shake my head. "What?"

"Couldn't hook up with a nice easy party girl. Oh, no. Had to go for the call girl with a heart of gold, like that cliché hasn't already been done to death." I'm about to remonstrate when he moves away. "The television was set on a timer. The video"—he holds a finger up when I go to speak—"which, before you ask, no I didn't watch beyond grabbing screenshots of their faces, it was stored in the memory."

Stefan wanders closer, joining in the summary. "The bodies have been here for three maybe four hours. Far longer than they were made to look. The rest of it was staged, the boiling jug, the missing cups, the text message to Rosa. Someone went to a lot of trouble to get information from these people—"

"No." I interrupt him before thinking, earning the glare that follows. "That's staged, too. Apart from the thumb—that, he needed—these people didn't know shit about Rosa. She'd never even met the younger girl."

He frowns, his face, already dark with facial hair, turns thunderous. "Then it's all staged. Who the fuck is this guy? What does he want?"

Caylon taps on his phone, the sound annoying as hell. I try to concentrate on Stefan but can't help but turn his way.

"Don't look at me like that," he says without glancing up. "I'm working on something. This is Andy, yeah?"

I glance at the screen and nod. "You saw him already."

"He looked different after you were finished with him. And this is the uncle from the video."

He extends the phone again and I nod, then frown. "I only saw him on the screen for a second."

"But it is. And this is a news article from his sentencing, after the automatic name suppression was lifted."

I take the phone, expanding out the details. "And what am I looking for here?"

"His name." Caylon points to it. "Andy and him. Their surnames are the same."

"Shit."

My expletive raises a smile. "Both of them are, by the looks of it, even though I'm not usually so judgmental."

My mind struggles with the ramifications. "Have you told Rosa?" He gives me an incredulous look. "Right." There hasn't been time. "Of course, not."

I pull out my phone, hands shaking with fury that someone this abusive, this monstrous, could still be in her life. When I call her number, it goes straight to voicemail. I try again, my hands fumbling so badly I could easily press the wrong thing, but this time I let the full message play out. It's hers but she's not answering.

Another call?

Surely, she wouldn't turn the phone off when we're in the middle of what feels like a war.

"Something wrong?" Caylon asks, reading my expression with the long ease of friendship.

"Are you any closer to finding an address for him?"

"Narrowing it down." He hooks up an eyebrow and I back off, dialling Rosa and hoping it's third time lucky.

It isn't.

A car full of Stefan's henchmen arrive and approach him for instruction. A nervous tremor wriggles up my spine, lodging at my brain stem, making me dizzy.

Then the phone rings in my hand and I eagerly check the number, my second of joy immediately stripped away.

It's Sashe.

Why the hell would my father's new bit of fluff call me?

With a sense of foreboding, I answer the call.

CHAPTER TWENTY-SIX

ROSA

THE MOMENT TRENT LEAVES, I WANT HIM TO COME BACK.
Waiting at his house is an exercise in torture. As much as I don't
want to place myself in danger, I also don't want to be pacing
back and forth, miles away from where my uncle is causing
havoc.

I don't want to lose someone I care about—no, someone I
love—as collateral damage to a madman whose sole target should
be me.

Finley is at Polytech, and I've warned her to stay there. Stay
in a protective cluster of as many people as she can until this
whole mess is resolved.

She'll do it. Out of the two of us, I might be book-smart, but
she's plugged far deeper into common sense than I've ever been,
letting my emotions rule my head.

I want my mother but she's safest where she is. The hospice
won't release details to anyone if they can't prove they're family.
My so-called uncle shouldn't be able to gain access.

It's the leeway in that 'should' that gives me vivid night-mares. A thousand scenes from a thousand slasher movies play on a loop in the back of my mind.

Real life should make things harder. It's not like he has supernatural abilities or a lack of appreciation for the laws of physics and biology my favourite films indulge in.

But harder isn't impossible. People slip up all the time. Human error is a well-known phrase for a reason.

I go into the kitchen just for something to do and find Sashe there, flipping through a magazine at the counter. She glances up in surprise, like I caught her doing something she shouldn't.

"You're home early," she says, then adds, "Sorry. I'm not used to having other people around during the day."

"Apart from all the staff?"

She wrinkles her nose, appearing playful. "My husband assures me they don't count."

"Right." I raise my eyebrows and she laughs.

"I know. I'm ticking off the minutes till I don't count either."

She smiles as she says the words, but I'm appalled. "That's not what I meant."

"No, I know." Sashes gives an indulgently long sigh. "But it's how I feel most of the time. Trent seems so used to the churn; he doesn't even bother to be polite."

I hesitate, unsure of how much of what's going on she knows. "He's got a lot of stuff going on at the moment. I'm sure it's nothing to do with you."

"Exactly," she agrees as though I made her point. "Nothing in this house seems to be to do with me at all."

The awkward conversation might be stilted but it's still a break from the turmoil going on inside my head. I grab a glass of ice and water from the dispenser on the fridge and take the stool next to her.

"You fit in here better than I do," I assure her. "And thanks for your help with my mother. You really tipped Trent's dad into helping."

"*Trent's dad*," she mocks, shaking her head. "I can't believe he hasn't even introduced himself. No"—she holds up a hand —"scratch that. I can *easily* believe it. He's called Anders, and I wasn't any help. He barely listens."

She looks so sad that I'm drawn to her. Curiosity firing on all cylinders. "That doesn't seem true from where I'm sitting. He only reacted after you appealed to him."

"Yeah. Maybe." She shakes herself, going from maudlin to cheerful in the flick of a switch. "Are you home for the rest of the day? I was thinking of going for a spa treatment. Massage, body scrub, mud bath, the works." She pauses for a moment during which I'm too gobsmacked to answer. "Or if you're home tomorrow, we could go then. Make a whole day of it."

"Tomorrow would be good." I don't want to explain too much, definitely don't want to frighten her, but keeping her within the house seems like a smart idea. "Can you show me how to work the television? I'm not used to something so fancy."

"Yes!" Her overenthusiasm makes me wonder how lonely she gets during the day. "Would you like to watch the new Jane Austen adaptation? I've heard the newest Mr Darcy puts the others to shame."

"That sounds good."

She leads the way into the entertainment room, glancing at the security screen as she does so, then frowning and moving over just as it buzzes. "Do you recognise that man?"

Dread encases my feet in treacle, every movement slowing to a crawl as I turn. The three steps to join her take an hour. Millenia pass as I squint at the tiny screen.

For a second, my mind overpaints the camera feed with my uncle. The same way he looked in the video that I would have traded my next decade in earnings to prevent Trent from seeing.

Then I blink and the image resolves to a hunched, battered man, wearing a crumpled suit.

My body relaxes with the recognition. "That's Trent's private investigator, Edwin. You can buzz him in, he's fine."

That he's here instead of Trent could mean anything but I immediately seize on the most worrying. That Trent can't be here himself because he's currently having his fingernails ripped out, his teeth pulled without anaesthetic, his fingers chopped off to find one that unlocks his phone.

By the time I've reached the front door, Trent's died in a half dozen awful ways; his friends meeting the same dreadful fate. All of them deaths that can be laid straight at my door.

The moment I yank the door open, I scrutinise Eddie's expression. Trying to work out how bad it is so I have a split second to prepare.

"Hey, Rosa. Can I come in for a second?" When I don't immediately step back, he adds, "Trent sent me to collect you."

"Collect her for what?" Sashe asks when my mouth doesn't work. "Where's Trent?"

"He's..."

Edwin's gaze turns to me, eyebrow hooked up, asking how much to divulge, and I finish, "He's involved with a job right now. Where are we going?"

"To the hospice."

My stomach drops to the floor. "What? Is my mother—"

"She's fine. It's a precaution." He tilts his head to the side. "Trent said something about your uncle having an issue with her, too."

An issue.

What a polite way to say that, working together, we put him away for over twenty years.

Not that it was just us. There were others. A cabinet full of recordings and only a few of them mine.

Girls who were just as easily talked into doing things that didn't feel good, didn't feel right. Girls who also had mothers too distracted by the constant battle to earn enough money they didn't ask what their boyfriend pimp was up to when he offered to babysit.

Questions they couldn't afford to ask.

"You have your phone on you?" At my surprised expression, he explains, "He could use it to track you. Just like he did with your computer."

I nod, handing it over. He switches it on, sees the lock screen, and turns it over, popping out the SIM card and battery before passing it back. "That should help but you'll be better off leaving it here."

"Okay." I feel naked without it, but I pop it on the sidetable and grab my jacket from the hook near the door. "Do you mind if I take my car? I don't want to be stranded anywhere."

Eddie stares at me with a frown, shaking his head. "Isn't your car still over in Sydenham?"

Fuck. Yes, it is. Parked a few doors down from the murder house.

"Yeah, sorry."

"You're going with him?"

I twist back to face Sashe, nodding. "We'll have to do Austen another time."

She pulls me into a hug. A gesture that surprises me until she whispers in my ear, "I don't think you should. Especially without your phone."

"It's okay," I reassure her. The warning doesn't really surprise me. After all, on our first meeting I'd stolen his keys, assuming he was a pervert. "I know him. He's safe."

"Knows me." Eddie rolls his eyes. "You also whipped my arse at poker."

"That was Finley," I snap back with a smile, detaching

myself from Sashe and following him outside. The wind has picked up, sending a chill straight to my bones. "Trent didn't say..." My throat clicks and I have to clear it before continuing. "He said nothing else, did he? About catching my uncle?"

The investigator shakes his head, pressing his fob so the car beeps unlocked.

It's a different make and model than the last one he was in. This one is a far superior upgrade, a roomy sedan rather than the beaten-up litterbox I last saw him driving. I stifle a smile of amusement that this is the car he drives to Trent's house but the one he drove to mine was markedly worse.

"Get in the back," he says when I try the passenger side door. "It'll be easier for you to duck down if you need to hide."

I follow his direction and he slams the door shut for me. Once I've done up my seat belt, I wait for him to finish fiddling with the multitude of buttons, bringing up a large screen of the surrounds while he reverses out of the driveway, then turning to a GPS map once we're heading forward.

"There's water back there," he says like he's a courteous Uber driver. "Snacks in the back of the seat if you're hungry."

"I'm good." My stomach is so tightly knotted, I doubt I'll be eating anytime soon.

I stare out the window, the afternoon weather turning worse with every passing moment. Specks of graupel hit against the window with increasing regularity. Even with my jacket on, I'm cold.

"Could you turn up the heat?" I ask, and Eddie stops watching the road while he searches for the right button.

Not his car, then. I file the information away, my eyes flicking towards the GPS, used to staring at screens so often that they miss the comforting glare of my phone.

We're heading along Glandovey Road, and I frown at the slowly moving map, then turn my attention out the window again. I don't have an internal compass—or, if I do, it's broken—but this doesn't seem like the right way to reach my mother's new hospice.

I lean forward. "Are you sure you typed in the right address? We should head north. Her new place is out towards Belfast."

"We're just taking a slight detour first," he says without concern. "Then we'll swing by your mother's place and make sure she's safe."

I sit back in my chair. The words sound innocent enough but there's still a growing lump in my throat. I pluck at the skin of my neck, rubbing against my windpipe, trying to shake the sensation. Part of it's just the healing bruises from Saturday. More of it is a reaction to his tone.

"What's the detour?" He doesn't answer and I shift in my seat, leaning forward to examine the contents of the pocket, before leaning back again. "Edwin? What's the detour?"

"Just to drop something off. Don't worry about it."

"But are we—"

"Sorry, I can't concentrate when I'm talking. Just relax, yeah? We'll have you to your mum's place soon enough."

Now all my senses are tingling, blaring out a multitude of silent alarms. The map shows us driving farther away from my mother with each passing second, farther away from Trent's, farther away from help.

My phone's in pieces on a sidetable. All Sashe knows is that I left with someone I trusted.

This car isn't his. Trent won't know the right licence plate to track even when he sees the front door security camera footage and identifies Edwin.

Other cameras might have caught the plate... or not. Even if they did, there's no reason to think the ones currently on the car match to the record.

My heart hammers and I grip the doorhandle. The road

outside is blurred from the speed we're travelling, but there's a lights-controlled-intersection approaching. He'll have to stop for the red light.

As I look ahead, the colour changes to green. I count the cars between us and the crossroads, trying to calculate the chances. But I don't know this side of town well. Hell, I don't know this side of town *at all*. It's afternoon and they should be on high rotation given we've passed three schools in as many minutes. But what's that? Thirty seconds? A minute? Two?

"Can we pull over?" I blurt, holding a hand to my mouth. "I'm sick."

"There's a bag in the seat pocket," Edwin states calmly, eyes focused on the road ahead. "Use that if you need to."

My skin is clammy. The chill coming from the window is far more powerful than the weak warmth the air conditioning blows into the back seat.

I lean forward in my seat under the guise of hunting for the bag he mentioned. Once I have it, I continue to stay there, using my body as a shield so he can't see my hand resting on the door release.

The light's still green.

Still green.

Fuck! It's *still* green and we're only three car lengths away now.

Amber.

Thank fuck.

But the cars ahead decide that's just another shade of turning signal, sneaking into the intersection as though the road rules are more like relaxed guidelines.

Then Edwin brakes as the vehicle directly ahead obeys the sign like a good citizen. My hand tenses, ready to go.

Ready.

Set.

I lift the door release, but nothing happens. I jerk at it, pushing the button in the opposite direction—an action that should roll down the window—but also does nothing.

"They're disabled," Edwin remarks mildly from the driver's seat. "The only way you can get through the doors is by someone outside opening them with the handle."

His smug face rubs me the wrong way and I spin my legs up, kicking between the gap in the front seats, aiming for his head. The blow lands mostly on his headrest but he gives a yelp that fills me with a warm glow.

A short-lived affair as a Perspex divider lifts, cutting off access.

"Try sitting back and doing what you're fucking told," Eddie yells, his cool knocked away with the feeble kick. There is a network of holes in the divider, right near his head, meaning I can hear him clearly. "You're not in any danger—"

"Is that what he told you?" I let out a grunt of disbelief. "Drive to Sydenham and I'll introduce you to the three people he murdered this morning. Maybe you can keep a straight face while you're giving the same lecture to them."

Edwin shoots me a concerned glance in the rearview mirror, then his eyes return to the road as the light changes. I try to remember the damsel-in-distress signals that were making the rounds on social media earlier in the year, some gesture I should make out the window, but my mind is a blank.

I turn and hammer on the glass, opening my mouth to scream as loudly as I can.

"If you make me stop this car to deal with you, you'll fucking regret it."

"Make your mind up. I thought I wasn't in any danger."

"You're not escaping so you might as well settle in for the ride," he mutters.

I close my eyes, my mind churning through scenarios at a million times a minute. "What're you getting out of this?"

"Stop talking now. I don't want to hear another word out of you."

"If it's money, I can get you money. Trent has more money than God."

He leans forward, turning on the car radio and cranking it up to full volume. The speakers vibrate with the overload, making the tune crackle until it hurts my ears.

I slam my palm against the glass behind his head. "Nobody wants to come after you. Drop me anywhere you like, and I'll make sure you're never prosecuted, never attacked."

"Shut your mouth."

"Take me to my mother's hospice. We can both pretend this bit never happened. You turned up, and you drove me to be with her. I can say that the hospice rang me with an emergency."

He's not listening, and I slam my hand against the divider again and again, releasing my frustration. My increasing sense of despair.

"Do you know what that man did to me? Is he really a person you want to associate with?"

He ignores me except to put his foot down, the car moving so quickly that I reach for my seat belt, scared he's riled enough to make a mistake.

I stare at my sneakers. Wonder if I could kick the glass out with them.

With a pang of instant regret, I see I could have taken out the laces while he wasn't looking. Taken them out, tied them together, then dropped them over his head and choked him against the head rest.

Too late now. The divider put paid to that.

My hands scrabble through the seat pocket, searching for something, *anything*, I can use to fight him.

A few packets of crisps and a water bottle.

Perhaps MacGyver could fashion them into a tool to escape or a weapon to fight but I can't. The only ideas my brain produces are visions of myself, dead.

The salt from the chips could go in his eyes? That would sting a bit.

Pathetic.

I lean my head forward, my aches and pains growing, pulsing, pushing me from discomfort into misery.

Those injuries will be nothing compared to what my uncle will do to me. I see Ceecee's ruined fingers, see Harry's gouged eye, and draw in a breath that's mostly a sob.

That's what he did to people who didn't mean a thing to him.

I crossed him. I testified against him, landing him in jail. Not a place known to treat paedophiles with respect.

And Andy. Dead because of me. Andy who I don't remember from back when I was young but who must have been there, on the periphery, the whole time.

Who was working for my uncle back then and now? Who must be close to him to do the things he did. To take the risks he did.

Close enough that a man who's been sneaking around, planting cameras and tracking software, sending cards that could look innocent to anyone else, has now flipped out, escalating to committing torture and mass murder.

The car slows and turns into a long driveway, shielded on each side by dense rows of poplar trees. It pulls into an open garage, the door trundling down the moment we're inside.

I undo my seat belt, shrinking away from the door when Edwin comes around the vehicle to open it. Shrinking back until he grabs my arm and drags me out.

"Don't play silly beggars," he snaps. "Just do what you're told."

Do what I'm told. Like I'm eight instead of eighteen.

Like I'm a small, frightened child with no good options.

I fall into step with my head bowed, waiting until we're near the door to slam my palm against the door release, jam my elbow back into Edwin's stomach, spin on my heel and run.

A metre away from the door it stops, reverses direction, and crashes back down to the floor, sealing my exit.

Harsh breathing comes from behind me.

I turn, already knowing who I'm going to see.

The years have weathered his face, but he's still easy to recognise. His hair's receded, now mostly white, his wrinkles are deeper than ever, but the same smirk twists his lips, the same glare is in those muddy brown eyes.

Jerred Loughlin.

My 'uncle.'

"You fucking bitch," he spits at me without preamble. "You killed my son."

CHAPTER TWENTY-SEVEN

TRENT

I'M TRAVELLING SO FAST THAT WHEN I HIT THE CORNER, the wheels threaten to skid out on me even with the four-wheel drive. With some fast reactions, I quickly recover control, but my heart beats a little faster, and it was speeding already.

It's been going a mile a minute since Sashe rang, concerned that my girlfriend had left with someone who looked like they'd just come off a three-day bender. The description of the investigator had reassured me for a split second, then spiked my fear.

Edwin might be working on someone's instructions, but those directions hadn't come from me.

"Why can't you track her? You're the one who installed the device in her bracelet to begin with."

"And it worked when we tested it," Caylon calmly responds.

Usually, I find his quiet confidence endearing. Right now, it makes me want to wrap my hands around his throat.

"What could block it?"

"The tracker is the size of an impressive grain of sand. There could be a million things in the way. It doesn't like metal or concrete. If she dropped it inside a toaster, that'd be enough to block most of the signal and my phone isn't as sensitive as my equipment at home."

We're taking the chance that driving while tracking will get us to Rosa faster than depositing Caylon in front of his extensive collection of souped-up computers at home and working from there.

A decision that satisfies my need to be doing something, going somewhere, taking action to get my girl back to safety.

A decision that could be the stupidest one I've ever made because the flip-side could be us taking so long to find her with the substandard phone software that Rosa winds up dead.

The choice roils my gut, making my head dizzy and my fists ready to smash through concrete.

Another corner. Another skid.

"Maybe slow down," Caylon says, then hunches in the corner of the passenger seat when he clocks my face. "We don't even know we're heading in the right direction."

His perfectly rational explanation makes my temper fire up another notch, now able to melt steel.

"You said it was most likely the north side of the city."

He opens his mouth, then snaps it closed, turning his full attention back to the phone. A scrap of wisdom I wished I possessed.

His phone beeps. "Zach's coming in from Rolleston. We'll meet up near Avonhead."

A small part of me opens in gratitude. For the past few months, everyone in my life has been drifting out of reach. Now, when I need them most, they're encircling me, supporting me.

Even Sashe called with the news that has currently shattered my world but is a thousand times better than not knowing anything is wrong.

"Do you know anything more about the investigator? Stefan's not getting back."

Stefan had already packed up and vacated the house when Sashe's call came through, leaving his men behind to sort things.

I'm scared that he recommended this guy and now he's conveniently out of touch. I'm not close to the man—I don't think he *allows* people to get close—but I know enough about him to understand that his focus is always on the power, the money. If it profited him to place a double agent in the role of private investigator, he'd do it without a thought.

There may be people in his life to whom Stefan is loyal but I don't qualify. My guess is the only reason he's helping us out now is because it ties us to him. It extends my part-time job—something I could have moved on from in a year or two—into a lifelong career.

That and we're less likely to name him while being dragged from cage to court by the police.

"He looks like he's sleeping rough and isn't well acquainted with showers," I say when a change of lights forces me to a standstill. "Apart from that, who knows?"

Caylon's wise enough not to remonstrate me for my lack of knowledge after the fact.

"Finley talked with him one afternoon." I grab my phone and dial before I can finish the whole thought.

When she answers, she sounds surprised. "You're not calling to evict me, are you?" she babbles in her joyful tone. "Because I got to say, I could live with you and your dad forever."

"The investigator," I say, nearly dropping the phone as I have to hold it between my ear and shoulder while taking another skid-worthy turn. "Did he tell you where he lives or where he works or—"

Caylon rescues the phone before it can drop, putting the call on speaker, resting it on his knees while still working on his own device. "Was Rosa wearing her bracelet this morning? Do you remember?"

"The swanky could-pay-my-rent-for-a-year bracelet? Yeah, I'm pretty sure she had it on. I don't think she's taken it off for a second since he gave it to her." There's a pause. "And your name is?"

"Rosa's in trouble," I blurt, earning a stern glance from Caylon. "We're trying to find her, but I think the PI might have picked her up in his car."

"His car? You'll probably find it broken down on the side of the road, then." Her voice takes on a sharper edge. "And why do you care why the investigator you hired to protect her takes her on a drive?" And sharper still the demand, "What's going on?"

"If Rosa gets in contact, call this number," Caylon says. "We really need to get hold of her."

"It's not her mother, is it?" Finley's voice chokes a little. "Oh, god. Should I cut my classes? I can get home and see if she's there." Then her voice breaks again. "Where are you?"

"Her mother's fine," I tell her but one glance at Caylon tells me he's thinking the same. "We'll get back to you if we hear anything and you do the same, yeah?"

"I... of course... but..."

He rings off and I grab my phone back, dialling a new number from memory before tossing it in his lap. "That's the hospice."

The receptionist sounds wary when Caylon asks for her room, and I comb my memory for information. "I'm her daughter's boyfriend," I tell her, not bothering to hide the panic from my voice. "That counts as family."

"We haven't got your name on an approved list."

"You haven't got a list at all because we only just moved her in there. My dad's the one footing the bill. That should be proof enough of our relationship."

It's not.

"Put her on the damn phone or the next call to your facility is going to be from the police, informing her that her daughter's dead."

Perhaps it's the panic. Perhaps it's the money. Perhaps it's close to the end of the shift and the poor woman can't be bothered dealing with any more bullshit.

She connects through to the room and a male voice answers. Her nurse.

"She's not really in a well enough state to—"

I'm about to yell again when I hear her in the background, fighting her own battles. The strident notes in her voice are so similar to Rosa that it twists something painful in my chest.

"What's wrong?"

Caylon and I fill her in, minus the murders, long past the point of easing into the subject. "Anything you can tell us about him could be helpful," I end with. "I know we asked you questions already but is there something more? Anything. Please."

My voice cracks on the last word and I have to concentrate my attention back to the road before tears can mist my vision.

Stay in the moment. Emotions can wait.

If things go wrong, I'll have the rest of a long, lonely life to indulge them.

"What about his son?" Caylon asks when she sounds close to breakdown, not able to provide more off the cuff. "Did you know Andy?"

"Drew? He called him Drew when we were... when we knew each other." She coughs to clear her throat, then can't stop, descending into a fit that takes a minute to resolve. "He adopted him but when they split, his mother got custody. Once he reached eighteen, the kid reached out again."

"Where was she?" I call. "Did she live in Christchurch?"

"She had a lifestyle block just out of the city." Her voice

dials farther into panic as she adds, "I can't remember where. I'm not sure he ever gave me the address. Do you think...?" Her sobs come over the line. "She's a fighter, but he's already in her head. I don't..."

The nurse steals the phone from her. "I think that's enough."

I'm about to burst out with a string of invectives, when Caylon says, "Finally! Here we go."

He tilts his phone towards me, the tangle of black spaghetti on the screen soon resolving into a map. "She might have been in an armoured car. That's the kind of thing that can block the signal."

An armoured car. Not something you usually pick up from your local dealership.

Another sign that whatever torment Jerred has in store for Rosa, he's been planning it for a while. Planning it, and now we've increased his impetus to hurt her by killing his son.

A deep sense of guilt fills me.

This is down to me. I'm the one with the weird proclivities. I'm the one who needed something from her she couldn't provide. Something she still tried to cater for because she's special, she's wonderful, she's kind and thoughtful and considerate and currently being transported far away from me by a man who's hurt her before and won't hesitate to hurt her again.

I stare at the tiny blinking dot. It's hard to believe the enormous outpouring of affection I have for Rosa could be encapsulated by the small collection of pixels on the screen.

"Zach?" Caylon asks as my eyes snap back to the road, my foot pressing harder on the accelerator, looking for any break in traffic to take advantage, to get us closer towards where we need to be. "I'm sending you a location. Meet us outside."

"You need firepower?"

"We need anything you can lay your hands on immediately. Anything that takes time is ruining her chances."

"It's on the way," he says, then I have to concentrate because I'm speeding through a red light and dodging the vehicle that correctly thinks it has the right of way.

"Try not to kill us before we get there," Caylon says, grabbing the handle above the door as I continue onward, pushing the car to the max as I hurry towards the girl I love, hoping I'll make it in time.

CHAPTER TWENTY-EIGHT

ROSA

I FIGHT.

Elbows, knees, teeth, anything goes in my mad burst at freedom. I run straight at Edwin, but he doesn't move aside like I'd hoped, instead turning himself into the rumpled equivalent of a brick wall.

Jerred waits, ready to intervene at a moment's notice. When he grows sick of me squirming and wriggling and kicking, biting, scratching at any bits of the investigator that come into view, he walks over and punches me in the face, punching again when I sag.

He grabs me in a headlock, hauling his bent arm against my throat until the room goes dark and a high whine sounds in my ears, then he drops me. The world feels so far away, my body so resistant to movement, that I can't get my hands up in time to break my fall.

I break it with my face instead. Slamming against the hard

concrete of the garage floor. There's a white-hot blast of pain, rousing me only to make everything hurt.

"Get up." Jerred kicks at me with the steel toe of his boot. "I'm not paying him to carry you."

Up is such a long way I don't think I'll make it, then a burst of anger propels me to my knees and from there, it's not such a stretch.

My uncle walks over, stopping an inch away. I could attack him, he's close enough, but I already know how that goes. I'm better off preserving my strength.

"Look at you," he says with a curl of his lip. "To think we went to all this trouble to track you down and now you look like absolute shit."

I run my tongue around the inside of my mouth, wincing as it travels near the incisor that was floor side down when I fell. It doesn't feel like it's long for this world and it's sure screaming bloody murder about it.

My mouth is full of blood, the taste of it nauseating. I spit a mouthful to the side and my uncle grins.

"Get a small taste of your own medicine, did you?"

"My medicine? What the fuck did I ever do to you?"

His fist smashes into my ear before I even see it coming. No time to move. No time to soften the blow.

Pain explodes from the side of my head, my right eye flooding with tears like it can wash away the sharp ache if only it produces enough.

He bunches the front of my blouse and drags me closer. Close enough his foetid breath wafts across my cheek. Close enough to see the ravages that time has clawed into his skin. Close enough to turn my stomach as I smell his scent, the same stench that haunts my dreams.

"You think you did nothing to me? Because you got the police and the courts to do your dirty work. I still rotted in that jail cell. I still had the living shit kicked out of me every time the guards turned the other way."

My body's already twisting in so much pain. A little more won't kill me.

"Sure, and I'm the one who forced you to break the law, is that right? I forced you to do all the disgusting perverted things you were doing. A man so low the only people he could find to believe his shit were kids."

He laughs, pulling me near and licking me from my ear to my eyeball.

The rush of nausea is immediate. I clamp my lips shut, bite down even though my tooth shrieks with renewed pain.

I will not throw up. Not here. Not now. I refuse to show this man any further weakness.

"Is that what you tell yourself? That it was something I did to you." That laugh again, drilling into my aural memory with all the elegance of a buzzsaw. "We both know how it really worked, you little tease. Dancing around with your short skirts and your bare midriff showing. Who's the one who couldn't wait to bounce on my knee, who was panting for everything she got, you fucking slut?"

"I was a child."

"You were a whore. It's baked in your DNA. Don't expect me to shed any tears when you got everything you wanted."

"And you got everything you fucking deserved. Did someone make you their pet in prison, hm? Someone like curling up with you at night. Someone like fucking the shit out of their good old paedo mate, Jerred?"

He roars and stamps his boot on my foot, so many bones snapping under his heel that I can't count.

Waves of hot pain radiate from the injury. I try to move it, lift it, get it to a safer position, but the agony reaches into my core, bringing my organs to a screeching halt, nothing moving, nothing working, until the first wash recedes, and I can gasp in a breath, still reeling.

"Get her inside," he barks at Edwin. "Onto the bed."

He grabs my chin, tilting my face towards him. "I've got one last starring role for you, my dear. One last shot at earning a reward for every piece of shit you put me through."

"Let me guess. You're going to dig up your dead son and make me fuck him."

His fingers dig into my jaw, twisting my face until my gaze locks to his. Holding me steady while the contempt filters into each line of his expression.

"You're not good enough to fuck my son, even when he's dead."

I think that's it, that he's about to move on to whatever's next in his horrifying plan. But he stops, the fingers holding me soften, become gentler.

A trap. One I know from the good old days. His good cop side, always coming out to rescue me from his bad cop. Except they're all the same, flip sides to a singular coin.

"Maybe if you're good, I won't kill you at the end of this one. Maybe I'll keep you until you've got my child in your belly. Would you like that, sweetheart? Want to give me a replacement kid since you stole the first one away."

There's something more deeply terrifying about that suggestion than any other he's put forward. That he could replace his child so easily. That Andy didn't mean enough for him to even truly care.

His only son, just more grist for his mill.

"He couldn't even get it up," I tell him, eyes narrowing when I see the twitch of his cheek muscle. "That's what you taught him. I seem to remember you having the same problem often enough."

Jerred turns and grips my throat, squeezing, his face contorted into a snarl.

"Hey, man," Edwin calls out, voice trembling with nerves. "Maybe ease up a little. You said you wanted her for a movie. You didn't say nothing about hurting her."

Miracle of miracles, the words strike home. Jerred pushes me, his smile spreading as I scream at the renewed pain from my shattered foot.

I turn to the investigator. "You know he's going to kill me, right? That's what you were paid to do. Bring me here so he could kill me."

"What he does with you is nothing to do with me."

Edwin's eyes shift to the side, seeking escape. His hands clench into fists and relax, clench and relax. His torso turns to the side, towards the car, subconsciously seeking an escape.

"It's murder. You kidnapped me and brought me here. When he kills me, you're part of it. You're the reason I'm here. It's murder."

"Like you haven't murdered someone already this week, you bitch," Jerred snaps, losing his patience and grabbing me firmly by the upper arm. "Same as your mother. Always pretending you're so high and mighty when you're really living so deep in the muck, you'd have to burrow upwards for a day to see daylight."

"Ooh. How poetic."

He slaps me, then slaps me again. My face is already so swollen from his earlier blows that it's numb to the pain.

"Trent is going to track you down," I say, staring at Jerred but speaking to Edwin, trying to play on the tiny connection we forged on the day we played cards. "He'll find you and he'll find anyone you love, and he'll show you what it means to be hurt."

"Or your rich boyfriend will buy himself a new playmate." Jerred's gaze traverses from head to toe, then flicks away in dismissal. "Maybe he'll find himself a matching heiress. One who hasn't spent half her life being fucked for cash."

My fist shoots out, catching him high on the cheekbone. The pain in my knuckles is immediate and intense, taking me by surprise. I haven't thrown a punch before, except in play. I didn't know how much it would hurt.

The blow won't win my freedom, but the satisfaction is immense. Until he stamps on my injured foot again.

Everything in the world greys out and I wait, holding my breath, thinking it will come back.

It doesn't. I tip forward, falling through time and space, falling into a deep dark hole that never seems to end.

———

I COME to with a bucket of icy water in the face. My wrists are bound, tied above my head. I'm lying on the right side of a bed, the left covered with an assortment of tools that I don't want to think about. Rope. A hammer. Some sex toys.

Jerred barks out a laugh at my distress, and I match with one of mine when I get my first sight at his face.

His eye is swollen and watery, a thin tear trickling from the corner.

Pretty sure he's winning the beating-the-shit-out-of-your-opponent challenge, but it's deeply satisfying to see the results of my one blow.

"Are you winking at me or are you just a pussy who doesn't know when to duck?"

"And it speaks." He shakes his head. "At least, it speaks until I decide to shove something in its big fat mouth."

"Better not be your dick or you're losing it." I conjure a sweet smile up from some deep reserves I didn't know I had. "I wouldn't mind having something to chew on. Nom. Nom. Nom."

There are too many points of pain for me to number. My foot is the worst, each slight change in position sending bolts of agony straight up my leg, biting nerves along the way.

"You want to fuck her, now's your chance," Jerred says, turning to Edwin. "Later on, she won't look nearly so pretty."

He reaches over me, picking up the hammer and hefting it in his hands while I try not to think of where it might land, how it might feel, what damage it might do.

"Better wrap it up before you do. No telling where this one's been."

Edwin shakes his head and Jerred narrows his eyes at him. "What's the matter? You don't fuck girls?"

"Not like this."

He's shaking and I wonder if something more happened while I was knocked out.

"Can I go?" Edwin asks. "You told me—"

"I told you once you finish the job, you'll get your kid back. Not before."

With a sickening jolt, I understand the impetus that turned the wary but borderline friendly investigator into the man who wouldn't listen, wouldn't help me, wouldn't *stop*.

I already know my uncle has no qualms about hurting children. Quite the opposite. I can't blame Edwin for capitulating, not if his child's life is on the line.

There'll be no help from his quarter. I'm back to relying on myself.

Jerred nods as though someone just gave him an answer. He turns to glance at me again, licking his lips as he stares at my nipples, hardened from the cold, pressing against the wet fabric of my blouse.

The sight turns my stomach. A tremor of fear twists and

turns inside me. I don't want to give into it. I'd rather spit invectives in his face and take the consequences; rather force him to kill me quickly in a furious rage than suffer through his plans.

"You used to be so pretty," he says, reaching out to trail the hammer along my leg, bumping along my shinbone, putting me on edge. "So pure. Now look at you. Can't even get a guy to throw you one for free."

His smile oozes wider, menace dripping down his face. He raises the hammer and I tense, watching his eyes burn with delight, cringing away from the expected pain.

Then he swings it, not down onto my leg, but sideways into Edwin's face. The investigator crumples to the floor, screaming, holding a hand to his mouth and nose, thick rivulets of blood flowing through his fingers.

"You really don't understand ingratiating yourself with your partners, do you?" Jerred says in a teasing voice. "When I offer you something, something that will incriminate you as much as me long after your kid's safely back home, you do that. Otherwise, I look at you funny. I get the idea that you might be working an angle, readying something to make you a profit at my expense."

He advances on the cowering investigator, tossing the hammer from hand to hand.

Edwin shakes his head, speaking with a voice that sounds mushy. "N-no. Believe me, I would never endanger my daughter like—"

The second blow of the hammer cuts him off, Jerred apparently not interested in what he had to say.

Now I only have myself and the man who hates me. Who blames me for ruining his life. Whose only son was beaten to death less than a metre from me for daring to touch me the wrong way in front of someone who cares.

I've never felt so much love for a boy before as I do for Trent.

And now I'll never get to tell him because I don't think he'll find me, not in time. Not before this wretched excuse for a human does everything he wants to do to me.

"Tears, is it? Oh, boohoo, baby. They didn't work on me then and they're sure as hell not going to work on me now."

He wipes the hammer against the bedclothes, smearing Edwin's blood over the happy design. One where cartoon characters cavort among a forest setting. The sort of thing you'd use to distract a child from their fear.

"And what's the plan now?" I ask, not caring for the information but wanting a way to anger him so whatever he does, he does it quickly. "You're going to drag out your substandard noodle and try to make it hard?"

"Watch your mouth, cunt." He taps the head of the hammer against my knee. "First, I'm going to film a nice video to sell to an overseas buyer who's expressed an interest in seeing how much pain a young woman can endure, then I'm going to film your unfortunate demise for a buyer who just wants to see someone die in agony on tape. Sound good?"

That he has buyers sounds terrible.

Not just for the wretchedness of being a valueless thing that can be disposed of in agony for some rich wanker's amusement, but because he won't stray too far from the script. I likely won't be able to tip the scales into him killing me early, killing me before the pain is so great, I'll be wishing I were dead.

He bumps the hammer playfully against my body.

"Don't you need to set up?"

"Already done. There are cameras everywhere, capturing your every movement, every emotion. They've been doing it from the back of the car, down in the garage, now on the bed. The same tiny little cameras that were tracking your every movement in your flat."

His smile is so large and oily, I expect it to slide right off his face.

"My buyers have loved the little tease of your daily life, but it's time to move to the main event. You ready?"

I clamp my mouth shut, fighting for control.

He lifts the hammer and I force my blazing eyes to stay open, glaring at him. If it's all I can do, I want to burn my image into his blackened soul.

The room explodes with sound, the heavy door slamming inwards, the tramp of heavy boots on concrete, gunfire pounding and ricocheting through the cavernous space, the hard walls echoing it, amplifying it. A chaos of noise and motion working upon my overactive nerves until they force my mouth open in a scream.

My world is confusion. So many sights, sounds, sensations I can't untangle them, make sense of them.

I jerk around, staring towards the door, see the men standing there, the rifle flashing with gunfire. The bullets tear at my uncle's flesh, the noise wet as they puncture his body, firing again and again into his bleeding frame. His body jerks with the impact, the hammer falling uselessly to the floor, barely audible in the continuing racket.

The gun stops.

For a long second, the only sound in the room is my scream.

My uncle falls, landing on the hard floor with the same noise as someone dropping a wet towel. Gurgles sound from his open mouth, blood filling it so I can't see the white flash of his teeth.

His dull eyes stare blankly at me, not focusing, not seeing, no person left behind them at all.

Something wet drips into my eyes until they blur.

When I blink the world is crimson. My brain misfires for long seconds, insisting to me it's glitter.

Crimson glitter, painting the entire world with its sparkling scraps.

"Rosa!"

Trent runs to me, stops short, staring with anxious eyes until I smile. Smile and sob and say his name, over and over like a mantra to bring good fortune.

He bends to cup my cheek, gathering the edge of his shirt to wipe my face, pulling a pen knife to slit through my bindings, smiling as I throw my arms around him, hugging him too tight, panic still working through me.

"You came," I whisper, squeezing my arms to remind myself he's real.

Zach stands behind him, by the door, still holding the modified weapon that is, for sure, illegal as shit. He looks slightly stunned as though even being the one firing the weapon, he hadn't expected it to be so effective.

Caylon hangs back, his eyes resolutely fixed to the floor.

"You're alive," Trent drags me onto his lap, kissing me, touching me, stroking my hair back and kissing me again. "I'm so glad you're alive."

His arms are around me, hugging me so tightly it's like we're becoming one, our bodies melding together. Then he draws back to lift me from the bed, igniting the broken bones in my foot, the horrendous swelling in my face, my ear, the hundred and one smaller injuries that want to lend their voices to the growing choir of shrieking nerves.

"You're hurt. Where are you hurt?"

Trent changes direction, ready to lay me back down on the bed and I throw my arms around his neck. "Don't you dare set me down," I warn. "It's just a few scrapes and bruises. I'll live."

"One day," he says to me, his voice rich with promise. "We're going to stop just living and actually enjoy ourselves for a change."

"You don't think I enjoyed all this," I say, smiling with so much love and relief that I can't contain it to a more suitable time or place. "Thrill a minute. Five stars. Especially the ending."

He tips his head, so it touches against mine, then curls me so close to his chest that my face vibrates with the beats of his heart.

"Another mess," Zach says in a tone that borders on impressed. "Hope this multitude of dead bodies won't continue or I might have to cut you loose."

"Like you'd last a second without both of us to back you up," Caylon mutters. "Just because you're holding a gun doesn't make you a leader. If you're cutting Trent loose, then count me gone as well."

"Jesus. What's crawled up your arse lately?"

"Em," Trent says with a wink to Zach. "Or at least, that's what he's hoping."

"Get her name out of your filthy mouth."

"See?"

The momentary distraction over, Trent nods to Caylon to open the door and whisks me through to the outside driveway, carefully tucking me into the car.

"I've just got to have a quick chat with—"

"I love you," I blurt, not caring that this isn't the right time or the right place or the right head space to get the words out. A few minutes ago, I was scared I'd never get to say them to Trent and damn if I'm going to let another opportunity slip away. "From the moment you pushed me out of your dad's study, I haven't been able to get you out of my head."

He crouches next to the car, taking my hand, staring up at me with eyes so sweet and full of wonder that I have to bend across and plant a kiss on his mouth, curl my hand around his neck, no matter how much it ignites all my aches and pains.

"All the time he was threatening me, all I thought was that I'd missed my chance, that I'd never get to tell you."

"I love you, too."

The declaration makes me snigger against his cheek. "I already know that, silly. You told me when you were trying to convince me to take your diamonds and your car."

"Did I?" He takes my hand from his neck, kissing my knuckles. "Well, good. Wouldn't want any of these deranged lunatics turning your head."

"Do you mean Jerred and Andy, or do you mean your friends?"

He bursts into laughter, and I treasure that as much as anything else. His calm manner. His solidity. His beautiful, beautiful strength.

We breathe in sync for a moment, then Trent reluctantly releases me and stands. "Come on," he says with his beaming smile. "Let's get you home."

CHAPTER TWENTY-NINE

TRENT

TEN MONTHS LATER

I stare across the table at Rosa, then can't resist taking her hand. We're sitting outside, taking advantage of the early summer with a barbeque at Zach's house. A place that puts even my dad's mansion to shame.

She glances at me, smiling as her eyes glow with happiness, and squeezes my hand before turning her attention back to Zach, who's pontificating about something. I lost track about ten minutes ago and haven't found my place since.

"That's not the way I remember it," Lily says darkly, then immediately brightens as he drops a kiss on her collarbone, manhandling her into his lap.

"Where's this baby?" Finley complains. "I seem to remember that was the only reason I signed up to this barbeque. I demand you produce her at once."

"Caylon's probably still manhandling baby seats and bottles and spare nappies and god knows what else into the car," I reassure her. "It's different from lugging around a few laptops."

"I could've been home having fun," Finley complains, pooching out her lower lip.

The home in question is still mine, even though the threat that first installed her there is long past.

It might not be a place we're sharing for much longer. Increasingly, I feel that Rosa and I could benefit from having our own space.

Her flat is long gone, rented out to new troublemakers. We combed through the place so many times, ensuring any equipment was found and destroyed, that I felt a strange goodwill towards the house on the day we finally packed all Rosa and Finley's supplies to leave.

Not that I'd settle for something like it. Not a chance. Even if we rely on my wages from bouncing at Stefan's club instead of handouts from Dad, it's still enough to find far more opulent living conditions.

"Missing Sashe, are you?" Rosa asks with a twinkle of mischief in her eye.

Finley shoots back an innocent expression that isn't fooling anyone.

She's been spending an increasing amount of time with my new stepmother, and I have caught her escaping from my dad's bedroom on a few mornings, looking very pleased with herself.

Sashe is also far happier than she had been. Dad, too.

Whatever arrangements they're currently entangled in, I wish them good luck. I'm not sure how happy I would have been about the situation pre-Rosa, but with her by my side, it's become easier to take everything in my stride.

"That's them," Lily shrieks, scrambling upright and bouncing on the balls of her feet. "Should I go down to the car to greet them? Or is that too pushy?"

"They're probably lugging fifty kilos worth of stuff out of the back seat," Zach's dad says, coming onto the lawn beside us. "But I'll go see if they need a hand."

Lily looks amused and exchanges a secret glance with Zach. His dad's been dating a lovely woman from a rival law firm lately. I wonder if that silent exchange means things are progressing faster than I thought.

"When's the food going on the grill?" Sierra asks, so much a mini-me of her sister that I have to look twice to convince myself I'm not staring at Lily.

"You can start it if you like," Zach says. "Zelda's laid all the food out, ready. You just need a pair of tongs and an apron and you're good to go."

She claps and launches herself at the barbeque. "The cook also gets a beer, doesn't she?"

"The cook gets a weak shandy if she's lucky," Lily tells her, rolling her eyes as she goes to monitor her sister's efforts. "And no putting chilli onto the sausages again. You nearly killed me last time."

"Baby mouth."

"Someone's talking herself out of that drink."

"Fine." Sierra's bumps her sister's hip with hers. "But maybe on Trent's?"

"Maybe not," I say with a chuckle, glancing over. "The only thing I'm having from the grill is corn."

"Rugby season's over," Rosa chides me. "Live a little."

"Having corn from the grill is me living," I tell her. "That and the protein ice cream I have waiting in the freezer at home."

"Wow, Trent," Finley jibes. "Way to make us all jealous."

Then Em and Caylon arrive with the baby and all our conversations stop in favour of making collective oohs and aahs over the little sweetheart.

"Can I hold her?" Rosa asks, then radiates nerves as Em carefully transfers the bundle to her. "Isn't she precious?"

She rocks her, jiggling a bit when the girl makes a late objection to the change. The baby soon settles and she shoots me a glance full of wonder as she lifts her tiny hand and plants a kiss on it.

A muscle in my chest tightens as I stare at them, a swathe of emotions catching me as they storm by, spinning and twisting me in their wake.

"Not until she gets her degree," Finley says through narrowed eyes, pointing a carrot stick at me. "I'm not ready to be a godmother. Not just yet."

"Wouldn't dream of it," I tell her, knowing that's a total lie and the image I just captured is probably going to play out in my memory every night for the foreseeable. "But let me know when you are ready, and I'll put some effort in."

The baby moves from Rosa to Lily, Em growing so nervous that Caylon puts his arms around to stabilise her, planting a firm row of kisses along her neck.

She goes back to her mum while Sierra serves up sausages and chops that are crispy black on the outside and pink and raw in the middle. Zach's dad finally wrestles control of the grill from her while she sulks, complaining that she'd just got the coals the way she wanted them as he turns out portion after portion of perfectly cooked food.

I think of how much things have changed since Rosa came into my life. The beast still lurks inside me, twisting its lithe body as it paces back and forth in its cage. I've grown used to its presence, understand now how to let it loose when I need to, how to keep it restrained before it goes too far.

Every step of that journey has been taken with Rosa beside me. And under me. On top of me. Many more positions that it's not good to name in decent company.

No matter how bad I think I am, she's never shocked, never taken aback. She listens, thinks about things, then comes up with solutions.

Not just in the bedroom but with everything. The most steadfast companion I could imagine having in my life. A joy to work alongside, a greater pleasure to hold.

Speaking of which... I reach out and tug her chair closer, close enough that I can lean over and take her into my arms, lifting her onto my lap where I can play with her hair and luxuriate in her warmth, and maybe, if she has a rug handy, indulge in a languorous bit of foreplay.

"Not in front of the children," she immediately scolds when my hand goes wandering, pressing her face against my chest to stifle a laugh.

A lazy afternoon with friends has never felt so perfect, and like all perfect things, it comes too quickly to an end.

As I drive Rosa and Finley home, I feel warm contentment that the group I thought was breaking apart into disparate pieces are now back together, with newer and better members, forming an extra layer of social glue to tie us closer. A perfect balance to everything.

At home, Finley immediately heads off to track down Sashe and fill her in on the afternoon's entertainment. Meanwhile, I trap Rosa against the kitchen counter, remembering Augie and his long-ago coupling on the same stretch of bench.

"No sex in the kitchen," my dad announces to my embarrassment, walking in on us doing nothing. Not a *thing*. "Unless it's me and my wife."

"And Finley," Rosa murmurs, earning a sharp glance followed by a contented smile.

"Don't worry. Your friend is in very safe hands."

She stares at him, her brow furrowing in concern. "Is she?"

Her glance swivels to land on me. "Have you talked to your dad about what you saw when you were younger."

I glare at her, appalled. That's not the kind of thing...

"What did you see?" He frowns at me. "What's she talking about?"

I grimace with discomfort. Of all the conversations I don't want to have, this one rates at the top of the list.

But I can't take it back. Not when Rosa is arching her eyebrow at me like that. Not when the expectation is written large across her face and my dad is staring with open curiosity.

"When I was little, I saw a woman being... well, I guess... sexually assaulted is the word." I close my eyes, faltering before I've really started. But if my girlfriend can be brave, so can I. "She was being attacked and then raped and I..." My words dry up and I shake my head.

"You can say it," Rosa says with confidence, nodding at me.

"At the end, the man strangled her."

My father's still staring at me with confusion clouding his eyes. "And where did you witness this cinematic delight?"

"On the security cameras. In the room at the old house."

"A redhead?"

My eyes spring open. "You saw it, too?" My heart pounds in my chest. Please don't let it have been him. Please don't let my dad be that monster.

"Saw it half a dozen times or more," he says with a nostalgic smile. "I loved those grubby old horror movies. Whoever woke up one day and took all the sex out of them deserves to rot in the bowels of hell."

"A movie?" I tear my gaze away, frowning at the floor, thinking furiously. "No. No, it was on the security camera monitors."

"It wasn't," he says with confidence. "Those camera feeds were in black and white. If you'd really been looking at those images on the monitors, you wouldn't have a clue what colour hair she had."

I open my mouth to argue, then slowly close it again.

"You shouldn't have been watching that," he says, shaking his head. "I'm sorry you saw." He turns to Rosa when I can't say anything. "He used to wake during the night, for years after Meg died. He'd get so tense I'd keep him on my lap while I was watching shows late at night. But I must've thought you were asleep, otherwise, I'd never have put it on."

"A movie," I repeat, feeling how differently shaped the memory is already. "On a video."

"Yeah. I can probably hunt it down for you. I've still got all the old tapes stored in a box in the garage."

A movie.

I close my eyes and feel Rosa's hands snaking around my waist. I lay mine on top of hers, leaning backward into the embrace. Another piece of my life twisting around, rearranging itself, slotting into the new space and finding a much better fit.

Her mouth rests against the back of my t-shirt, breathing warm air through the fabric while she jiggles with laughter. "Oh, you think that's funny, do you?"

"Yes," she says, the word barely audible through the mirth.

I spin around, hugging her face on, my hands dropping to cup both cheeks of her delicious arse.

"You want to go perform a re-enactment?" she asks with a delicious naughty smile.

And yes.

The answer to all her requests is yes.

***

ROSA

Six months later

My mother slips into a doze while I'm lying next to her. I stay in place for a few minutes, smiling at the peaceful sound of her breathing. Smiling at how much better she's been lately, and hopefully for a long time to come.

Anders contact in oncology turned out to be a life saver, literally. After examining my mother and combing through her copious notes from long years fighting her disease, he enrolled her in a trial, utilising her genetic profile to tweak the medication on offer to fit her particular situation.

The difference was spectacular. Instead of her treatments knocking as much out of my mother as it did the disease, the personalised medication stomped the cancer into immobility while keeping her strength intact.

For months after, each time I visited, I noticed an improvement. It was like scrolling backwards through a photo album, with each new turn of the page showing a younger, fitter version of the subject. Winding all the way back so that soon she might live independently again.

Not that she has to. With the generous access to Anders' money, we can provide people to wait on her hand and foot for the rest of her, hopefully much longer, life.

The cancer is still there, but it's more like one of those ailments you die with rather than from. Even if things revert tomorrow, I've already had far more time with her than I'd dared to hope.

Enough time with her to talk about the ghosts from our past and finally put them to bed. Enough time to know for sure that neither of us is holding onto guilt that belongs to someone else.

I ease myself off the bed, nodding to the nurse who pops his head around the corner to check on us. Outside, I rush to my car and get behind the wheel just as my phone beeps with a call.

"I'm coming," I shout, not even checking the screen, I'm that certain who the call is from. "Don't leave for the show without me."

As a treat, Trent bought us tickets to the World of Wearable Art awards. Knowing his contacts, the VIP table is probably going to be in the very best seats.

But we're not going to sit in them unless I move my arse. We're using a private jet to get up to Wellington—courtesy of Anders—but I still need to get to the airport and get onboard quick as possible for us to make the opening time.

"Don't bother coming home first," he tells me with a laugh. "I've got a dozen different outfits waiting for you on the plane."

"Okay. Wait! You're on the plane already?"

"Yes," he says, and I can hear the eyeroll in his voice. "Right where you should be."

I scrabble for my seatbelt, tucking my phone away, and set a course on the GPS for the airport. Once there, I toss my keys to the valet and jog for the private suites where an employee escorts me the rest of the way to the plane.

"Swanky," I tell Trent once he breaks our greeting kiss long enough for me to draw air. "How come I've never been on your private jet before?"

"Because we have everything you need at home."

"Ah," I say with a nod of agreement. "That sounds like the sort of stupid thing I'd say."

"When we get home, I have another surprise for you."

I examine Trent's face closely but when the boy wants to keep a secret, he keeps it. Luckily, I know a secret weapon. Five minutes after take-off—safety first—I tickle him until he begs for mercy.

"Okay, okay. I've found a small apartment that I think would suit the two of us. It's near the university and close to Stefan's main club, so we'll both shave hours off our commuting time each week."

"But I enjoy driving."

I'm only halfway through testing the fleet of sports cars that Anders keeps in his three garages. The excess is disgusting until I'm behind the wheel of a gorgeous gem that can go from nought to a hundred with barely a squeak.

"Then you'll just exchange driving for necessity with driving for pleasure."

"And how small is small?"

"It's only two floors."

I give him a cautious glance, wondering what else he's hiding. "And would they be close to the ground?"

"They'd be the penthouse and the demi-penthouse."

"Of course. Can't have you slumming it."

He yanks me across his lap, digging his nose into the curve of my neck and snuffling, then helping himself to a generous bite.

"Oi," I protest. "I'm getting all gussied up for the main event."

"Right." He tosses me into the window seat and walks back a few metres to grab dress bags from the hanger. "You'll have to get naked first."

I'm already working on it.

"Here's the one the shop assistant who hates you picked out."

I glance at the chartreuse colour, wondering why the woman dislikes earning a commission, then shake my head. "Next!"

"This is the sales lady who thinks you're an Eliza Doolittle project."

"I am," I say, my interest perking when I see the beautiful dark green in lush velvet. "Okay. That's my new favourite."

"What about...?" He produces the next garment in gold lame with a flourish.

I spend the next twenty minutes happily trying on one dress after another, deciding to keep at least half of them, even if most of my days are spent at home or at uni, alternating with visits to Mum and an occasional venture into the great outdoors to rage it up at a party or three.

"You look good enough to eat," Trent announces as I test the roominess of the gold number by straddling him in his seat.

I grab handfuls of his hair, sucking on his left earlobe before whispering, "No one's stopping you."

In a second, we're flipped, me relaxing on the seat while Trent is on top of me. He slides onto his knees before me, rolling the gorgeously coloured fabric up to my hips, then tugging my lace underwear down, slipping it off and pocketing it.

"No underwear on the private plane," he murmurs, the vibrations from his words spiralling across my skin like the sweetest caress. "Or at the show," he adds. "Or while walking around home."

His words muffle as he turns to kiss the inside of my thigh, gradually working his way up, taking my hips and tugging me until I'm perfectly positioned for him to spread my legs wide, and bury his face for a feast.

The gentle lapping of his tongue is a tease designed to make me crawl with desire, and I clamp the arms of the seat so hard I'm sure the imprints will remain visible the next time someone takes this recliner. At first, his thick fingers clamp around my thighs, the rough pads of his fingertips and thumbs in constant motion, creating an orchestra of delight and need across my skin.

Then he moves his right hand, running his thumb along my lips, then again, the second time applying enough pressure to spread them gently apart. He slides the thumb inside me, the rest of his hand playing with my perineum and sliding up to tease my hole while his tongue rejoins the festivities, licking me with long smooth strokes from bow to stern.

I close my eyes, delighting in the flood of sensations that ripple through my body, spreading myself wider so his access is unrestricted, giving him carte blanche to do whatever he feels.

"Such a pretty pussy," he murmurs, moving his thumb to circle my clit gently while his fingers take prime position, slotting in to the first knuckle, the second, finally getting its neighbour to join in the fun. "You taste so good."

A retort springs to mind about boys and their diets but I push it aside for later. Right now, takes too much of my attention to devote any to foolish words and silly teases.

"Are you going to come for me?" he asks, his tongue darting and retreating until I want to grind myself hard against his face.

When I lift my hand from the chair, needing to grab handfuls of his hair, to control him, to put him exactly where I need him, he clicks his tongue.

"Naughty girl. Do you need me to restrain you?"

And it's that tease and everything that floods into my mind at the suggestion that sends me catapulting over the edge. Trent opens his mouth, pressing the width of his tongue against my clit to capture every convulsion as I spasm around his fingers, as my hips jerk until I'm pressing harder against his tongue and his fingers and anything, any friction my greedy cunt can find to prolong the glorious sensations.

When Trent withdraws, my fingers seek the buttons on his shirt, fumbling to undo them until he lifts my hand away.

"No time," he whispers, the guttural tones sending a new ripple of pleasure vibrating down to my bones. "You'll have to store up every impulse, every dirty thought of what you want to do to me until after the show."

I hum in agreement, so relaxed that I couldn't protest even if I wanted to. "I can do that."

The steward comes out to tell us we're close to landing, and I tug my dress down, hoping he doesn't know what we were just up to from the guilty expression on my face.

"Hey," I say as we dismount after landing near the terminal. "Does that qualify me for the mile high club?"

"Oh, I doubt it. If that's on your bucket list, we'd better try harder on the flight back."

"Can we dismiss the staff?"

He scoops me against him, lifting me so I don't have to walk in heels, not a favourite activity even before half the bones in my right foot were broken. "But what if we get thirsty halfway through? Who'd bring us a light refreshment?"

I'm laughing as he sets me on my feet right next to the door of the limousine, beating the driver to opening it for me.

"Have I told you tonight how much I love you?" I ask him as he joins me on the bench seat, tucking me under his arm. "Because it's at least this much." I spread my arms wide.

"That's good," he answers, his voice wavering a little, like he's nervous. "Because there's something I want to ask you later and I really hope you'll say yes."

My mouth goes dry, eyes wide as they stare at him.

"Later," he reiterates. "I don't want it to interfere with the show."

I turn to stare ahead, mind blossoming with possibilities, all of them utterly scrumptious to think about. "It's not a pair of golden handcuffs, is it?"

"Later," he repeats, pulling me against him and wrapping his arms around me. Strong and secure, my big blond boy and his big blond heart making me feel as safe as ever. "We've got a whole evening to enjoy before then."

My skin flushes pink, my heart full of gratitude as I turn to look ahead, aiming to please, aiming to be the good girl he thinks I am.

Thanks for reading!
If you enjoyed this series, you might also like:
YOUR LOSS: A DARK HIGH SCHOOL ROMANCE

It's meant to be one night

The arrangement isn't something I sought. Not something I wanted. It's a means to an end, nothing more.

And yes, I enjoyed myself in his stupidly wealthy household, however shameful that is to admit. But it doesn't *change* anything. A little unexpected pleasure doesn't alter the fact that Lachlan's father is the largest crime boss in the city. It doesn't stop my dad from being an addicted gambler unable to pay his debts. None of it rewrites our agreement or renegotiates the terms.

Once it's over, I expect us to go back to normal. Two teenagers who exist in different social circles, ignoring each other inside the high school walls. Him with his clique of elites, running the place more efficiently than the principal could ever dream of. Me, a girl who comes from nothing, facing a future that's equally bleak. I'm situated so far below him he shouldn't even know my name.

One night. Whatever he wants. Done and dusted.

A pity Lachlan didn't get the memo.

ABOUT THE AUTHOR

Layla Simon is a fictional entity writing dark romance stories because she keeps running out of books to read.

(and please don't tell her TBR I said that)

She enjoys writing about large dangerous men and tiny feisty woman, possibly because she is neither of those things.

You can check out her available and upcoming titles on my website: https://laylasimon.com

Stay up-to-date with every new release by joining my newsletter: https://subscribepage.io/LaylaSimon

Or investigate my link tree:
https://linktr.ee/laylasimon

Printed in Great Britain
by Amazon